The Tarnished Cross

Romantic – Mysterious - Inspiring

by Alan Updyke

Is he guilty as charged?

Trapped in conflict, wanting mercy but fearing a harsh sentence, Sam and his girlfriend Jodi must prepare for trial. Will they believe in the advocacy of love or succumb to the condemnation of religious authority?

He is the people's judge and it is his constituency that will hear the accusation.

Harsh judgment breeds resentment, but mercy – forgiveness. And it is from these contrasting principles that a greater truth is revealed.

Battle lines are drawn. A game of war for their souls is about to commence.

...MERCY TRIUMPHS OVER JUDGMENT.

The Tarnished Cross

Text copyright © 2026 Alan Updyke

© 2026 Status

© 2026 Updyke Books

All Rights Reserved

Please give us a review: If you find this book insightful, please know that our success depends on your review. Go to Amazon.com and search the author's name, "Alan Updyke," or title,
"The Tarnished Cross - Romantic"
or simply scan this QR Code:

He is unseen. His message is often unheard, his presence undetected. But behind the scenes, the Advocate is working in your life, and He has a reason for doing so: untold mercy.

"Religion is regarded by the common people as true,

by the wise as false,

and by the rulers as useful."

Seneca

DEDICATION:

In memory of:

Samuel Wade Wardrop

April 17, 2019 - September 15, 2022

Forever with Jesus!

TABLE OF CONTENTS: Chapters

PROLOGUE

Because of his foolish and immature actions, it has been said of Samuel Urban that he is lucky to be alive. He *is* still alive, yes, but should he be forgiven of his sins to live freely without consequence, or accountability, for the awful things he did?

The victim's scream: it is intensely shrill and unnerving. It was *her* cry for help, *her* pleading for life.

It is something Sam will never forget, unable to erase from his troubled mind, a flashback that often replays as his thoughts drift back – a torturous daydream, an instant mood changer, bringing with it a flood of guilt.

It is the collision he remembers. A terrible crash that he holds himself responsible for.

Seventeen years before... Stunned, at first the trauma hadn't registered in a mind clouded with questions. Where was he? Where did that other car come from?

He felt pain in his leg.

Was he injured? Who else might be hurt?

He was at first overwhelmed with uncertainty.

The sounds of the crash, jarring motions, reflections of light, impacts on his body – so much happened so fast, he just couldn't comprehend it all in that crucial moment.

His vision blurred – sounds became momentarily distant – and pain surged. Fear was rising. Sam suddenly felt nauseous, then dizzy.

There in front of him he saw a crushed car and a young woman sitting upright in the driver's seat with blood streaming down her face. He heard a hissing noise and then one sound became more recognizable – a baby crying. There was a loud popping and a sudden flash of heat. Flames began licking at the edge of her car's crumpled hood. Shattered glass was everywhere.

And then the screaming began.

The torture of a human being unfolded in slow motion before Sam's eyes and consumed his bewildered mind.

Next, he heard someone shouting at him. It was Faith. She had opened the passenger door and was pushing against him. But what did she want?

The totality of that scene would haunt Sam continually, even affecting the rest of his life. Yes, it was a terrible, unfortunate *accident*. But how did it happen, what was the cause, and who was to blame? And what happened to the young child in the car?

Answers to these questions would be revealed over time, climaxing in a convergence of events and lives that would change his forever.

But the immediate consequence of such a tragic accident, a legal response, came first. Someone had to be held responsible. There was an arrest and a trial. But the result of those proceedings was unacceptable to some, requiring additional action of their part, even revenge, and that is where our story begins, many years later.

CHAPTER ONE: Vulnerable

Wednesday, May 8, 1985 – day one.

In Walthem, Pennsylvania, the young Samuel Urban was known as the people's judge, the District 12 Magistrate. The small town nestled in a narrow valley along the Susquehanna River had a population of 11,398 at the time of the last census. A handmade plaque hung in Sam's office to remind him daily of his purpose. It stated, "Rule – with diligence. Show Mercy – with cheerfulness." The sign arrived unexpectedly in a padded envelope. There was no return address and no note to identify the sender. It seemed that someone was observing Sam, watching him very closely from a safe distance, anonymously. He and his office staff waited for the author of those words to identify him or herself. Eventually they lost track of the time that elapsed, but it was more than a year, the mystery remained, and soon enough, the need for the sender's identity was forgotten.

Sam looked at those words frequently and reflected on them. His was a difficult job that required political finesse. The system often required one thing while his heart urged him to do another. This happened as he heard the plight of those who were downtrodden and most often already strapped financially. They could not afford to pay another fine or lose time from work. Even worse would be the effect of a recorded conviction on them.

These were past friends, the kids he went to school with, the gang that he conspired with to steal beer, the ones he partied with on weekends. Good times, fondly remembered.

Yes, everyone got older, some matured, and each took a different path in life. Sam knew he got some lucky breaks, but not so with the familiar but aged faces he saw in his courtroom. He couldn't help but to feel pity on them.

This judge felt like he lived in the middle, somewhere between justice and required retribution. And if his clients felt scorned by his rulings, they would soon have the opportunity, as his constituents, to vote him out of office. That was the system.

But worse, Sam now faced a former classmate and girlfriend, Faith Culver, who targeted him, accusing him of a crime he believed he was innocent of – there was a blank spot in his memory. Still, he didn't understand why she was doing it. How could she, a longtime friend?

And this wasn't the first time he had been in trouble with her and the law.

Sam mentioned the incident involving Faith to his present girlfriend, Jodi Culp, but didn't elaborate. He knew that an investigation was underway, but hoped that the whole thing would just blow over, and rapidly.

Relationships: surely, they are complicated. As a young man, Sam already felt the weight of the world upon his shoulders. His past was always there to chastise him, like an unwanted blob of ink dried upon a marriage certificate, it marred and could not be erased.

Sam's father hadn't been one to offer loving advice, and most of the time was self-consumed and uncaring toward his sons. But he once told Sam, "Marriage is that way. It becomes full of regrettable criticisms, harsh words that won't be forgotten. Watch what you say. The fewer grudges, the better chance you have of surviving it." Of course, his wife, Sam's mother, was in earshot of the comment that was actually meant for her.

As he neared the end of the term of his elected office, Sam's future felt uncertain. He expected a challenger, someone to go after his job. He dreaded a campaign of lies and counter lies. It dirtied everyone so that no one else could know the greater truth. Gray matter. It would result in everyone having their own version of a truth, a compromised truth, a story they were willing to accept and believe, at least somewhat so. But where is truth in that?

Suspicions would linger, easily revived. That was the truth Sam already knew, and knew all too well, from a time past. It was when he stood before a judge, under arrest, and faced serious charges.

Now, not to be naive, Sam also knew about Jodi's discontent, as he was well aware of her desire for a greater commitment from him, but his life felt like he was standing on quick sand. He knew the parable: the wise man built his house upon the rock. He often caught himself feeling uncertain, insignificant, even doubtful of his ability to establish a safe home and a secure future, especially when he drove past the mini-mansions on Bluestone Avenue, with their professional landscaping and perfectly manicured lawns. Their driveways, walls, trees, and shrubs cost more than the modest one-story ranch house he could afford. Their elaborate residences with storied foyers, great rooms, balconies, and fireplaces were symbols of perfection and success.

Surely his wife and children, the family he would have if he stayed with Jodi, deserved the same; but how could he achieve it?

And then, suddenly, out of nowhere, and completely unexpected, came the call from the local police chief. He had questions about that night, the time he recently spent with Faith.

So, Sam was very nervous right now.

Laughter was fleeting and silence imposing as these concerns pressed upon him, even during the precious moments he spent with Jodi, the woman he wanted to marry *someday*. And making things still worse, despite his efforts to conceal his thoughts from her, he knew that she knew all too well, that something was wrong.

++++

Jodi: Sam and I have been dating for nearly four years. Yes, I know that he had some trouble in his past, but the criminal record was supposedly expunged. My guy is thoughtful and kind, sometimes too serious, but can also make me laugh at the drop of a hat, that's when he isn't overly concerned about a problem. Lately though, something is bothering him. He seems distant.

He's the kind of guy that you believe in and hang on to. He has a good heart. So, I have remained committed to him, though sometimes I wonder why he hasn't proposed… yet. It's been good, mostly good…well, in reality, if I were to be honest with myself, I'd have to admit that things are going just a little better than okay right now.

I'm tired of the daily grind. He has his work and I have mine, but not the job I wanted, and often I feel insignificant. Yeah, he's kind of a big shot, and sometimes I think he gets off on it. But he's entitled to it, right? It hasn't always been easy for him.

But what about me, does he know that I am feeling impatient – getting older? Does he even care? With a proposal we could begin to finalize our future, nail things down with a firm commitment, even if the big day is still a couple of years off. As his long-term girlfriend, I need that – a firm commitment. A feeling of finality. Certainty.

++++

And then the events of that fateful morning, Wednesday, May 8, 1985, came upon them like a sudden and unexpected storm of huge proportions – a personal tsunami! They were about to be swept into a sea of uncertainty and be lost, drifting about without an anchor or sail to be steadfast or directed.

Sam intended to go to the office late that morning. It didn't open to the public until 1PM. He just stepped out of the shower and was drying himself when the banging began. Jodi was pounding on the back door of his upstairs apartment.

"Hold on, just a minute," he shouted as he wrapped a towel around his waist. He darted for the kitchen, water dripping on the linoleum floor, his hair wet and disheveled.

++++

"Sam! They're coming for you!" I yelled through the glass of the door still closed. My words smashed through the quiet of his morning.

"Jodi, slow down. What are you talking about?"

I observed as Sam fidgeted with the deadbolt that seemed to be stuck, then rubbed the sides of his forehead. His stress was on full display. It was obvious to me. His face turned bright red as his heart pounded hard, his blood pressure surging.

"Sam! They're out for you. With a warrant. They are charging you… again!"

As Sam unlocked the door I barged through, accidently slamming it against the side of the refrigerator. "My friend at the

13

newspaper, Susan, she called me. It came over the scanner there as the police sergeant was calling her boss to inform him of your arraignment. They want lots of press. It's all set up."

Sam looked puzzled.

"You're going to be arrested!" My voice began to quiver despite my shouting. I felt a bit nauseous. Panic was beginning to overwhelm me. "The cops will be here any minute!"

Sam stood in the center of the room motionless; his gaze fixed upon the window in the side wall behind the dinette table. It afforded a view from his second-story landing. Time stalled as I observed him. He was watching something outside.

"Sam! What are you doing?" I bit my lower lip hard enough to taste the bitterness of blood and squinted to hold back the tears that were beginning to overwhelm me. I was losing it. "Sam, are you okay?"

I turned to see what was holding his attention. Beyond the glass, a squirrel scampered along a tree limb that wobbled under its weight. Its quest portrayed a carefree life. In that moment, the scene felt sarcastic, even ironic. But I couldn't begin to know what he was thinking.

"You have to do something. Sam! Wake up!" I felt a tear as it trickled down my cheek. Another ran to the tip of my nose. Suddenly, he realized that he was naked.

"I have to get dressed."

He turned, and without another word, walked to his bedroom. When he returned a few minutes later, I was standing near the kitchen sink, an empty coffee mug in my hand. The faucet was running. Tears welled in my eyes. "Where's the coffee?" I asked.

He placed the filter in the coffee machine and spooned out six heaping teaspoons of ground Columbian beans, a robust brew. As he held the carafe under the running water, I observed his hand as it began to tremble. He steadied his arm with his left hand and turned the faucet off at the indicated measurement of seven cups.

Several minutes passed and he didn't speak a word to me. I sat at the table, my face buried in my hands. My body shook slightly and I sensed that Sam knew I was crying. I tried to hide it, to not be intrusive.

"Here, this will help."

As I raised my head, he poured the freshly brewed, hot coffee into my mug. Its steam burned in the tip of my nose, a welcome, needed stimulant.

"Tell them to wait," he instructed in firm monotone as he stood beside me. "I'll be back in ten minutes. And I don't want them coming to my courtroom. But before I see them, I have to get something."

"Okay, I'll try to hold them here," I volunteered, but inside I was feeling reluctant and uncertain. Not seeing a box of tissues, I wiped at my eyes with my sleeve. "I'll tell them that I just talked to you. You were at your office… But you're on your way back here. You've already left, so they may as well wait… Right?"

"Good. That should work. I'm headed out the door right now."

Fear was obvious in his tone.

"Thanks, Jodi."

The words fell behind him as he bolted for the exit. Suddenly, he stopped in his tracks.

"Can I take your car? Mine is parked out front."

"Sure." I tossed my keys to him. "It's around the corner on State Street."

"Thanks, mine are on the hook where I always keep them."

"I'm sorry." My statement seemed out of context, but still, I felt it was necessary.

He paused and our eyes met, connecting on a deeper level. I felt desire for him – but was it that of a lover, or maternal instinct?

"I'm so, so sorry," I repeated.

He nodded and then, without another word, Sam disappeared as he jolted through the rear door.

I wondered when I would see him again, and under what circumstances. "Sam, be careful." I felt empty, knowing that my words were inadequate for the moment. The predecessor of loneliness gripped me. Fear, doubt.

++++

But Jodi's farewell was like a distant echo in Sam's ears. More relevant questions were pressing upon him. *Arrest? What is the charge? Sexual assault – it must be sexual assault. But a rape charge from Faith Culver? How could she?* The primary question plagued him. *Why?*

Expecting to soon be incarcerated, he was beginning to realize the inconvenience, the restriction, the loss of freedom he faced. There was a letter he still needed to read. It remained on his desk at the office. Now, with the proverbial stopwatch ticking, the race was on. He had few precious moments of freedom remaining. But in his mind, the intrigue, the mystery of that note unread, drove him onward. He just had to have it.

The sign's appearance is abstract. Its words are something that would be out of place in Sam's world, in 1985, its message inappropriate for *that* time. But it is prevalent nowadays.

"Back the Blue."

The words are etched on an unusual rendering of our national symbol of patriotism and unity. The stripes of the flag are few, and they are blue and white.

But back then, the police were Prima donna, their authority unquestionable and rarely challenged, especially when their arrest warrant was cited in a courtroom. And the State Police, they were the "crème de la crème," their uniform, and wide (flat) brimmed hat with the chin strap, intimidating symbols of the power of the law. (There was always a stern, mean, even angry face peering out from under the visor that shadowed their piercing eyes.) Their brawn was enough to restrain you and take you away, enough to publicly charge you and place you before a throng of salivating reporters, enough to ruin your reputation and your life. They could simply seize it all. That kind of power demands respect.

They could put you behind bars, pretty much at their own discretion, because the courts would back them up, that is, until Sam came along.

Still, Judge Urban, (Sam), often rejected their traffic citations, whenever it was possible, sometimes citing a technicality. When the "Force" complained, the "People's Judge" refused to concede. In retrospect, one would wonder at his tenacity, his unwavering determination. Did he have the bliss of a fool, not comprehending the consequence of his actions, or did he possess the might of a superhero?

Resentment was brewing and it was becoming rank, like the rotting potato under the kitchen sink. And so, it finally stunk and came to this…

Sirens wailed as the state police cruiser raced down Route 11. They were sent to get their man, the one they despised. Their retaliation was, in their opinion, long overdue.

An officer smiled with glee, riding shotgun and holding the arrest warrant. "Are you sure he will be home?" he asked the other trooper.

"Should be. Neighbor said his car is parked on the street." The cop was happy about their plan to remove the liberal judge. Urban often embarrassed them in his courtroom. "Can't wait to see the look on his face. He's had this coming for a long time."

"Yea. Think I'll address him as 'judge', just to emphasize the farce that he is… 'Judge, you're under arrest… again!'" he rehearsed. "Has a certain ring to it, don't you think?" He raised his hand for a fist bump. "Let's get him."

"He's going to be arraigned today?" his partner inquired after a moment of silence and continued, "hope the press has been given ample notice to attend all the festivities."

"Oh yea. Sarge took care of that. It should be a real picnic! I can't wait to see the front page of tomorrow's paper."

When Sam returned to his apartment, Jodi was gone, and the police were waiting for him. He surrendered without resistance. The events that followed later became a mishmash of fast-moving images and loud sounds in his memory bank: angry faces, threatening words, handcuffs, a siren, strobing lights of red and blue, people pushing and shoving, shouting voices with insinuating inquiry, the white explosions of camera flashes, accusations, arguments, and finally the hammering of the judge's gavel.

It was that final courtroom sound that crashed in Sam's brain and lingered there.

He was arrested and arraigned by a colleague, another magistrate he knew all too well. Sam wondered how his friend could do it, but realized that he had no choice.

Sitting alone in the holding cell at the rear of the municipal police station it all swirled in his head, aching with pain. Sam vaguely recalled the proclamation of bail temporarily withheld and the hand to shoulder hug of his dear friend and defense attorney, Jared McCabe, promising to have him released by morning.

"Poor Jodi," he mumbled to himself as his mind shifted. He longed to hear her words of comfort. She was always sympathetic toward his concerns, even patient with his mood swings. "My god," he whispered, "what must she be going through?" He last saw her at his apartment, just before he ran out, headed to his office.

Sam had gone there to retrieve the note that arrived the day before. It was one in a series of notes that he held in confidence. Even Jodi didn't know about them. He kept them stored away and hidden in a small box placed in the back of his desk's filing drawer. It was disguised by the clutter of other items that lacked relevance – old seals and notary stamps. But this note arrived only yesterday. Recognizing the handwriting that addressed the envelope, Sam quickly slid it under the mat on his desk, intending to open it at the end of his work day, but was then distracted and left for home, leaving it unsecured there.

Now, he wondered why and how another note would have arrived just before his arrest. It seemed an unlikely coincidence. Did someone know more about what happened than he did? Could that person help him understand or expose the truth about the events described in the arrest warrant, the accusations of Faith Culver? The night of the alleged assault - much of it was still a blur – as he had limited recollection of it.

As he stood quickly and searched the front pants pockets of his jeans, he recalled emptying them onto the counter just before his mug shot and fingerprinting. The note, folded in half, had been pressed tightly into his left rear pocket. He was processed and surrendered his wallet and comb. He was then patted down, but the note remained, momentarily forgotten and unnoticed.

As he sorted through these details, Sam reached for it. Like others received in recent months, words were simply printed in black ink with block letters on a plain sheet of white paper.

"My life is as a role that I am playing in a skit – a certain time and circumstance in this world. It is where I live now, but like an actor in a TV movie, this show will soon end, and the influence of it will quickly pass away.

How truly relevant is it all?"

Sam could relate. Tears welled in the corners of his eyes. He continued reading.

"Loved ones: how I long to see joy dancing in their eyes once again. As I consider the loss of such, I am overwhelmed with sorrow. Their pain hurts me even more."

Jodi's smile flashed before his mind's eye. A sob burst out of his throat, unsolicited.

The note was signed as the others: *"Your Advocate."*

Whatever was to happen to him, Sam knew that he had to protect the woman he loved.

"This too will pass," he softly spoke words of assurance to himself. "But there is going to be hell to pay, I just know it. I have to survive – but how? I'm only human." Self-pity charged in.

But who was this "Advocate"? Was he trying to encourage Sam or redirect his thoughts, and did he know in advance that Sam would be arrested?

It was well into the twenty-third hour of that first day as Sam rolled on the cot in the holding cell. He experienced a fitful, restless attempt at sleep and the torment he felt was relentless.

++++

I was beginning my second movie after taking a sleeping pill, and still experiencing insomnia. That was after I cried on the phone with my best friend, Susan Kasper. We first met at work, at the **Morning Herald**, Walthem's daily newspaper. Susan was an apprentice reporter. I worked in the art department, composing display ads for local businesses who spent their hard-earned dollars on the **Herald**, believing the salesperson who promised to drum up more business, much more in profits than the newspaper promotion would cost. Hard to believe, but that was their pitch.

You had to be a "looker" to work in the sales department, and the office manager tried many times to persuade me to take the job, but I declined, again and again. That's probably why I was stuck in my present position for many years without a promotion and hardly a raise. You are wondering why I stayed – but that is a story for another time. Although in brief, I was waiting for Sam.

I heard the other girls telling stories. They flirted to get the ads and it seemed that they had to keep pushing the envelope further and further. Sexual harassment was part of the job and to be accepted. I just didn't want to play the game.

One salesperson was groped by a client. The advertiser had an annual contract, was current in payment, and considered important to the paper's income base. The publisher refused to file a complaint. The account was transferred to a recent hire on their staff: a new victim.

Now, back to my story… I knew that trouble was brewing for Sam, and that it was potentially serious, but I was surprised when he was arrested, and I wasn't prepared for his incarceration. When I heard he was locked up, I had a meltdown, and that's when I called Susan. She was, of course, obliged to fill me in on some of the details related to the charges against him.

She has a unique point of view and usually makes me laugh, although that night her attempt at the absurd, even her innocent and indiscreet half-witted observations were unable to jiggle my funny bone. Susan always has a story to tell, the account of a silly incident, the kind of thing that could only happen to her.

Too late. A desperate discouragement had already begun to grip me. Sam was sitting behind bars. This was public. I felt shame, but still, I didn't want it to be just about me. Sam must have been devastated.

And something else was happening. I had a wrenching feeling in my gut that we were in trouble, as a couple, in a way I thought could never happen to us. Infidelity? I was beginning to doubt him and the authenticity of our relationship. I knew that Faith was an old flame. So why would he go to her apartment to be alone with her? Wasn't that like tempting the devil? Was he two-timing on me? I needed answers. And I needed them quick.

A pint of chocolate chip mint ice cream and half a pack of Oreo's later, I was just beginning to feel numb. The blinking images and noise coming from my television set didn't register. I had no idea who was stalking the young woman portrayed on the boob tube, or why. I decided to stop at the liquor store tomorrow, to be better prepared for my next binge.

++++

Four Days Later: A man is feeling that all is lost. Hope is fleeting. The threatening reality of his present situation is closing in around him like a hangman's noose. Suicide tempts. Death is imminent.

CHAPTER TWO: Defenseless

Thursday, May 9, 1985 – day two.

HEADLINES: **"Local Magistrate Jailed On Rape Charge"**

All was peaceful at Jodi's home until the minute hand jumped to the 12th numeral for the start of the seventh hour of the day, and the speakers on her clock radio began surging with the sound of bass and a snare drum. She moaned, rolled away from the morning racket, and pulled a pillow over her head. She wasn't ready to face the challenges of another day. Her reprieve from the trauma of the day before had been much too short. But the call of morning was unrelenting. Her alarm was set for 7 A.M.

++++

Slowly, my mind began the process of recollection. *Today is Thursday.* I became concerned for a moment and then remembered that I had already called in, to take the day off from work. My boss told me to take as much time as I needed, but of course, it was without pay. Like an old computer searching for data, my mind stalled. I just wanted to stay in bed.

"Don't you forget about me. Don't, don't, don't, don't. Don't forget about me." The lyrics of the most popular song caught my attention and my heart broke as I thought about Sam. With a "hey" and "ooh-woah", **Simple Minds** was droning on and on.

"Come on, call my name. Will you call my name? I say: ooh la, la-la-la-la…"

My eyes grew wide with recollection. "Sam," I whispered.

"Come on, call my name. Will you call my name?"

"Sam," I spoke louder. "Samuel Urban!" I declared, but then my demeanor dropped like a lead balloon. "Sam, are you okay?" I mumbled between hushed yawns. And just then I decided that the second thing on my agenda for that day was to go and see my boyfriend, the man I still cherished, despite all that happened the day before.

But first, I was already committed to an appointment with his lawyer, the busy professional who was reluctantly sparing a few moments of his valuable time that morning before supposedly venturing out to the courthouse for an important hearing. Attorney at Law, Jared McCabe, knew all the morbid details of the events leading up to and resulting in the arrest warrant filed against Samuel Urban.

In the bathroom I contemplated my age as evidenced in the mirror which I had begun to resent.

++++

Although a vivacious and beautiful woman in her prime, Jodi was three years past that eternal age of 29 claimed repeatedly by a young female concerned about the years accumulating to quickly and anxious to move on with her life. She was an attractive five-foot, eleven inches tall with thick reddish, strawberry blonde hair that she quickly gathered and anchored at the back of her head with a clip. She had large hazel blue eyes that reflected her sensitive, caring nature. Her mouth was perfectly formed, shaped like a heart when she freely laughed, and framed by thick, lush lips. She pulled high leather boots over her long slender legs and pushed her tight denim jeans, size 6, inside them before closing the side zippers.

She looked in the mirror again and frowned, an unjust critic of her natural beauty. She really didn't need makeup. A little mascara, some penciling to darken her eyebrows, blush on her high cheekbones and light brown lipstick were quickly applied before she sighed with hesitant approval. Stepping quickly, she headed for the door.

Across town, the reputation of Jared McCabe, the busy lawyer in Walthem, was synonymous with success, his practice growing with additional clients and adding revenue to his business each year. A native of the town, he had many contacts, and most were repeat customers.

There is something women desire even more than good looks and physical prowess in a mate – the financial means for a comfortable life. In a single word: security. Now Jared was not the best-looking guy, but still, his prosperity was beginning to attract members of the opposite sex.

He looked at his watch and ducked into the lavatory to check his appearance for the third time. Jodi was expected to arrive within the next few minutes. Remaining single, Jared had been through several short-term relationships, but nothing serious. It was because he still longed for Jodi.

Jared, Jodi, and Sam were college friends, before he entered grad school. No one was formally dating back then, but Jodi and Sam were often goggle-eyed with each other, making Jared feel like the third wheel. Many times, he tried to capture her attention. To his eyes, she was smoking hot, and he often told her so, but his flirting didn't score. Perhaps this would finally be his chance to make a real impression. Afterall, Sam was losing now.

He pushed his glasses up high on his long, thin nose and patted the hair on the sides of his head, above his large ears. Too much bulk. He pushed a comb through and pressed it down again. He checked the part that was low on his scalp, allowing for a convincing comb-over, hardly noticeable to the undiscerning eye. Now, he would attempt to charm her with his smile, big gaudy, yellowish teeth.

A medium size sweater vest with a diamond pattern complimented his blue plaid shirt, highlighted by a navy neck tie. He pulled at it to loosen its choking grip on his throat.

A voice came from the intercom on his desk. It was the lobby receptionist. His 8:45 appointment had arrived. "Please, send Ms. Culp in. I'm expecting her."

++++

He met me with an exuberant greeting, "It's so good to see you again," and leaned in for a kiss. But I quickly ducked to avoid it. "You look great," he said.

I frowned, already feeling uneasy with the meeting.

"Can I offer you a drink, a coffee, water or…"

"I'm good. I'm a little pressed for time." I felt uneasy standing there and looked for a place to sit. An armchair was located in front of his desk.

"Yes, of course," he agreed, as he stepped toward his high back leather recliner. Pausing at the end of his desk he motioned toward the chair I should occupy. "Jodi, please, make yourself comfortable. I appreciate your promptness. I have a couple of big hearings. A hectic day."

"Thank you for taking the time to see me." I wanted to speak as a client, not as a friend. "I know you are a very busy lawyer."

"Yes, well, the work comes with the success I have achieved," he boasted. "But I am in control of my schedule. You know, I can take time off when I want to… to enjoy the good things in life."

I wondered at the implied meaning and his braggadocio's manner.

"I mean for pleasure. Dining. Travel. Entertainment."

Beginning to get his drift, I felt the need to use a little finesse at that moment. After all, this was Sam's attorney, his best chance. And I needed to motivate him.

"I'm happy for you, Jared. I can see that you have done well for yourself."

"Thank you," was his quick reply. "A long way from our college days."

Despite his self-centered nature, he stopped talking for a moment and looked at me with an intensity that immediately made me feel uncomfortable. I quickly glanced at the floor, needing to break his gaze, a connection I regarded as inappropriate and unwelcome. I wanted less lingering eye contact. As I studied the bottom of his desk I shifted in my chair and tapped my forefinger against the open palm of my left hand. It was more than a nervous twitch. But Jared, distracted by his own desire, missed my signal.

"I'm sorry," he offered after the pause. "How is Sam doing?"

That was my cue. Back on track. "Okay, I guess. I'm going to visit him at the jail soon. But why is he still there? In a jail cell, I mean." It was the question that dominated my mind all morning.

Obviously caught off guard, Jared stammered with his first word in reply, "D-d-delayed. They delayed the bail hearing. Judge Wilson, the magistrate assigned to Sam's case, tells me it is pressure from higher up."

"Higher up? What does that even mean?"

"I'm not sure. But it was within their prerogative to request a postponement. I think they can only delay for a few days," he offered. "Wilson did give me some assurance though," he looked at me, but I wasn't feeling positive about Sam being incarcerated. "They're keeping him safe at the local police station, using the holding cell there," he continued. "I'm sure he will be alone," he reached for better words, "I mean it will be private – that he won't have to share that space, or the building for that matter, with anyone else."

I wasn't getting his drift.

"Other inmates… perhaps even someone he sent to prison previously."

As I weighed the advantage or disadvantage of the situation, Jared continued. "You know Ken, and Chief Sabol. They're good men, as well as the other officer, Barney Billings – they will keep him comfortable. Probably doing take-out from Deb's Diner," he kept talking. "She's one hell of a cook… you know."

"Yeah, sure," My response was flat, monotone. "Sounds great." The sarcasm must have stung, because Jared was at a loss for words just then and the tone of the conversation shifted.

"I'm sorry."

"How bad is this, really?" I demanded.

"Rape is a first-degree felony. Twenty years."

I shifted in my chair and placed both feet firmly on the floor. The accusation was very serious.

"But highly unlikely," he interjected. "Even with his prior record, I believe they will be lenient."

"What are you saying," I nearly shouted. I felt an emotional surge and anger, but tried to remain calm. "His record was expunged. He is clean, totally clean. Not even a parking ticket."

"Oh yes, good. That is definitely in his favor."

I observed this lawyer looking long at his law degree, framed and hanging in a prominent place to his right, within my view. I wondered what he was thinking, or deciding in that awkward moment. What he said next was surprising.

"The Assistant D.A. who is prosecuting has already dropped an idea this morning," he paused to be sure I comprehended what he said. "They're just testing the water, mind you, nothing definite."

I felt another surge of emotion. What was he suggesting? It sounded grim.

"A plea bargain, you see. If they reduce the charge to sexual assault, it becomes a second-degree felony…"

"No!" I interrupted, surprising myself at the volume of my single word protest.

"Only ten years," he quickly interjected. "Probably out in five with good behavior."

There, he finally said it, and I was crushed. I wondered: *Am I meeting with a coy, arrogant lawyer who really doesn't care, or is this an old friend that we can trust? Aren't they all bottom-feeders anyway? Has our comrade been corrupted by the evils of the system he practices?* "No!" I shouted and clenched my fists instinctively. "Absolutely not!" After a pause to gain control, I continued, "I hope you're not serious about this?" Jared looked away. "Jared!"

"No." He spoke softly.

I saw him swallow hard, and strained to hear what he said next.

"I don't think Sam will go for it either."

"Jared! Whose side are you on…? Jared!?"

"Yours, I mean, his, of course?"

"Are you sure? Why would you even suggest such a thing?" His eyes became steely cold, almost enough to be intimidating.

"Well for one, I'm obligated to!" he asserted as he raised his voice.

"This isn't your idea, is it?" I focused my gaze, penetrating as a laser. I knew that my next shot had to hit the target. "You are on *our* side. You're Sam's lawyer, and his friend. For god's sake, Jared, we are counting on you!"

He nodded in agreement. "Of course."

"And Sam is innocent! You believe that, don't you?"

"What I believe really doesn't matter."

I sensed a tone of insincerity.

"I will do everything in my power to represent him brilliantly," Jared continued, "and establish his proclamation of innocence in a convincing legal defense for the verdict he deserves."

Deserves? I was disturbed at what became obvious to me just then: Jared's lacking of a deeper conviction. Innocent or guilty, it did matter what he thought. For me and Sam this was so much more than a legal procedure. Not just another case.

My mind reeled as I looked at Jared with a blank stare, and a memory came as a sudden flashback – another time when he was too close, arrogant, and offensive. It was back when we were still in college. I was alone with him then too, and felt trapped. I trembled slightly as I vividly recalled that uneasy feeling.

Sam and I had made plans to see a movie. I was new to Walthem, and he promised to surprise me after the show. I expected him to reveal a secret place from his past. I hoped it would be romantic. My expectations were high.

I remained on the sidewalk in front of the theater, near the ticket booth, long past the time Sam was expected. When it became obvious that he would be very late, I was disappointed but decided to enter the auditorium where I could wait a little longer.

A few minutes later, just before the movie began, Jared, Sam's roommate, stumbled in and sat next to me. He explained that Sam was stuck in the bathroom, sick to his stomach. Jared leaned in close. His breath smelled bad.

It was a disparaging evening, trying to maintain distance from an uninvited companion. Jared's intention became obvious: at one point he took my hand, then tried to embrace me, and hit on me repeatedly. I struggled to remain calm and be cordial, but nearly lost my patience.

Now it felt the same.

I spoke first.

"Do you have a copy of the complaint, the detailed arrest warrant?"

"Yes, of course." He reached toward the front of his desk and picked up a folder.

"May I see it?"

"I will make a copy for you. I already have one for Sam, for our next session."

I eyed him, wondering if he would provide the papers at that very moment.

"I'll have my secretary make a copy," he clarified, "but I can tell you what's in it. Do you have any questions?"

"Yes. Loads of them."

"They met at Sal's Alehouse," he hesitated, "you know the basics, I assume."

I nodded, although what I thought I knew was very sketchy.

"Well, Faith…"

He cleared his throat and I could see that he was becoming uncomfortable with dictating from the report.

"She claims they went to her apartment together to look at an affidavit from her brother who resides in Westmoreland County," he offered. "The guy is in some serious trouble."

I didn't care about her brother. I needed more on Sam. What did he supposedly do, once he got there?

"Faith claims she was drugged and fell asleep after a struggle."

He hesitated again, I sensed his reluctance to continue, but then kept reading, silently. He seemed to be searching the document for a specific detail. I waited impatiently.

"Sam was choking her, or something like that, before she lost consciousness, or awareness."

"Now Jared, you can't believe that!!" I interrupted. "Choking - Sam? Come on now, you know him better than that."

"I'm just telling you what is in the arrest warrant."

He paused and I realized that I had to calm myself. I had to take it down a few notches.

"Faith woke up and realized she had been assaulted, sexually. Sam was still sleeping, so she fled."

"Yeah, right!"

"Before she left, she saw a pill bottle that apparently fell out of his pants pocket."

Jared grimaced at the next detail. Finally, I realized how difficult this was for him.

"Sam was unclothed. The bottle lay on the floor next to his pants. She grabbed it and took it with her to the police station," he swallowed hard again. "Guess she figured she needed it for evidence."

"Oh, the poor thing!" I exclaimed, "Traumatized but acting so precisely. A bit of a contradiction, don't you think?"

"Maybe," Jared admitted, "it does seem a little suspicious, but his prints are also on the bottle."

"I think she used the drug on Sam! Did you consider that?"

"But why would she do that? It doesn't make any sense. And, they have been together before…"

"I know that! I already know, Jared, that they were dating once before."

"Maybe…" he hesitated and swallowed hard again, "Maybe it was just an indiscretion on Sam's part. I think he still has the hots for her…"

"You're saying that he is two-timing… on me?"

"It could have been mostly innocent, then somehow got out of control," Jared suggested. "And the drug… I don't know, maybe they both wanted to get high… but she must have gotten really pissed off, or jealous about you, to yell rape."

I wasn't buying it, and by my response, Jared knew that he was losing the argument.

"Maybe she wanted a commitment from him and by refusing, he insulted her?"

"Really?!?"

"Jodi, she had some rough sex. The evidence of that is indisputable. The police took her to the hospital where she was examined." He blushed. "I, I don't want to get into the details of their report. But they said it looked like an assault."

"No! No, no, no. I don't believe any of it!"

"So… what are you suggesting?"

"That he was framed! Isn't that obvious to you? Sam was framed; he had to be."

"You're saying that Sam is the victim?"

Jared was shaking his head slowly as he squeezed his chin between his thumb and the forefinger of his right hand. "But why? And framed by Faith? I don't get it – what does she have to gain?" He dropped the report onto his desk. "Sam isn't saying much. He isn't giving me anything to work with… says he doesn't know."

Jared saw my glare and relented from the criticism.

"If it's blackmail," he suggested, "well, how does that work, now that everyone already knows… but I guess she could withdraw her charge if he pays."

"He doesn't have any money! And what do you mean, he doesn't know?" I wanted to call him an idiot, or something worse just then, but bit my lower lip instead. I was thinking out loud, my thoughts racing for answers. I needed something to reassure, more than that, motivate that attorney for my boyfriend's defense, because he just didn't seem to be convinced of Sam's innocence. But in truth, and I hate to admit it, the seeds of doubt were planted in my mind just then. I pushed them back, into the recesses of my brain. I wasn't willing to give Jared's suggestion of Sam being unfaithful any real consideration, at least not yet, not then. "What if she is working for someone else, someone with a grudge against Sam?" I blurted, surprising myself with the suggestion.

++++

And their questions hung in the air heavy with contention. Sam – an aggressor or the victim? Faith – a former lover rejected anew and once again full of rage, or, something else? These questions simply lingered there, unanswered.

There was the "why" and the "who," the reason for the charges against Sam and the question raised by Jodi's new suggestion, the possibility of a third person being involved.

The inquiry remained unanswered, a lingering mystery to their defense.

++++

"Faith was tested," Jared continued. "A tox screen. There was still a minuscule amount of the drug in her system, along with alcohol and a little tetrahydrocannabinol. That's cannabis," he informed.

Again silence.

"And did they test Sam?" I finally asked with a glare that penetrated through the fog of my despair. Another moment passed with no response from Jared. "I better get going," I blurted. "When can I pick up the papers?" I stood, waiting for the answer that would conclude our stressful conversation.

Jared darted from behind the desk. "Jodi, I really am very sorry. I wish I had better news. It's her word against his. A 'he said - she said'. And they have evidence."

I could no longer contain my emotions. Tears welled in my eyes, blurring my vision.

"Don't worry," Jared offered, "we'll beat this."

He reached for a hug and I pushed him away. I wasn't convinced.

"I'll get the papers you requested, and, I'll bring them to you," he suggested.

With a huff I began to turn away.

"Let's meet for a coffee, or lunch," he offered next. "Someplace less formal, relaxed, I mean more casual."

He seemed to be rambling on and on. I had lost my concentration.

"I want to hear more of your ideas. Maybe you know something I don't."

The comment was meant to challenge me. "Maybe," I answered with regret. I turned for the door.

"I'll call," Jared said.

I stiffened my back, raised my firmly set jaw with clenched teeth, and departed, anger obvious in my stride. At least I hoped that my disgust was fully on display. I had had my fill. This guy was obnoxious.

I grabbed some groceries and returned home before going to see Sam. I considered taking a quick nap but when I got the mail an unusual letter, a small envelope, aroused my curiosity. It was addressed to Samuel Urban, C/O Jodi Culp. I decided that I should take it to the jailed magistrate. It might contain information relevant to his arrest.

The police station was housed in an old cinderblock building with a new facade. Years past it was used as a garage, but had been remodeled several times since then.

Officer Ken Kapish, the newest recruit on the force, was sitting at a large gray metal desk and greeted Jodi as soon as she opened the front door. He appeared to be alone; a scanner chattering in the background. In this small town he knew just about everyone.

++++

"Hi Jodi. You doin' okay?"

"Best as can be expected." I was not about to expose myself and wasn't in the mood for conversation.

"Here to see Sam?"

 I nodded.

"I was expecting so. Tell you what… I've got an extra chair. How about we just take it into the cell room. You two can have a private chat that way."

"Thanks, Ken. I appreciate it."

When the door to the cell block opened Sam looked up quickly. It seemed that he was hoping for a visitor. He smiled broadly as soon as he set his eyes on me. His thick, dark brown hair was a little disheveled; the shadow of a light beard outlined his square jaw. Even at his worst, I thought he was very handsome. His forehead was one of distinction, framed all around by a prominent hair line, including long sideburns. His torso was triangular, broad shoulders, small waist. This young man was buff in all the right places. Even there, in that forlorn place, I felt a connection, and the heat of passion.

Ken unlocked the door to his cage and the bars swung outward. I stepped inside and Sam grabbed me in a tight embrace. I stiffened and looked away.

I saw Ken flush with envy. If I could read his mind, he was likely feeling jealous. I had seen that look many times before. It may sound a bit vain, but I know that I have many young male admirers and apparently, Ken was secretly one of them.

He placed the metal chair in the hallway, the cell door remaining open. As he exited the cell block, the deadbolt on the steel entry door clanked loudly.

I sat on the cot next to Sam and was the first to speak. "How could you?"

"I didn't touch her. Really! I didn't do it."

"Tell me what happened."

"She left the room. I felt groggy. I sat down. The lights went out."

I frowned with displeasure at the lack of detail. I wanted to believe him, but he wasn't giving me enough. "Sam, do you still care for her?"

"What?! You've got to be kidding me. No! No way!!"

But I sensed that he was hiding something? I needed to know more, a concise accounting of every minute while they were together. "I mean, maybe she still means something to you… Does she still love you? Sam, was it consensual?"

"Come on Jodi," he was beginning to get angry. "I already told you. I didn't have sex with her." He cleared his throat. "When I woke up, she was gone. I got dressed and went home. I didn't know what happened, so, I figured I'd just wait for her to call me."

++++

Sam avoided saying *her* name, so that he wouldn't establish a connection to *her*, the other woman, at least not then, in the presence of his 'sweetheart'. But Jodi was already feeling suspicious of him and Faith, a former girlfriend.

++++

"Did she?"

"No, two days later the police called instead. At my office."

"But you really don't remember what happened?" I persisted.

"I guess there is a blank spot. But I think I just fell asleep."

"But you must have thought something happened!" My temper flared. "Why would you just walk away?"

"Jodi, I didn't know what to do. I know it looked bad. But I would never be unfaithful to you. I needed time to figure it all out."

"How much did you have to drink that night?"

"No," he paused, "No! Only a couple of beers."

"You sure?"

"Yes!"

He nearly shouted at me, his eyebrows raised, his face contorted.

"Jodi, I wasn't anywhere near being drunk."

Then he became quiet for a moment. I held my breath, expecting him to admit something terrible.

"Sal's daughter was serving that night. I bet she can verify it."

Sam's expression grew distant and I suspected that he may have remembered more, or was finally willing to be honest. Faith was a former lover. Had he hoped to hook-up with her again? Was he telling me the whole truth? I was beginning to have my doubts.

"You know, it was a little strange," he continued. "She, I mean Faith, approached me to ask for help with her brother's court case. I noticed that she had a glass in her hand but wasn't drinking. I finished one and offered to buy her a second, but she hadn't touched her first one yet. I bet the bartender noticed that too."

"I'm not sure that is relevant."

"Maybe not, but out of character for her," Sam suggested. "She wasn't her usual self. Seemed a little nervous, or something."

++++

The natural light in the narrow hallway dimmed as a thick cloud covered the sun outside. With it, hope was fading for the couple inside. They sat there, loosely holding each other's hand, not knowing what to say next. Jodi's was slipping away.

++++

"What am I going to do? How am I going to get out of this?" In his despondency, Sam seemed even desperate.

"I went to see Jared." I tried to sound cheerful. "But I'm not sure he's got you covered."

Sam returned a blank stare.

"Really! … I have my doubts about him."

"Oh no," Sam disagreed. "Jared knows the law. He's good." He raised his head to make eye contact. "Yeah! He's the best. I trust him."

"Well, I'm glad you do." I said with sarcasm.

"What do you mean?"

"Well, for one… I am sick and tired of him hitting on me!"

As Sam looked away, our dilemma became empowered by an awkward silence. Uncertainty and separation.

Then, I suddenly felt sorry for him and my mood shifted. Negativity was getting us nowhere. Jared was just being a jerk, no, more than that, a scoundrel. I didn't like him, never really did.

I knew that I had to stay positive. I quickly decided to reaffirm my commitment, take Sam's side, and stay faithful to him. It was natural. We had history. They had little proof. I wasn't ready to condemn him, no, not just yet. We had been close, still were. I always knew him to be a truthful and sincere person.

"You're a kind, even merciful man, Samuel Urban," I attempted to raise the bar. "God has not abandoned you. He has your reward."

"I don't think so," Sam replied. "I only wish that I could believe that stuff. I don't think there is a god that cares two bits about me."

"Yeah, I know the feeling…" I had to be honest. "But I thought it was worth a try."

"Thanks. Guess it was a good attempt at optimism. But I'm not feeling it.

Sam smiled, but the moment of relief was fleeting. He hesitated and spoke with greater intensity.

"I've had some time to think in here. It doesn't look good for me… maybe I deserve to be punished."

His eyes became dull, almost lifeless.

"What do you mean?"

"The life I took. It was reckless, irresponsible. Yeah, I caught a lucky break back then, but I didn't deserve it. What does the Good Book say? Whatsoever a man soweth, that shall he also reap."

As he looked at me, I sensed the terror that gripped at his soul.

"Something like that," he concluded.

"Come on, you don't believe in that stuff either," I said somewhat teasingly. "Karma, maybe."

"You see, that's what I mean."

"Sorry my friend, I'm not going to join your pity party. Come on, you know the law. You have to figure out how to help yourself."

He didn't answer.

"Come on, Sam!"

"Yes, you're right, I have to get my head straight. So, what's next?"

"I'm going to go and see the district attorney. I'm not giving up. I will do anything, and everything I can do, to help you." But I wasn't sure of myself. Was I lying? Exaggerating?

"But the D.A.? Do you think that is a good idea?"

"I don't know, what do we have to lose?" And then I remembered the note that came in the mail. I dug through my purse until I found it and handed it over to Sam.

"Another one." He seemed to recognize it. "And this was sent to you?"

"Guess you can't get mail in here."

"True enough. Did you read it?"

"It's addressed to you."

"No, it has both of our names on it."

And Sam began to share his confidential mail with me. As I watched him open the envelope, many questions formed in my mind. *He has others like this? Why hasn't he shared them? Do I deserve this revealing? Relationships are so complicated. Is this because I'm being affirmed by him, even as his soul mate? Can he truly trust me?* I didn't know the answers – I didn't even know if I could trust myself. How could he?

++++

It said:

"Allow unanswered questions to persist, but quiet their demands. Be humble, not dogmatic."

"Rejection comes when we listen to man. Healing comes when we return to Truth and are fulfilled in the companionship of its spirit. Seek intimacy, not authority."

"To be lost is a state of dwelling in anxiety and fear. To be found is to have calm, even if you still do not have all the answers you need."

"Find mercy to triumph over judgment – it always wins in the end."

"Your Advocate."

Two Days Later: A young woman lies on her sofa, crying softly to herself. She is in a fetal position. All that she has hoped for seems to be lost. She is full of regret. The many decisions that brought her to this point seem ill-fated.

CHAPTER THREE: Prosecuted

Friday, May 10, 1985 - day three.

HEADLINE: **"Urban Still on Ballot – Voters Will Decide"**

Alone in his cell, with nothing but time on his hands, Sam began thinking about those who might want to have revenge on him. Was he framed because of a grudge nurtured by someone he sent to jail? Sam knew that hate was a powerful motivator and could be the reason for the attack, planned by someone wanting war, driven by scorn. He began to take inventory of his courtroom cases.

Domestic disputes and civil suits were the most difficult to resolve. The law was often vague, although its intent obvious: a resolution agreeable to both parties. Plaintiffs pressed hard. Much seemed to hinge on the judge's opinion. Sam always tried to lead the opposing parties in a case to an amicable compromise. But for those that stood before his bench, it was an emotional game of cat and mouse. The question was: who would get caught? Sometimes common sense prevailed, but often someone's feelings and their reaction to an accusation from the other side clouded clear thinking. Negotiations stalled. The person offended in court usually felt scorned. He, or she, then became stubborn, obstinate, and immovable. Many blamed the judge for their misfortune as he decreed with an outcome they refused to accept.

Mr. and Mrs. Peterson were among the worst. It was rumored that he had had an affair with her sister, out of town. Their marriage was in divorce court. He pressed for his property rights and she filed a restraining order against her estranged husband. They both broke the rules and their war raged on and on. They owned a small business in town on Main Street, a nostalgic movie theatre. Legally they were partners. That was more fertile ground for dispute after dispute, suit after suit, and many hostile arguments before Judge Urban.

He sincerely tried to remain neutral but Mr. Peterson eventually concluded that Urban took his wife's side. The disturbed man even made threats. And Peterson was a councilman who held the seat for many years. He had the resources to hurt Sam if he so desired.

But now, the couple's war seemed to have stalled, or they were observing a cease fire of some sort. Sam had not seen either of them for many months.

Obviously, there was Faith to consider. How did she get involved? Sam attempted to analyze the facts he knew to be true. Did her beau, Luke, her live-in boyfriend of the past five years, put her up to it? But why would he?

Faith and Luke were also frequent flyers in Sam's courtroom. They were brought in on a charge of possessing an illegal substance, less than an ounce of marijuana. Judge Urban slapped their wrists and sent them to clean the town park. Next, Luke began to deal narcotics and was arrested for selling pills to high school students. Sam's hands were tied. The accused had been caught red-handed and the evidence against him was overwhelming. Sam's role was to rule if the case had enough merit to continue to county court. If it were only possible, this judge would have given his old friend yet another break. Even Luke seemed to understand Sam's predicament, but Faith did not.

After Luke was sent to prison Faith attacked Sam, accosting, and assaulting him publicly. With words and fists.

She accused him of driving drunk, said he was a threat to the public, and that he was addicted to pot. Her criticisms were loudly stated, for all to hear. It was another memorable evening at Sal's.

Everyone watched intently as Sam tried to quiet her. He approached her gently but when he got close enough, she slugged him, a fist punch to his face. Sam's nose began to bleed and he grabbed for the napkin holder as panic began to rise in the pub.

Faith shouted that Sam was not qualified to be the judge of them, or to send Luke to prison.

To Sam's merit, he kept his cool. Once he realized that Faith would not be managed, he made a quick exit.

That incident busied the townsfolk who talked about it for many months. Sam even became the target of some teasing and cat-calls, labeling him as a traitor, chicken, or lover boy. ("Ha, ha.")

Now, some were saying that he assaulted Faith to get even for the public humiliation he suffered that night.

Luke began serving his time, but with an endorsement from a prominent clergyman in town, Father Jacob Jackson, the convict quickly got out on parole for good behavior. It was a year ago when Luke and Faith quickly reunited.

Everyone involved in the case now seemed to be amicable toward Sam, but was an old grudge reason enough to frame him? More prominent in Sam's mind was: *why would anyone, especially the authorities, believe her?* Luke and Faith were generally considered with ill repute, and were disrespected by the police. *They aren't capable of pulling off such a scheme,* he reasoned.

And so, their quest began. Sam and Jodi needed to learn how and why he became vulnerable to be charged with sexual assault, if was he framed, and who was the mastermind behind it all.

Sam needed to be exonerated.

Then suddenly, he had a thought. He shared secrets with Faith in their past, the time of their youth. She was vulnerable too. Sam grabbed his notebook and jotted down a few words, and circled them. Faith would know what they meant.

++++

I greeted the morning reluctantly, facing another day of stressful meetings and interviews about Sam's case. I felt a tinge of resentment, knowing that I was doing all the hard work while Sam sat on his butt in the police station. It seemed that everyone was catering to him now, and he better not be enjoying it!

I faced the mirror of horrors once again. Never my friend, I secretly longed for a peaceful resolution of my battle with the reflection of my face, self-esteem losing badly at that moment. But age, well, it is a formidable foe and I knew that it is a young woman's worse adversary. And this day I would contend with one superior to myself, a female working hard to climb the ladder of success.

++++

This person was ruthless, and winning was the only acceptable outcome for her while building a stellar reputation. She clenched the authority of her office with a firm grasp for the power it provided. She battered her opponent, showing little concern for justice. She was outcome driven. Truth was not her ally. It didn't matter.

She was the District Attorney.

She aspired to someday be appointed as a judge in the Federal Court. Who could know, maybe one day it would be the U.S. Supreme Court!

Sam often talked about the process. A two-term district attorney, that person elected by a huge majority, was in line to fill a vacancy in the county for the position of judge, the person that oversees jury trials and rules on cases sent there by the magistrates.

++++

I sighed as I dropped my lipstick, realizing that that was where Sam would end up, in full view of the public, in a major trial that would get lots of publicity. How could I bear it?

I reached into my closet for my best suit, a tight skirt and well-fitted jacket that came to the waistline, all in a navy pinstripe on beige. Thankfully, it was there, hanging against the wall. I yanked the hanger off the rod to examine the outfit. I wore it once since it was laundered; I think it was to a class reunion. I brushed some lint off the shoulders. It probably needed dry cleaning again, but I could get away with using it one more time.

I'd seen the D.A. on tv many times. She is a looker, tall and beautiful, a brunette with long hair and eyes that match its color. Intelligent. Accomplished. But Sam always said that physically I was her match, a contender, and now I was determined to rise to the occasion as I confronted the captain of our adversary's team.

I reached into a small jewelry box that sat on top of my dresser and lifted out my gold necklace, a small cross dangling on a thin chain. I always regarded the necklace as a personal reminder of one's beliefs, a symbol of their faith. But the necklace was popular among more than the religious types, and for others, the Christian implication might not be relatable, maybe even offensive.

I wondered what the D.A. would think about it. Would it send a subtle message?

The clerk at the jewelry store where I bought it said it was for those who believed in saving power. Surely, we, I mean Sam and I, needed that.

She said the cross necklace was therapeutic for those oppressed with heavy hearts. Surely, that was me.

"Take up your cross, and follow Me."

They are God's words. As I placed the chain around my neck, I paused to reflect on their meaning.

"Deny yourself."

I am hoping for a better life… a new life. I think the cross is the gateway… *But how can I attain it?*

"I am the resurrection and the life."

Could it be Him? It must be a gift from the Savior.

I decided to wear it. Perhaps it means that the Lord is with me… or that I am, or should be, dependent on Him?

After struggling with the clasp, I glanced once more into the mirror. Well, it is what it is, that is, I am what I am. But the necklace looked nice dangling on my green turtleneck. Seeing it there, I felt a tinge hopeful; perhaps I wasn't all alone after all.

I turned for the door.

My car, a 1982 Oldsmobile Cutlass Supreme, was parked in the large lot reserved for townhouse owners, in my usual spot, number 27. The sun was shining brightly, the buds on the dogwood were swelling, and off in the distance I heard the sound of a lawn mower, executing the first cutting of the season. In that moment, as I paused to absorb my surroundings, all seemed peaceful. What could go wrong with this delightful day?

It wasn't long until I found out.

I placed the key into the car's ignition and turned it. **Click, click**. "What's this?" I turned the key again as I pressed harder. **Click**… and then one fainter, …**click**. "You've got to be kidding me." I turned the key again. This time, nothing. No grunt, no grind, not even a click. My car was dead.

I let loose a long sigh while I squeezed the steering wheel with both hands. I looked out the windshield and noticed a robin carrying a twig to the nest it was constructing in the flowering cherry tree that blossomed in a grassy plot, the space between the rows of cars. An expectant mother… humph!

I looked to my left. No one. Then to my right, I observed a young man in tight jeans and a sleeveless t-shirt opening the tailgate of his pickup truck. I exited my car as quickly as possible and ran to him. He looked like a shady character, a brute. But what choice did I have?

"Excuse me," I pleaded.

He stopped and glared at me. I felt his assessment, checking me out, his eyes moving up and down. He paused at the slit in my skirt and licked his lips. But I'm sure that wasn't intentional.

"I'm sorry to bother you," I continued with a flirtatious smile. "My car is dead."

He returned a look of bewilderment, like what was *he* supposed to do about it.

"It's right over there." I pointed to the light blue sedan. "It's the Oldsmobile."

He nodded.

"I think I need a jump." My mind reeled when I realized what I had just said.

Come on Jodi, you have to do better than that. Like, ask him to help you restart your car because the battery is apparently dead... or something less suggestive.

He was smiling. I waited anxiously for his answer. "Do you have jumper cables?" I added quickly.

He finally broke his silence. "I think I know you. You're in the end unit, aren't you?"

I nodded reluctantly. Why did he have to know where I live?

"And your boyfriend is the magistrate?"

I didn't answer. I didn't know where he was going with that question. Maybe Sam had thrown him in jail. I began to panic.

"And he's the one in big trouble, isn't he?"

"Yea. I'm on my way to the courthouse to see the District Attorney," I fussed. "He's innocent, you know…"

"Oh yeah, I'm sure he is."

The guy began warming up to me, although, I wasn't cherishing the chance to get to know him. If he was a neighbor, I didn't care.

"I've heard that he's a good judge. Got my buddies off."

Thank goodness – a positive outcome from Sam.

He stood for a moment and looked toward my car. "Yeah, I can jump start your car. Go get into it," he instructed. "I'm going to pull alongside, close, so the cables will reach. Roll down your window so I can tell you what to do."

"Thank you." Luckily, he was a gentleman, of sorts. "I really appreciate it." I was relieved to return to the driver's seat. I heard his Ford F150 roar to life and watched in the rearview mirror as it approached my vehicle. With the truck vibrating on its chassis nearly close enough to bump my door handle, I saw the driver jump out and come to the front of my Oldsmobile. After some fiddling, he lifted the hood. It screeched as it went up, blocking my view.

"No wonder it won't start," he leaned toward me from the front fender. "Your battery cable is loose." He mumbled something more.

"What did you say?"

"Looks like sabotage. It's obvious that someone has recently had a wrench on this battery."

"What? Really?" I returned the innocent look of one not responsible for such misfortune. *Play the role of the victim.*

"Hold on, I'll get the tools I need."

My car wobbled and after what seemed like a long time of near silence, I heard him mumble something again.

"Try it now."

I turned the key and the engine of the Cutlass roared to life, purring immediately.

"I think you're good to go." The hood came down with a loud thud that shook my car.

I was already rooting through my purse and found a five-dollar bill. I held it out the open window. "Here, take this for your trouble," I offered in reward as he stepped away. "I really appreciate it." I hoped he would take the cash. I didn't want to owe him anything. No paybacks.

"No problem," he paused at his door. "I really didn't do anything. You have a good day now, Miss. And good luck to the judge."

"Thanks again."

"I mean it. I really hope he beats it. A bum rap." He hopped into his truck. "I voted for him before, and I'm going to vote for him again."

"Thanks," my voice trailed off, drowned out by the rumbling of his v-8 engine as he backed away.

I looked at my wrist watch. I intended to see Sam for a quick visit before going to the D.A.'s office. Now, the remaining time was short. I knew that if I was late, I would miss my chance to meet with the D.A. Yeah, it was going to be too close. Poor Sam.

I decided to stop downtown at a boutique store that carried Avon cosmetics. Its location was less than two blocks from the courthouse. But I had to be quick. Eighteen minutes later I was looking for a parking space. I slowed my car to a crawl and coasted past the store. The driver behind me laid on his horn and swerved to pass abruptly, nearly clipping my rear bumper. *What the hell?* I ignored his rude gesture. There, three cars ahead, was an empty space. Relieved to be parked, I stood at the meter and searched in my purse for some loose change. *Why can't you ever find a quarter when you need it?*

The boutique was already busy with several customers and the owner was intent on convincing a large woman with auburn dyed hair to buy some collector bottles of cologne. I looked through the rack for the foundation I preferred. They were sold out of my color. *What the...?* My patience was wearing thin. *Well, guess I will have to settle for the next closest thing.* The register rang and we completed the transaction without exchanging a word. Her other customer was relentless on dominating the counter.

When I returned to my car, I noticed it leaning toward the street. I went to the rear of the vehicle and sure enough, the driver side tire was as flat as a pancake.

"This is unbelievable." I referenced my watch again. *"What next?!"*

I went back into the store and stood behind the auburn woman, impatiently waiting for a break in their conversation that was now seasoned with local gossip. Finally, the owner/clerk looked at me.

"Can I use your phone?" agitation was evident in my voice. "I have a flat tire. I'd like to call for a tow," I paused, "or whatever." I was fuming now.

Without saying a word, the nice lady slid a countertop phone toward me.

I found the card in my wallet for roadside assistance, AAA, and reluctantly dialed the number.

"How long will it take?" I blushed as I listened to the reply. "I can't wait that long."

I listened again.

"Well, what do you suggest I do?"

The clerk looked my way, curious about what she was overhearing.

"What if I leave my car keys here in the store?" I suggested with an inquiring look to the clerk who nodded with approval.

"Now wait, you're going to do what?"

Another pause.

"So, you have to tow it then?" I shook my head in disapproval. I asked for a pen and pencil and wrote down the address of the garage. But I'd have to get a cab if they towed my car. Unbelievable!

"Jodi. My name is Jodi Culp. Yes, an Oldsmobile… yes. Light blue. A Cutlass Supreme… yes," and I listened some more. "So… why can't he just change the tire here? I have a good spare in the trunk, and I'll check in with you after my appointment."

A long pause.

"I have to get to the courthouse very soon. I have an appointment, an important meeting…. Yes, I can walk from here," I informed reluctantly. "Listen, I'll leave my membership card with the store clerk."

With one ear on her customer, the store owner again nodded in approval, interest rising, obvious by the look on her face. Her glances were shifting back and forth now, between auburn and me.

"I'm at 554 Summit Ave. My car is parked out front. Okay, yes… Okay!" and I rolled my eyes in frustration. "Thank you. Yes, that should work quite nicely. Thank you!" I quickly placed the handset on the phone.

"Did you get that," I asked the clerk, interrupting auburn, and not caring if I appeared to be a little rude. I couldn't wait any longer.

"Excuse me," the clerk said politely to her talkative friend after the other woman huffed loud enough for me to hear her expression of disapproval. The clerk remained calm.

"Yes," she answered as she turned toward me, "I'll watch for the tow truck. You go now. I'll be here when you get back."

"Thank you. Thank you, so much…" I whispered in her ear as she patted the top of my hand. "This day is just unbelievable. First, my car wouldn't start. My neighbor said it was sabotage. Now this? Doesn't seem like a coincidence…"

"Try to relax," she interrupted. "It's my pleasure, Honey. I want to help. I know who you are."

"Really?"

"The district attorney's office is corrupt. Political. Power mongers."

She surprised me with the assertion.

"I hope Urban humiliates them all. It is wrong what they are doing to him."

Dumfounded by her comment, I smiled as I placed my membership card and car key on the counter and gathered myself. "Well thank you. Again, thank you so very much!" I was touched by her kindness. I squinted to hold back tears. The trauma of just getting to the courthouse had nearly beaten me, but the words from this stranger bolstered my confidence. Still, could it really have been sabotage? Could this delay have been someone's intention?

Now my appointment was in just ten minutes. I sprinted across the town square. *Damn. What the hell is going on?* I quickly stepped aside to avoid a collision with another pedestrian. *How could this happen to my car... two times broken down!? This just cannot be coincidental.*

++++

The courthouse was the only building positioned in the center of the city block at 100 Main Street. It was surrounded by lawns and landscaping, had a walkway around the perimeter, and memorials on each side. The architecture was gothic and from a distance the appearance of the building resembled a church. The stone and granite cathedral had an elevated section angled on one end, perhaps originally a steeple, but after renovations it resembling a tower, more like that of a castle: a bastion of justice, dictating legislative authority. Or so it seemed.

I charged up the granite steps and through the huge brass doors. The D.A.'s office was located on the ground floor, among other agencies designated by plaques that protruded from above large wooden, paneled doors.

I paused at the reception desk. Standing there, I shifted on my feet and looked at my watch once more. Only two minutes late.

"May I help you?" the receptionist finally asked without lifting her head.

"Jodi Culp. I have an appointment with the DA... Ms. Conway."

She sorted through an array of stick-em notes at the edge of her desk. "Okay, I have your name here. The waiting room is on your left," she instructed in monotone, still not making eye contact. "Ms. Conway will meet you there."

The greeting was so impersonal that it made me feel insignificant, even slightly intimated. I had to admit to myself that I was out of my league. I didn't care what Sam said about me being a contender.

Six minutes later, an attractive tall woman, probably in her early thirties, approached without swagger, a hand extended. She wore a black pants suit and a white silk blouse opened immodestly. She acknowledged me. "Ms. Culp, I assume?"

Her hair was thick and parted on one side, combed over her forehead. First impression – good: successful, capable, wealthy, educated, strong, refined, resourceful – yes, very intimidating.

I accepted her handshake, limp as it was, swallowed hard, and answered, "Nice to meet you."

"Please, come into my office."

I followed her into a large room with huge windows that afforded a pleasant view of the gardens outside. The D.A. gestured toward a wooden chair as she stood behind her desk, arms folded.

"Ms. Culp," she began, "I reluctantly agreed to see you. You know, there isn't much I can tell you. Details about our prosecution are confidential… you understand?"

"Yes, of course. I just have a couple of general questions."

"If I can."

"Well, for one, are you aware of the history of the accused… Sam," I cleared my throat, "has with the alleged victim?" I paused as I wrung my hands. They were sweaty. "Faith is his former girlfriend."

"What exactly do you mean?"

+++

Jodi began to feel nervous, her face burning, over-heated after being slapped by the unwelcome tension already evident between them.

++++

"They were together in the past. They were a couple," I explained, as if she didn't already know.

"And…" Conway, still standing, shifted on her feet, spread apart in a bold stance. Battle ready. "Please be clear. Just what are you implying?"

"They had consensual sex," I nearly blurted.

"And how do you know that?"

"Sam told me. We don't have any secrets."

"Do you mean before, or now?"

++++

She grinned, but the look on her face was sly, that of a master manipulator. In the courthouse, she was their queen.

++++

"At least you hope that he is telling you the truth, and telling you *all* of it… even some of his dirty little secrets?" she suggested.

Yeah, she was smug. I took offense and had a difficult time concealing it.

"Ms. Culp, I have another meeting. If you have some relevant information, then please, stop beating around the bush."

My response was at first non-verbal and the resentment I felt was showing. I thought the meaning of my statement was obvious. Guess not. "They were active for many years before," I bleated.

"Oh, you mean that it was consensual in the past?"

She raised her voice. Her tone was stern.

"Consensual, you say… that they were welcoming to each other… is that you're meaning?"

I nodded reluctantly.

"So, your premise is that it also had to have been consensual on the night of," she paused and looked at a paper on her desk, "the night of April 29, the time of the alleged crime?"

"Isn't that obvious? That is, if they even did have sex that night."

"No!" she shouted. "It isn't obvious."

The D.A. paused, and I could almost sense the engine that worked in her head accelerating, its pistons ramming fast and hard against the valves and everything heating up.

"Does past privilege give license now… when he is in a relationship with someone else?"

She paused again for emphasis and her technique was having an effect on me. Unnerving. My pulse quickened. I felt the accusation and could not answer – I only glared in return.

"And I believe that *someone else,* is you? Is that correct?"

She raised her right hand and pointed directly at me, her left hand on her hip, appearing like a Mama scolding her child. It hurt. Again, I couldn't speak as great humiliation fell upon me.

++++

And there it was: the insinuation that Urban was a predator, that Jodi knew it and that she was letting him use her for her own benefit. The insult hurt like hell.

++++

"Ms. Culp, are you aware of the brutality of the crime that the victim endured?" She continued without waiting for my response. "The victim, I can tell you, without divulging anything confidential… it's all in the arrest report… had contusions on her face, consistent with a blow to her head, and on her neck, indicative of strangling. And, had marks on her shoulders as if she was forcibly held down! I believe she put up a fight in her defense as she resisted his sexual assault."

The D.A. looked intently at me and mercilessly continued her prosecution of the case.

"After a thorough examination by medical professionals it appears to not, I repeat, not have been 'consensual,' in fact, it looks like a violent act… and there is bruising in the vagina."

She pressed the point, running fast for her homerun.

"It was a criminal act, a brutal assault, **rape**! And the state intends to fully prosecute the person guilty of this horrendous crime."

"He didn't do it," I whimpered. "He said he didn't touch her."

"What? What did you say?" she cross directed. "Excuse me. **I can't hear you!**"

She was yelling at me now. "I said," I nearly shouted in return, "I said, **he didn't do it!**"

Her response was quick, even impulsive. "He's lying!"

+++

A tenuous ceasefire halted their arguing momentarily. The two women paused there, face to face, scowling at each other. It might have been one heck of a catfight, but they were too dignified to become physical and restrained themselves to heckling with words that cut deeper than claws.

++++

"He is falsely accused then?"

She wouldn't let it go. My lips pursed, I took a deep breath and blew it out of my nostrils with an obvious sound of frustration. But it had a calming effect on me. "He was framed," I said, almost polite. My adrenaline had surged and I was already headed back down, a crash imminent.

"Framed!? Is that your theory? That's what your defense will be? And framed by who?"

++++

A big cat on the prowl, the kill was within her clutches, the reminiscent taste of blood already tantalizing her senses. It was the demise of her opponent she enjoyed even more than the spectacle of the drama.

++++

She demanded more information, but I had none. Now completely rattled, I looked away. I had the thought, a fright, that maybe I was saying too much, giving them something that would assist them in their prosecution.

"So… he gets *another* **free pass**!? That's what you're willing to give him?"

That statement was obviously cloaked in malice. "No!" I stood to my feet. "He didn't do it. He was framed!"

Conway shook her head. "No. That isn't indicated by the testimony of the victim, or the evidence. Besides, who would frame your boyfriend, and why?"

"I don't know."

"Motive!"

She shouted at me again. She was a merciless creature full of anger and hate. But why did she despise *me*? A feminist, yeah, but willing to viciously attack her own kind? Why did she have to degrade me so?

"I need motive before I will even consider it for one second."

"I don't know who, or why, but someone framed him…" And that was all I had. Turning toward the door, I glanced back and meekly concluded, "Thank you."

"Yes, we are done here," she confirmed. "Thank you for coming in today."

She smirked at me again as I ran for the door. I stumbled but caught my balance before falling; a full face in her plush carpet would have been most gratifying for the bitch. It was dirty, just like her. And more so, that would have been humiliating even beyond the devastation I experienced in that horrific moment.

I made it to the portico and found a bench before nearly collapsing. I sat for a moment and tried to gather my thoughts. Inside, I was full of rage, ready to explode. I had not known about the victim's injuries. How could Sam not know what happened?

It was worse than I could have imagined. The insults cut deep, taking me to a place where my heart was about to burst. I felt like I was bleeding out, as if my life was draining away. I cried softly, knowing it was for my loss.

One fact seemed irrefutable just then. I was in serious trouble because of my connection to Sam, my needs and expectations. And I was seething with anger toward him. I was so mad! If he was innocent, then surely, he was a fool! Yes, stupid – and guilty as charged - by me!

How could he have been so dumb, so reckless and irresponsible in his actions? I needed to hit, throw, or smash something.

But I was all alone in my despair. Looking across the square, humanity, nature, even life-force seemed to be working together harmoniously. It was a glorious spring day, despite the dark clouds that hovered in my soul.

I realized that my body was shaking. Then I saw someone, a few feet away, staring at me. I had to get control. *Please, no panic attack. Not now.* I jumped to my feet and quickly ran around the corner. Another bench was there.

I blinked and wiped away some tears. A pigeon swooped down and did a perfect three-point landing nearby. It began pecking at a few crumbs someone littered there. Was the sparrow also a hopeless victim of circumstances beyond its control? I wondered. But God promised to take care of them. *Bullshit! The birds were starving.*

"God, where are you?" I whimpered. No answer. My doubt was confirmed.

+++

Jodi began plodding slowly along the path that took her back to her car. Her mind was reeling, stuck on one idea until it smashed into a dead-end, did a U-turn, came back and throttled down another one-way street. Crash - another barricade. No conclusions. Nothing was making any sense.

She saw her car and there was a strange man lifting a wheel into the trunk. As she got close, she noticed that his name was Clodd Henry, according to the embroidery on his blackened and soiled, blue stripped shirt. She stopped a few feet away but seemed unable to put words together for a proper inquiry. After all, she was demolished.

++++

Noticing me, he simply said "Hi," and smiled. "You the owner?" he asked after closing the trunk.

"Yes, I am."

"Caught a nail in your tire," he explained. "Good thing you didn't drive on it too long."

Unable to get his meaning, I simply stood there with a blank look on my face.

"I can fix it," Clodd informed.

"Oh, you can?" I noticed the confusion on his face.

65

"If you'd like, I can take it back to the garage and put a plug in it for you," he offered. "Still has some good tread."

"Okay."

He began to reopen the trunk of my car. "Okay then, I'll take it with me. You can pick it up tomorrow. Should be done by noon." He stood the tire on the pavement, closed the lid and handed me the keys.

I was still blank. I barely comprehended what he was saying.

"Miss? Miss, you okay? You don't seem to be quite right."

I trembled as a shiver ran down my spine and forced my consciousness unto the matter at hand. "Yeah, I'm just fine," I noted with sarcasm to myself. "Just fine… and dandy."

"Tomorrow then?"

"Yeah, tomorrow." I forced my thoughts into submission once again. "I'll see you tomorrow… But where are you at?"

"Our address is on the receipt." He reached for his clipboard. "Okay then. Before you leave, I have some paperwork for you to sign.

"Oh yeah, sure."

I drove to the local park and stopped my car under a shade tree. I rolled down my window so I could feel the gentle, cool breeze – and hear the sounds of earth, seemingly in predestined motion. It all spun around me, consuming my senses. I closed my eyes and hoped for relief, or sleep, or something akin to calm. In that desperate moment, even death seemed appealing. I heard its call. *Escape!* I needed a way out.

For a few fleeting seconds the hum of Mother Nature's presence was all I comprehended. Sovereign, but still, it did not offer any resolution for an abiding peace.

++++

Not wanting to see Sam now, not after the humiliation Jodi experienced from the District Attorney, she considered cancelling the plans she made for that evening. She was to meet Jared and then coaxed Susan to also come, not wanting to face that flirtatious scoundrel privately, again.

Being truly alone was what she desired most at that moment. Then again, maybe it was not the best thing for her under those circumstances – the despair she felt, the lack of direction that nagged at her unrest. A broken heart. Torment. Yes, she had to face it – the terror of Sam's crime could not be denied.

But she needed to talk to Susan, so she decided she would go. First, she would have to get home and change into something much more comfortable – a favorite, a well-worn jogging suit. She just had to ditch those heels as soon as possible.

++++

I arrived at Ben's Burger Barn five minutes before the appointed time of our meeting. I parked my car and walked to the diner, hugging store fronts along the way, wanting to not be seen by anyone. I peeked around the corner. Yes, Jared was already there, sitting alone at a table, visible through a large window.

He wanted to meet me at a fancier place, suggesting a swanky Italian Ristorante, but I didn't have the appetite for it, or for him. Especially, not him.

I decided to wait for Susan.

67

Ten minutes later I saw her walking briskly as she rounded the corner. She seemed to be dressed up and I immediately noticed that she was wearing more makeup than usual. She looked good in her tight jeans and boots. I peeked inside again. Jared seemed to be settled in, sucking on a plastic straw in a paper cup.

"Susan!" I called to her, just a little louder than a whisper. My friend was startled and missed a step, stumbling on a crack in the sidewalk she fell forward. I caught her in the nick of time.

"Oh, hi," she bolted. "Oh, it's you."

"Susan, we need to talk. But we don't have time now. Jared is already inside. He's been waiting awhile, maybe fifteen minutes or more."

"Oh…"

She paused and I sensed that she was deep in thought.

"Am I late?"

"Susan, I had a terrible day. I'm having second thoughts about Sam."

"Oh?"

Another pause and a surprised look.

"Really?" she asked.

"And I think someone is following me. Or sabotaging my car… or something."

My friend returned a blank stare.

I tugged on Susan's sleeve as she stepped backward. "We don't have time now," I repeated. "We have to get in there, but we still need to talk… later."

Susan pulled away. "And I have some news for you."

Despite the urgency I was showing, she paused for emphasis of her revelation.

"What, what is it?" I wanted to shake her to release her words, but hesitated. "Susan, quick!"

"Karen Jackson, the state representative, is giving a big interview. Maggie Johns got the assignment."

"So…"

"It's about Sam!"

"Oh, no!" I swallowed hard. "Well, we'll just have to talk some more later… or tomorrow morning." I waited for Susan to acknowledge my suggestion with a nod. "Okay, let's go in."

++++

The two of them quickly gathered themselves to gain the composure and display of a royal entourage. They walked inside the Burger Barn with the stately demeanor of a princess escorted and intended for the attention of an anxious prince, a suitable suitor. Here was the eligible bachelor attorney in waiting. At least Jodi was hoping that he would take a second look at her friend, Susan.

As they approached, Jared rose quickly in greeting.

++++

"Hello ladies!"

I spoke first. "Jared, this is my special friend, Susan Kasper, reporter at the **Morning Herald** and next to win a Pulitzer." I turned to Susan. "And it is my pleasure to introduce you to attorney extraordinaire, one of the great legal minds of our time, Jared McCabe."

That was tiring. In my present state of fatigue, it was all I could muster. I hoped it would break the ice. Susan giggled as they shook hands. "Well, that was exhausting," I teased as the chairs screeched on the tiled floor and everyone quickly took their seats. I dodged Susan to place her next to Jared. He was still looking at her intently.

"So, Susan, you're a reporter?"

"Yes. Yes, I am. It's a challenging job," she smiled, "journalistic integrity… you know."

It suddenly seemed that someone spoke with an air of distinction. I turned to see if the body next to me was still Susan, the person I knew all too well. Impressive. I hadn't realized that my friend was capable of this. And Jared seemed to already be intrigued with her.

Susan was determined to dazzle. While making eye contact, hers wide, she watched to see if she was having an impact. I wasn't sure about him, but I certainly was impressed.

As their conversation continued, I was quickly becoming invisible and feeling like the third wheel. But for me, that was a good thing. I ordered a strawberry milkshake and began to look for the chance to make my exit.

Susan ordered what Jared was having, a bacon cheeseburger and fries. Without taking his eyes off her, Jared passed a manila envelope to me, the copy of the arrest warrant I requested at our previous meeting.

With a quick "thank you" I apologized and stood to leave, noting that I had had a long day and was feeling very tired. Neither of them seemed to care.

Arriving home, another letter was waiting. It had the familiar address that included Sam's name. I decided not to wait this time and without another thought cut it open.

It said:

"What will you, the downtrodden, know at the realization of your defeat? Let go of it to experience the power of healing, wholeness, and even happiness."

"We must first have acceptance before going deeper. Apologies are immediately acknowledged."

"A quickening spirit, ministering to the meek, writes upon the tablets of their hearts."

"And mercy weighs heavy in the balance of judgment. This is justice – even our triumph."

"Your Advocate."

CHAPTER FOUR: Empowered

Sam's position as District Magistrate stirred resentment in one who became his archenemy, one he still had not identified, as this man's vexation lingered for many years undetected.

And the reason for the anxiety of his nemesis: it was a mystery to even those who knew him well, except for one, a younger sister.

At 64 Church Street a widow, Jen Foster, had just finished a conversation with their older sister, Karen Jackson, one of the bigwigs in town. They talked about Sam, the young judge taken into custody. It had been the day's hot gossip that rang many telephones in town.

The sisters agreed on the irony of it all, especially since Sam had been charged once before, many years ago. He faced a felony charge and jail time, but Jen thought he did not deserve it. Now, the news of his arrest was upsetting her once again. And, it was the memory of the accident victim, Darcy Rogers, that still haunted many people in Walthem, and in particular, the ghost that persistently tormented Jen.

In the months prior to her crash, Jen had received letters from Darcy, who was her close friend. The letters contained information that blamed someone else for Darcy's troubled life. Her demise was untimely and surely unfortunate, but Jen's anger was directed toward that other person, the one identified in Darcy's letters.

After ending the call with Karen, she went to find them. She wanted Sam to finally know everything about Darcy. Somehow, she hoped it might help him now.

They were stored, hidden away in a shoebox, on the top shelf of her bedroom closet. Jen placed them in a large manilla envelope, strode outside to her mailbox, straddled the deep mud puddle formed by the front tire of the mailman's jeep, left the package inside, and raised the sender's flag. Since he was once again incarcerated, Jen mailed the letters she had received from Darcy to Jodi, Sam's girlfriend.

Nearby, in a large two-story brick house, the rectory of Saint Patrick Orthodox Church in which Father Jacob resided, the telephone remained silent as the off-duty clergyman watched the evening newscast on his television set. He was dressed in his silk pajamas topped off with a striped smoking jacket. His vest pocket contained two Cuban cigars, still in their wrappers.

His housekeeper was busy in the kitchen finishing the dishes after serving him supper. Jacob looked toward her with contemplation as he closely observed the swaying of her body, but did not speak a word to reveal his lustful desire. She was as a professional to ethics, chaste as a woman, and uncompromising in her belief of the priestly vow, so he usually spoke to her fondly, in a tone expressing empathy. Sometimes he pushed it, and became suggestive. But she wasn't about to make the same mistake his former housekeeper had made.

The clergyman's advances went on, day after day, without acknowledgement from his housekeeper. When he touched her clothing, she promptly slapped his hand.

Jacob turned to look at a small framed photograph that stood among reference books and decorative bookends in what he referred to as his library with prideful acclaim. The photograph did not stand out, as if demanding recognition, but blended with its surroundings. Visitors seldom acknowledged it, and that was fine with this priest who didn't want to expound on its significance. Pictured was as an attractive young woman, a single mother holding her little boy, a baby riding on his mother's hip, and smiling broadly. The photograph expressed joy, and although the memory was fond for Jacob, it presently stirred anger within him. His dear "Janie" had suffered a terrible fate. The picture served not as a reminder of happy times, but as a directive for revenge.

The priest refilled his tall glass with red wine from a decanter kept on a mirrored tray at the sideboard and again looked at the telephone on the coffee table. He tapped his fingers there. He was becoming impatient, waiting for his call.

Finally, the cordless phone rattled and he grabbed it before the third ring.

"Hello, Father Jacob here."

"You can drop the formality with me," was the curt reply.

"Karen!" the priest acknowledged his sister's voice, "I hope it is good news. Are they keeping him in jail?"

"Surely. By now you should have confidence in me. I have clout." Karen Jackson was an elected official in the district and the eldest of Jacob's two sisters, Jen Foster being the youngest among the three siblings.

"Oh yes, I know that you are very capable."

"Sure, but now we have another matter of urgent concern."

"What's that?"

"Jen!" and she paused for emphasis. "Our dear sister is upset after a neighbor gave her the scoop on Sam - told her that he was setup." She sighed, "It's the local gossip!"

"Damn the talk in this town!" Jacob roared. "Why would she believe that load of crap? And what does Jen know anyway?"

"Beats me. She didn't tell me anything specific."

"She's got nothing."

"Really, how can you be so sure."

"Because I didn't do anything."

"Maybe," Karen asserted. "But I'm not sure. And apparently our dear Jen knows more than we think. She had been receiving letters from Darcy Rogers and has suspicions about you."

"What do you mean? What would she suspect me of?" The self-righteous clergyman cleared his throat and tugged on the front-bottom edge of his jacket to eliminate its wrinkles. He regarded himself as refined and superior to most others. He remembered his deepest secret and for a brief moment feared that he could be exposed.

"I don't know, but she knows you all too well."

The priest scratched at a sudden itch, the bald spot at the back of his head, and accidently displaced his glasses. They began to fall but were caught on the precipice of his large nose where his nostrils flared.

"What did Darcy say in those letters?"

"Jen didn't tell me! But now she is pointing a finger at you."

"For what? She's got nothing. There's no reason for her to suggest anything. Besides," he was quick to ask, "how do you know all of this?"

"She just called me, you big baboon! I just got off the phone with her. How else would I know?!" Karen raised her voice. "Jen called me early, just before I left for the office. She still trusts me and wanted to talk to me about her concerns."

"I don't believe it!" Jacob said flatly, in response to her irritation. "Why would Darcy write to her? She died seventeen years ago," he noted as he sought understanding. "So why would it matter now?"

"I'm just as bewildered about the letters as you are… I don't know what's in them." She redirected, "Well, maybe Jen was just blowing off some steam… but I'm sick and tired of her whining."

Jacob already knew that Karen brokered authority like Elizabeth, the Queen of England, and expressed disgust for those who showed weakness.

"But you didn't exactly do right by that poor girl," she concluded.

"Yes, I did!"

"In your eyes," Karen shot back. "It would appear quite different to a woman's perspective… overworked and under paid."

"So, what are you driving at? What are you trying to say in all this jabbering?"

"No loose ends!" she yelled, emphasizing her demand. "I mean it! I won't be complicit in any of your dirty doings. Get those damn letters!"

"And how do you suggest that I get them?" he demanded, continuing to query his bossy sister. "How do you think I can accomplish that?"

Jacob did not know that they were no longer in Jen's house but had already been placed in her mailbox, for delivery to Jodi Culp, the girlfriend, but intended for Samuel Urban, the troubled magistrate.

"Send your man, your janitor. Isn't he the one that does all your dirty work?"

The priest was silenced by the suggestion.

"Isn't he the one that okayed the rendezvous with the floozy?" Karen persisted.

"Floozy? Oh, you mean Faith… Faith Culver," Jacob clarified as he found his voice again. "She's my janitor's girlfriend. But hey, Urban has been charged. He took the bait and now he will lose everything… right?"

"Yes, well, I expect so. But I still don't understand why you have it out for him so much. You were hoping that he'd make a mistake when tempted… and, apparently, he did."

"He forced himself on that poor girl. He needs to be removed from the bench." The priest paused, "And he killed someone."

"It was an accident."

"He was negligent."

"But found innocent. Well," Karen had her own reasons for wanting to can the magistrate, "I don't get what your beef is about that, but from my perspective, he does not serve the Commonwealth very well. He is the worst judge in the state and the cops want him gone, so, I'm agreeing with you, at least for now."

"My sincere appreciation for your efforts," Jacob replied, attempting to change the tone of the conversation. "And thank you."

"Don't thank me. And remember, this conversation never happened. If you're accused… if Jen really does have some kind of proof, or dirt… I'll have nothing to do with you or your morbid affairs. All I can say is, I hope this will finally bring you some closure. You have been a mess, consumed by your guilt."

"What? I'm not guilty of anything!"

"You better not be."

"What about the election?" the priest sought reassurance hurriedly, as he sensed that the call was about to end abruptly.

"We will have a write-in candidate, probably a local cop who is adored by the people in his precinct. Besides," she continued, "it doesn't matter once Urban is convicted."

"No need to say more," Father Jacob felt gratified. "And again, thanks."

The other end of the connection was already dead. He placed the cordless back on the table, lost in the joys of revenge. Proud and arrogant as he was, Jacob quickly shunned off the idea of his younger sister, Jen, being a serious threat. Still, he knew that Karen would have to be appeased. She'd be checking in again and demanding more answers, especially in regard to those letters.

Nearby, on the wall, a plaque drew his attention to the words inscribed there. Its heading pompously announced **The Ten Commandments**, God's laws. Now, it seems unlikely, but Jacob may have noticed them this day because of a prick of guilt as he felt the need to take inventory of his soul; not that he really cared, but he had to be on the ready just in case he was required to defend himself. Surely, all his sins were justified as a high-ranking priest.

Regarding the list of laws: he was likely an offender of the majority of them, just like everyone else. More so, he was outright guilty in disobedience of some; but today, **The Ninth** annoyingly bothered his conscience with the most vengeance. But who would know, and why should anyone care? He peered at the list again. He thought about **The Sixth** with prideful assurance. *No, I'd never stoop that low.* Still, he wondered if he might be capable. *If it has to be done, I'll force my henchman to do the dastardly deed.* And in that moment, he was thankful for Luke, so Jacob went looking for his janitor.

He walked through the sanctuary before exiting the rear of the church through a supply room. Luke Stolarick was there, in the rear of the parking lot, burning rubbish in an old oil barrel. Jacob eyed him suspiciously and saw a frown of disapproval unfurl, eyebrows lowered, his forehead creased.

Without a greeting or explanation, Jacob stated that they needed to have another meeting. "Let's get together in your '*office*' at about nine tonight," he said, an insult intentionally insinuated. "We'll finalize details then."

It was an order more than a suggestion and Luke agreed quick. "Yes, Father. I'll be there, of course."

They stood equal in stature as the master with dark, lifeless eyes peered intently into those of his servant, expressing anxiety. The priest saw Luke tremble momentarily. *He isn't as tough as he pretends to be,* Jacob observed.

Hours later and always prompt, Father Jacob opened the door that led to the basement; it was five minutes before the appointed time of his meeting with Luke. He carefully descended the rickety old steps, holding tightly onto the handrail. Some of the treads were warped and uneven, due to age. Some even wobbled under the pressure of his weight, more than 300 pounds. Once on the concrete floor, the priest could see the large furnace, an old hand-fed coal firebox converted with an oil burner. A bright yellow light glowed inside, visible through the door vents.

In an area alongside the heat exchanger, Luke was allowed to create his lair. Father Jacob paused momentarily to take it all in. There was his rear projection large screen TV, a VCR, a collection of X-rated video tapes, an old upholstered sofa, its padding showing through the worn spots on the arms, and a dingy, old, overstuffed recliner that leaned slightly to one side. The janitor had a faded neon sign hanging on the wall, Genesee Beer, an outdated refrigerator, the kind with the rounded corners on top, and a small wooden table accompanied by two chairs. A discarded kitchen cabinet was his only place to keep things, personal belongings. It had two drawers above a single door. Luke topped it off with an old piece of plywood salvaged from a garbage dumpster - a slab of granite would have been better used there, but none was available. Several pasteboard boxes were stacked in a corner. It was all that Luke owned.

Jacob allowed Luke to run a long extension wire so that he could have a telephone there also. It was connected to the third line hookup, not used by the church, although the priest would have preferred to have a secret line for himself. Then again, he really didn't like to talk on the telephone that much and avoided it whenever possible, and he certainly didn't want to know about Luke's private matters. On Sundays and Fridays, a church secretary would answer calls and use an intercom to alert Jacob in his office if the caller persisted even after she made her standard response noting that Father was busy in a meeting. The problem was, he seldom spent time in his office, even on those days designated for receiving inquiries from parishioners.

Luke stood near the cooler with a brew in his hand. Jacob approached the recliner and paused there, scowling. He cleared his throat accompanied by a loud grunt.

"Oh, excuse me." Luke was quick to step forward to pick up a couple magazines, inappropriate literature to be found in a religious setting. He cleared the seat. "Want something to drink?"

"Sit!" the priest ordered as he lowered himself onto the chair. It groaned under his weight.

"I have been good to you, have I not?" Jacob began by setting the parameters for his lecture. "I let you use the shower in the guest wing, entering only by the rear door, of course. By the way," he asked with a second thought, "are you keeping it clean… and I mean spotless?"

The inquiry was unworthy of a response.

"I allow you to have your den down here and… I saved you from doing more time."

Luke had heard this speech several times before. He replied with a singular nod.

"You would be nothing without me," Jacob said mockingly, "I took you in and gave you a place to live. I made it possible for you to be paroled early." A long arching frown cut into his stone face as his brow stiffened. "Luke, you owe me," he lowered his voice, "you will always be indebted to me."

Luke returned a steady gaze.

"So, how is *she* doing?" Jacob asked with a false concern for *her* health. "Is she holding up?"

"Oh, you mean Faith?" Luke clarified. "She is resting in the hospital. They're keeping her pretty well drugged up. But I guess she's okay."

"Got her story right?"

"She will."

"Was she examined by a nurse for evidence of rape?"

In the 80's a rape victim was discretely examined by a female nurse for signs of sexual assault. DNA testing was not yet common place.

"Yeah, looked like some rough play... she kinda likes it that way."

The priest raised an eyebrow.

"We've done it before..." Luke intended to detail the tryst, but his remarks were cut short when Jacob raised his hand to indicate that he should stop talking. "That Urban... he must be a party animal. I'd say there's a side to him no one knows."

"Really?"

"Well, apparently he's still got the hots for her," Luke noted. "She said that the judge was really coming onto her."

"She must be enticing."

"Yeah, I know... and he wouldn't stop when she told him to."

"Good. But spare me the details... That creep needs to be removed from his office and kept in a jail. That's where he belongs!"

"Yeah... right."

"Now I need you to do another task for me," Jacob continued. "My sister has some letters and they must be destroyed."

"How am I going to do that?"

"I don't know, and I don't want to know how you do it… Wait 'till she is out of the house, break in, find them, burn them," he said thinking out loud. "I don't care what you do. Just so the letters are destroyed."

"I don't think so…" Luke replied. "Using Faith to lure the judge was one thing, but a break-in, well, that can be pinned on me," he sighed as he shook his head slowly. "I'm trying to keep my nose clean. I don't need any more charges thrown at me."

"Oh, right!" Jacob blurted with a cough. "You are exemplary. You should be a role model for our young people in this community," he mocked sarcastically.

"Father, please, there must be another way."

"If so, I'm not comprehending it," he was already standing. "Be a good boy," he admonished and paused. "Maybe in a few days we can watch a flick together. We've got a good thing going here. Now is not the time for you to start burning bridges." He looked long and hard at Luke and saw that he was still not convinced.

"But, but…"

"Oh, and you're keeping a close eye on the judge's girlfriend, right? I want to know what she's up to," Jacob interrupted. "What's her name – Culp! That's it, Jodi Culp."

"Well yeah… but…"

Jacob was already starting up the steps, leaving Luke silent in his wake. He stopped, "And keep her away from the hospital, you know, away from Faith. The last thing we need is those two conspiring with each other. I don't trust them. Neither one!"

Hours later… like a shadow in the dim light of night, the presence of an arsonist was evident but unseen, obscured from and mysterious to the conscious eye. As a sleuth of sabotage, he was consumed by evil. He advanced against his victim as a puma on the prowl, acutely aware of his surroundings and calculating each move.

He was a tall person, concealed by a hooded sweatshirt and a long overcoat. He exited his car parked around the corner from 64 Church Street, the home of Jen Foster. He wore smooth bottom shoes, with the intention of not leaving a distinguishable footprint. He looked up and down the street. No cars were coming. His gait was swift and purposeful as he moved against his target.

Just as he stepped on the front lawn of her modest ranch home, the electrical wires overhead began to glow with a soft light as the neighbor's house was illuminated by the headlights of an approaching car. He quickly retreated to stoop down alongside a vehicle parked on the edge of the street and concealed himself there. Lights flashed and shadows jumped as the unwelcomed car passed by.

He reached into a shopping bag and retrieved a glass bottle. It was filled with gasoline and its short neck was stuffed with a rag saturated with the accelerant. He sat the bottle on the sidewalk, removed one glove and felt for the lighter in his front pants pocket. He was paying close attention to details. He ignited the cloth fuse of the Molotov cocktail and quickly replaced his glove before picking it up. He darted toward the house and pitched it at the large picture window on the front of Jen's house. It shattered the glass and fell inside. One second later he saw a flame ignite on the carpeted floor.

His retreat was even faster than his advance. He saw no one. He believed that no one had seen him.

It was shortly after midnight that the intended fire began to grow. Residue of the homemade bomb burned on Jen's living room floor unnoticed as she slept in her bedroom, located down a hallway. She had taken a sleep supplement, melatonin, after feeling anxious all day about her decision to mail the letters to Jodi. The smoldering fire was almost out when a spark jumped and landed on a sheer window curtain. It lingered there for a brief moment before a tiny flame ignited. Within seconds the fire increased in intensity and climbed up the loosely woven fabric.

Jen's bedroom door was tightly closed. On the ceiling in the hallway a smoke detector remained dark; no small red light was illuminated. Its battery died more than a year ago.

The kitchen filled with smoke, and like a scout looking for the enemy, it advanced toward Jen, billowing and rolling along the hallway ceiling. It soon filled that small space and remained there contained as it summoned the inferno to remove the barrier, the door to her bedroom; for the monster desired a victim, even as it consumed the front room. It ate the thin wood paneling like it was an appetizer and then began chewing at the framework, charring the spruce rafters, now chomping on its main course. Ceiling tiles and insulation melted away and flames flew into the attic space where they found the oxygen needed to multiply, becoming a host of smaller dragons. The mother beast was now enraged, hissing and puffing vehemently. Even the plywood on the roof began to steam.

The fire dragon clawed at the floor in front of Jen's bedroom door, found a small space there, and pushed its fingers through.

Jen coughed. In her dream she opened the oven door to discover a burnt meatloaf. *Oh no, I forgot to set the timer.* She coughed again, this time stirring in her sleep. She rolled onto her side and coughed some more, aggressively. Now fully awake she sat up and spun on the mattress to place her feet on the floor. She instinctively felt her forehead. She was sweating. Her bedroom was unusually warm.

She darted for the door but paused there as she observed the smoke that was now seeping in all around, framing it in an eerie vapor. Confused and frightened, she reached for the doorknob and turned it. The door burst open and black smoke charged in, engulfing her. Coughing uncontrollably, her lungs were beginning to burn. Attracted by a glowing light, she stuck her head into the hallway. It was then that she saw the fire and became aware of her predicament. Her face turned bright red and her hair singed, melting away in the intense heat.

But in that crucial moment fate was determined to rescue this woman and gave her the good sense to flee in the opposite direction.

Or was it providence?

Jen turned back into the bedroom and ran for the window at the far side of her bed. She usually slept with it cracked open to have fresh air during the night. She threw up the double-hung glass frame and stuck her head through the opening, coughing continuously. She leaned out further and looked toward her neighbor's house. She saw a light come on there. With both hands she pushed and forced herself through the opened window, falling head first into a perennial bed of dried stems and leaves. That was her last conscious moment.

She was discovered by the assistant fire chief, the first to respond to the alarm sounded at the firehouse. His duty was to race to the scene of the reported fire in his personal vehicle and to quickly access the need for additional equipment and manpower. Flames were already shooting through the roof when he arrived. He ran around the tinderbox seeking a rear door, wondering if the house was occupied, and looking for propane tanks. That's when he tripped over Jen's unconscious body.

At 1:30 AM Susan Kasper, working the night desk at the **Morning Herald**, was assigned the story about the house fire. Her deadline was in one hour, for the morning edition. Knowing that she would be unable to reach the fire chief by phone she jumped into her Ford Escort and raced to the scene, with a hope and a prayer that he would still be there. Her editor, Franklin Strickland, reluctantly agreed to also let Susan take the pictures for the story, but they had to be good or she wouldn't be given the opportunity again. She craved the byline that was prominently displayed under the photo in print.

Chief Carson Donaldson was still there, a clipboard in his hand. Firemen were packing up their gear and checking the tanker truck.

"Hi Chief," she greeted the local volunteer. "I'm Susan Kasper..."

"With the **Morning Herald**," he interrupted. "I know who you are. We talked once before."

"Oh, did we?... Sorry. I know that you're real busy, but I have an early deadline."

The smell of industrial chemicals, plastics burned, hung heavy in the damp night air that lingered there. Susan coughed lightly.

A beam of light, a fireman's flashlight, cut through the smoke like a lighthouse beacon in the fog of a storm. Not purposed as a warning, it offered no hope for this sanctuary of human habitation which was already destroyed. There would be no safe harbor here.

A few charred timbers remained upright, glowing bright orange as they hissed, enveloped in the thick, toxic air that swirled around them. It appeared as an entrance to hell. The fire dragon's temporary lair. It would linger there until all was extinguished.

"A deadline? Don't we all?" he replied while looking at his watch. "I have an important meeting with my boss this morning. Everyone is always so rushed these days." Donaldson was watching something the other volunteers were doing. "Not that way," he yelled at a recent recruit. "Damn," he cursed under his breath. "Fred, can you show him the proper way to roll up the hoses… please." Looking back at the young woman with the press badge pinned to her jacket he said, "Well, I don't have much yet. Cause still undetermined. Owner, Jennifer Foster, suffered smoke inhalation and was rushed to the hospital by Medic One," he paused as he concluded his brief report. "You can call the hospital to check on her condition, but I think she is going to make it."

"What time did you get the alarm?" Susan interjected quickly.

"Eleven fifty-seven. Almost midnight."

"Address?"

With a shake of his head the chief furrowed his brow and turned away. Susan had seen the sign for Church Street as she arrived. Standing there, a strong current ran against her right foot as water splashed against her ankle. She was wearing low cut canvas sneakers. She looked down at her feet and there on the curb the house number was painted in large white numerals, 64.

After taking a few photos, she jogged back to her car and headed to the hospital for the chance of questioning the injured woman. As she rounded a curve, she was passed by a familiar vehicle headed in the opposite direction. The charcoal gray sedan had municipal tags on the front. She looked in the rear-view mirror. As she suspected, the trunk of the car read, "State Police Fire Marshal."

"Shit!" she hit the steering wheel with her fist. "He didn't say it was an arson fire." Jabbing the brakes, she turned into the first driveway for a quick turn-around. Going back, she would at least be able to verify that the fire marshal was definitely involved. No assumptions – only facts could be the basis of her report. She would try to grab a photo of him in front of the charred wall.

CHAPTER FIVE: Elected

Saturday, May 11, 1985 – day four.

HEADLINES: **"House Burns, Owner Hospitalized"** and **"Prodigal Judge Fails Us** – Rep. Jackson Calls for Justice After Urban Betrays Public Trust"

1985 was the year Pennsylvanians elected local municipal officials. Counting this day, there were only three until Election Day, the time when residents would cast their ballots: merely 72 hours for Sam to save his career, but more than that, his reputation, even his life.

Samuel Urban, District 12 Justice, was up for re-election, unopposed on the ballot, but present circumstances threatened to change that. It would be his second full term if he received the nod of the voters. Additionally, he had served to complete the remaining term of Judge William Williams who resigned due to a terminal illness.

Williams was the Magistrate who dismissed the original charges against Sam, and then, not only recommended the young man to be his replacement, but pulled every string in the book, using all the political clout he could muster, to get Sam appointed.

Williams was a good man, liked by the vast majority of the people in town. He was firm, fair, and predictable. If you had even a minimal understanding of the law, even what you were told by others, the street wise, you knew what to expect from Williams when you were forced to stand in front of him. The verdict -nearly always acceptable.

From the sidewalk, the passersby shouted to him. One called him "Willie," another "Billy," or the most endeared to him, "Billy Willie." It was an expression of respect and affection.

The magistrate never flaunted extravagance or isolated himself from the common man. He was one of them, and they appreciated his camaraderie. He served with the community's upstanding citizens in clubs and committees.

When struck with pancreatic cancer, he remained faithful to fulfill the duties of his elected office and seldom missed a day at work, unless hospitalized for a procedure, then finally, at the end, when his health had deteriorated and his weight dropped below one hundred pounds, his office was closed and Williams disappeared from public view.

Before he died, he became a phantom of his old self, the man that was plumped in size and jovial in expression. His life quickly slipped away and everyone who knew him felt remorse, for his suffering, and their loss.

We are a flower quickly fading, a vapor in the wind. In retrospect, life is short.

His funeral was attended by hundreds of admirers, those truly appreciative of his life's work.

There is no doubt that the old judge wanted his legacy preserved, but it would take a humble person to make that happen.

Williams adjudicated Sam's case during the last six months of his life, and Sam had certainly been humbled. But there was something more, and Williams knew about it, lending him to understand, to perceive Sam's character on a deeper level.

No one really understood Williams' reason for wanting Sam to replace him. Sam did not seem worthy. But the experienced judge felt that the aspiring lawyer was the obvious choice. And, he had that 'something more'.

Eight years later, the memory of the man was dim, a shadow from the past. The spotlight had been redirected to Sam. Now it was his turn to fill those shoes, but footprints had been left by a big man, a great man, and Sam struggled to meet the public's expectation.

From the rectory of Saint Pat's, the Reverend seethed with anger. The announcement of Sam's victory in the first election caused him to rage, and now, the thought of Sam's re-election, winning another full six-year term, was more than he could bear. It made him feel nauseous. Compared to Williams, Father Jacob was a vastly different kind of man. Angry, resentful. It was such a contrast, and a contradiction to the office Jacob served.

Still, Sam was unaware of the priest's desire to have him defeated. Everyone in politics had enemies. Even if Sam had known of the priest's opposition, he most likely would have given it little consideration.

This Saturday was a difficult time for everyone entangled in the web they spun: lies with many intersections and turns, accusations confounded by charges and counter charges, secrets that pried open locked closet doors leading to the darkest places within their hearts; it was there that their consciences died. Suspicion was increasing between them.

Jodi was beginning to doubt Sam's innocence. That was enough to force the winds of change.

Impatience was growing like a storm on the horizon, becoming a funnel, it was intent on pinpointing the one who was most wicked for eradication; but would he, or she, escape in a bunker of falsehood established for such an emergency?

At the burned-out home of Jen Foster, the State Police Fire Marshal was wrapping up his investigation. It was determined that the fire started in the front, living room. A bottle was found there with evidence of an accelerant that spilled on the floor. This was documented with photographs. The front window was broken – the firebomb's point of entry established.

Walking to his car, the investigator stepped on something hard and found a pocketknife in the grass on the front lawn. It appeared to be nothing special, a department store item, but when he turned it over, he noticed a name imprinted on it.

Such knives were manufactured with the names pre-printed on them and displayed on a retail rack in alphabetical order. It was a cheap way for the consumer to obtain a personalized gift.

On it was the name "Luke."

After a restless night, Jodi was moving quickly on the morning of the eleventh. Coming down the stairs of her townhome she glanced out a window and saw movement in her front yard. She halted, took a step back and gazed intently toward a large maple tree. Yes, there was someone attempting to conceal himself behind it. Part of his back and buttock was still visible on one side of the tree's trunk. He was wearing a black shirt and blue denim jeans. As she watched she saw a face peek around the tree from the other side. He was wearing a baseball cap.

Someone was stalking her.

"Hey," I yelled. The face pulled back. "Hey you!" I banged on the glass. The large window vibrated like the top of a snare drum and nearly cracked but somehow withstood the jarring force. I darted for the front door and threw it open with a single motion. "Hey you!" I leaped onto the front stoop.

The man was already running, probably 30 yards in front of me, toward the parking lot. I watched with panic as he ducked behind a large truck and disappeared around the corner, behind more townhouses.

"Damn," I cursed under my breath. "I knew someone was following me."

I picked up the newspaper lying on my walkway and read the headline on the front page. It was about Sam. My face flushed as the temperature of my temple shot up abruptly.

Once Jodi was on the road, Luke followed her to the police station and then made a U-turn to return to the church. Father Jacob had relieved his janitor of extra work for a few days and wanted to know what the girlfriend of the magistrate was up to. She was trouble and they hoped she would stay away from Faith. If she headed to the hospital, Luke would try to divert her again.

The police station seemed to be caught up in an unusual flurry of activity that morning. Chief Sabol was in his office talking to the fire marshal who was holding up an evidence bag for him to observe. I strained to see what was in it. A pocketknife.

"Can you dust it for prints?" I overheard the request as the door to the Chief's private space hung open.

Officer Barney Billings, the senior cop on the force, was on the telephone at his workstation and I heard him say something about election posters. This made me curious.

As I looked toward Ken's spot, I observed him holding a cream filled donut in one hand and a cup of coffee in the other. His eyes were glazed over as he lingered in a place unknown to me with donuts. Lala land. Pure delight.

Despite his mouth being full, he managed a muffled "Hi" and nodded at me. He opened a desk drawer and reached for the keys to the lockup.

Once inside, Sam quickly rose from his breakfast table. They had provided a folding card table and chair and he was eating a mushroom omelet served with rye toast. Fine cuisine in a lockup, but I wasn't happy for him.

My mood must have been obvious. I was so steamed that a geyser was about to erupt. Ken opened the cell door and quickly retreated to his messy desk without saying a word.

I held the newspaper in my hand, rerolled, and without a civil greeting I waved it in the air at Sam. "Have you seen today's headline?" I demanded an answer but didn't wait for it. "Oh, this is great, just great! Now we have a state representative campaigning against *us*."

Sam noticed and likely took some comfort in my use of a plural pronoun just then. My mistake. But his calm was to be quickly dashed. "Oh, for sure. Now *you're* in a world of shit!"

He stepped closer. "Can I see it?"

Smack!

I swung and hit him squarely on the side of his head. His ear turned bright red.

"Why…?" he started to ask but didn't have to wait for an answer.

"It's not just her," I began to scold him. "Other state officials too. And the D.A. really has it out for you!"

"I think she's considered a county official…"

I sighed, shook my head, and raised my fist - he got the message. His was an inappropriate response. Not funny. I meant business.

"She made me feel like a criminal," I charged again. "A brutal," I paused for recollection, "violent crime against women… and I am supporting it…?" I blurted, now nearly in a rage. "And I am giving you," again, I tried to remember the D.A.'s words as I waved the newspaper in his face, "a license," I paused, "that's it, a license to continue to take advantage of the opposite sex. 'Freedom,' that's what she said, to continue to hurt women even more! You've had a 'free pass!'"

"Jodi… calm down. Please, you have to calm down."

"How? How can I be calm?" I demanded and raised the paper as I thought about swatting him a second time.

Sam grabbed it out of my hand and stepped back.

Disarmed, I finally took a deep breath. I stood stiff, my fists clenched. Sam wasn't sure if I would strike again or relent of my physical attack. "Faith was beaten," I informed in monotone, as anger seethed between my teeth. "You! You beat her up?!"

"No, of course not!"

Sam seemed surprised at the accusation.

"I didn't even touch her."

Really? That was just too much. I couldn't even respond to his denial. I began staring off at something distant, my eyes dim and unfocused. I was overheated and I'm sure Sam could sense it. I was beginning to feel defeated. He had no credible defense. Just his word, and what was that worth? *He didn't even touch her... really?!*

"It's not true. None of it is true." He whimpered, appearing as one pathetic and hurt.

"Then why did she say those things to me?" I asked, my tone sharp.

"It's what they do. It's what *she* is trained to do. That's how she attacks a witness in the courtroom. She's good at her job."

Fair enough. I could see his point. I softened a little. But she was a monster.

"Don't take it personally," he advised. "Business. It's all business. Hit them where it hurts: where they are vulnerable. Knock your opponent off base. Hopefully they will reveal something they didn't intend to say, expose themselves. Make a mistake."

I was listening now. *Did I say too much? Did I give her some information to use against him?* But I still needed to be reassured and comforted, and Sam couldn't see just how badly I was hurt... or just didn't care.

"I see it in my courtroom all the time. I don't like it," he admitted, "but that's how the system works."

"Well, it sucks!"

"Yeah, it does."

"Why!? Why did you do it?"

"I didn't! You know that I am innocent...?"

But his statement seemed more like a question than a declaration. Something had changed in my perception of his guilt. "Why did you go there, to her apartment, where you would be alone with her?" I clarified, as I exposed my feeling of betrayal. "That was stupid! And why weren't you thinking about me – that it might not be the best thing for us?" I persisted, beating him down with my words even as the D.A. had done to me.

"I'm sorry. Sooo sorry. I just wanted to help with a legal problem… offer my expertise, if I could."

"Well, you're a real jerk! A total idiot!" I walked past him and sat on his cot.

Sam dropped to his chair. "You shouldn't have gone there, to see the D.A. This whole thing is a setup – they're not willing to listen to reason."

"Well, you sure made it easy for them. I don't know how you are going to get out of this one. It's going to be a real shit show!" And suddenly I felt like it was a mistake to get involved with a man who had a shaded past. I was tempted to leave him, right then and there, and for good. In that regard, he had no persuasion for me. The attraction I had felt for him was suddenly gone, now blocked by mental images of a contorted face, that of another woman, the district attorney, yelling at me and accusing Sam of a brutal crime. And then I imagined the bruises on the face of another woman, the victim of the crime.

Still not perceiving the gloom I felt, Sam smiled inappropriately and seemed to brighten.

"But I have an idea." His tone was suddenly more optimistic.

"You know… Faith isn't exactly clean," he began to explain, "I mean she has a past too. And it's pretty shady."

He reached across his small table to the back edge where a notebook, some papers and an envelope were cluttered in a small spot designated as his office. He handed me an envelope. "Do you think you could give this to her?"

"You mean Faith?"

He nodded.

"I don't know. I really don't want to see that bitch!" I was thinking about how she had ruined my life.

"Just hand it to her. Don't talk," Sam instructed. "She will know what it means."

"What does it say?"

"Not now… but I will explain it all to you later. Really, I want to tell you everything."

"Why can't you tell me now?"

"It might lessen the impact… of this note."

I sat and looked long at the envelope in my hand. It was addressed to Faith Culver.

"I believe she's still in the hospital," Sam noted. "But we have to hurry… she might be getting out very soon, maybe even today."

"And just how do you know that?"

"They talk out front. I hear things."

"I don't know…" I hesitated.

"This just might be our best chance. It may be *my* only chance."

"Really? It's that good?"

"I hope so."

"Well, you must really have some good dirt on her," I pried again.

"Later. I'll explain it all, later."

He searched my eyes for confirmation. But even with this news, I was mostly feeling loss and uncertainty toward his suggestion.

"Just hand it to her and walk away. I don't have any other way of delivering it. Faith doesn't even have to know who you are."

"Sounds like a hit-and-run."

"Well, not exactly... but yes."

I noticed that he stumbled on my application of a legal term, always the scholar unwilling to corrupt a principle and needing to correct others. I kind of liked that about him. He was constantly reminded of the higher calling he served, that which was established in his life. I knew that, but did not fully understand his conviction of compromise. He certainly wasn't – uncompromised, that is.

"Okay," I said with reluctance. His legalese was not the point and certainly not relevant now. I would not be distracted so easily. "This is it! Samuel Urban, you are losing more than you think," I threatened.

"Please, Jodi, please! Just a couple more days. I'm stuck in here. What else can I do?"

"I don't know," I was sharp. "Isn't that *your* problem – I mean after all; you surely brought it on yourself?" I circled back to my original point and the anger that lingered there reignited. "And why are you still sitting in here anyway? What is your attorney doing for you?" I sneered as I inferred more than I asked.

"I don't know."

He looked at his impromptu office and wrung his hands. "It's the weekend. Nothing ever happens on the weekend."

"Well, it seems to me that they've got this all figured out. They really have been working it for their advantage. And now you have this bad press," I returned his attention to the paper on the table. I still needed an answer that would suffice for the dread I felt.

Sam looked at the headline and shifted in his chair. He had no response. With that I stood abruptly and walked quickly for the door, the envelope he gave me still in my hand. "See ya," was my curt farewell, all that I could muster. The sarcasm evident in my voice was intentional. I carried myself in a way that was meant to be offensive. I knew that I was acting contrary to the tenderness he desired and still expected. Yes, I was smirking at him.

"Oh, almost forgot," I stopped and dug in my purse. "I have one for you too." I found the letter from the Advocate and held it outward, toward Sam. He hesitated for a second, not knowing what I expected of him, and then began to rise from his chair. I dropped the letter and watched it fall to the floor. Humiliation intended. "I don't know what it means."

As Sam retrieved the letter sent to him by his secret observer, I considered how long it would be until I opened the note not intended for my eyes to see. Would I even deliver it to Faith? Ken finally opened the door after what was a long, stressful wait for me. I pushed him aside and slammed it hard.

++++

Body language. Jodi made it obvious. There had been an affair. She was scorned.

Sam watched in quiet disbelief as she stomped through the police station and proceeded out the front door without looking back.

101

Her swager - it seemed dishonorable. It was an indignant display. Humiliating.

She trotted on scorched earth. What, or who, had she become?

If Sam was still too dense to realize what was going on, it should have been obvious to him just then.

He wondered what else the D.A. might have said and how badly it must have hurt Jodi, even while being disgraced by the accusation of his abuse.

Then it finally hit home, at the place where the force of the intangible clings to your soul. He had cheated on her. That was the misery she bore, the shame she wore.

Until then, a tidbit of optimism lingered for Sam with the idea of the note he penned for Faith, but after that stressful meeting with Jodi, the agitated girlfriend that struck with a blow that surely was a knockout punch, all hope was gone, vanished like the fresh aroma of her hair.

And Sam realized that he was involved with two young, attractive women – and just then, he surely must have known it, that two was far too many.

An affair is emotional as well as physical. In all cases, it is a breach of trust. The shun – it hurts deeply and rubs even more those who are sexually deprived. That was Jodi. At least it should have been... or, could she have, or was she capable of cheating on Sam?

Rejection is a tormentor. Fear, its colleague.

To say that Sam was discouraged is an understatement. He was obviously losing the only person he loved truly, the only one he could still depend on.

Despair came rushing in, the floodgates of negativity opened wide.

On the other side of town, Father Jacob was lounging in his library, looking for a book of sermons as he considered the need to copy a brief homily for that weekend's services. Plagiarism was of no concern to him.

The photo of Janie caught his eye once again. He picked it up and pondered on recent events.

"Janie, my dear… I wanted to do right by you," he whispered to his ghost. "I would have taken care of you…" his mind drifted to a time in years past, "if only we had more time." His thoughts shifted. "But I won't quit now, no, I won't quit until you get the justice you deserve."

Did his sister, Karen, have everything under control? She got Urban arrested on the word of a distraught woman, an alleged victim, but did she have enough power to follow through and get him removed from office? Would Luke and his girlfriend toe the line? Had the letters been destroyed?

A dark shadow clung to the clergyman's soul. After many years of waiting for the planets to come into proper alignment, the time finally came for his eclipse. The timing was right; the players were in place. The day of his revenge was now. Samuel Urban would finally pay for his crime – the fatal auto accident that killed a young woman.

This day, Luke intended to scrape some exterior woodwork to advance plans for restoration of the large stained-glass window that highlighted the altar in the front of the church. Seeing a delivery man pull away from the curb he went to retrieve the morning newspaper. Placing his tools on the stepladder, he walked to the blue plastic tube that was perched on a flimsy fence post, the receptacle for the periodical. He paused to look at the headlines. They told the story: there was more trouble in town - a house fire.

While beginning to read the cover story and return to the chapel, he bumped into something immovable. Jacob was standing there, already disgruntled, holding out his hand for the newspaper he subscribed to and paid for. The janitor flushed and quickly handed it over. "I wonder who set..." Luke began to question his boss when the man suddenly turned and nonchalantly walked away, also absorbed in the printed page. Jacob didn't care to converse.

According to the newspaper, the magistrate remained in jail.

As the priest paused there, he was still thinking about the case against Urban, wondering if the events that led up to the arrest of the judge would leave any doubts.

"Concrete," Luke had affirmed after orchestrating the event. "He took the bait." But Jacob had doubts and remained guarded.

Everyone already knew that Sam often frequented Sal's late on a Friday evening and sipped drinks as he jawed with the locals, sometimes well into the early morning hours. It was friendly, harmless banter.

Faith met him there, asking for assistance in understanding court documents that regarded her brother who resided in another county. Sam didn't deny her, a former classmate and friend, even though some stress still lingered between them.

Faith and Sam were at one time an item, real tight, for several years as they attended high school together. After they broke up, Faith bragged about dumping him when he two-timed with Nancy, the crush he had before Jodi.

That first-love flame between Sam and Faith was extinguished, but occasionally they still experienced some sparks. This was obvious to others who observed the way they talked privately in a secluded corner of the pub, that is, until Sam let Luke go to prison on a drug charge. That's when Faith became enraged and attacked him. Was it a lovers' quarrel – who could say? But to those who observed them, it appeared to be much more than a disagreement between two people casually acquainted.

Even though she had misbehaved, Faith believed Sam was still approachable. If she offered herself to him, he would likely take the bait. It would be enough to break up him and Jodi. After a few drinks he would drop his guard because of his false sense of security. And he liked the attention he received from the opposite sex. When it came to old pals, he was a softie.

And so, Sam's reputation, though not much different than that of his peers, preceded him for vulnerability. Perhaps his biggest mistake was trusting his school day friends to be discreet, even when he slipped a little. Still, the question of his intentions for visiting Faith's apartment that consequential night lingered in the minds of the townsfolk and was the hot topic on their gossip line.

In the General Hospital, Room 616, Faith, the rape victim, was arguing with the staff, demanding to see her doctor. She wanted more pain pills. Her nurse's notes stated that the patient was seeking drugs and likely addicted to narcotics.

With everything that was happening, Karen Jackson, the priest's sister, was working this Saturday. She pushed a stack of papers on her desk forward to make room for her briefcase. In the midst of all the clutter jarred by that movement, her desk sign fell to the floor with a low thud. The middle-aged woman stood and yanked at the bottom of her jacket to straighten her business suit, one appropriate for a female competing in a man's world. She pushed her long brown hair highlighted with blonde streaks away from her face and paused long enough to steady her balance on her thick, high heels. She was still an attractive woman and displayed much younger than her years. She had the curves that would catch a man's eye and she knew how to use the bait. Sexual harassment was her specialty, always welcome, because she was proficient at winning the game. Members of the opposite sex were her pawns. As she bent over, her tight skirt crawled up her legs almost to her thigh. She retrieved the sign. It said, "Karen Jackson, State Representative, 9th Legislative District."

The distinguished member of the House looked at the wall clock in her office. Time was sifting through her fingers, minutes wasted thinking about her siblings, Jen and Jacob. She intended to command every second within her grasp. Her first appointment for the day, the Commissioner of the Pennsylvania State Police Force, was due to arrive in twelve minutes. She had to compose herself and gather her thoughts.

Ms. Jackson had been hearing the police complain about Justice Urban, the magistrate commonly referred to as "the peoples' judge," for many years. Sam was too lenient and often made the cops look like fools. Traffic arrests were frequently dismissed. Speeders were not prosecuted. Revenues were down. Their system of ticketing for the dollars generated by fines became ineffective for municipal government. Their losses were all because of Sam.

Karen also received a call from the ranking member of the board that was appointed to oversee the state insurance commission. That industry depended on convictions from traffic violations in order to justify charging their clients more. High risk insurance - it was their gravy. They needed points against their drivers. The system was established after many years of lobbying for legislation in their favor. It ran like a well-oiled machine until Urban came along and jammed the gears of their revenue generator.

Karen Jackson looked at her notes from the last meeting with the Commissioner and the fine points they agreed upon. Urban would be arrested. Some of the best troopers would be briefed on how to establish a solid case as they investigated the sexual assault charge against him. Sam would be denied bail. As soon as possible, he would be brought before a judicial disciplinary board and the outcome was easily predetermined: he would be removed from the bench. Of course, it would be her task to plan and oversee the kangaroo court, wielding her strong arm of influence.

Now she had to be sure they weren't overlooking anything. Were they controlling the press? Who would be their candidate in the upcoming election? Should she give an interview to introduce him?

She asked Councilman Peterson to recommend a candidate for district magistrate, the seat currently held by Samuel Urban. Peterson was too dirty, with his shaded past. If he stepped up for an election, his ex-wife would accuse him of abuse during their troubled marriage.

No, her candidate had to be squeaky clean, although it was unlikely Urban had the means to dig up dirt on an opponent. In this town, everyone's reputation was already known, documented by the gossip that was so common. All it took was something to spark their interest again. Just the mention of a person's name would open the door for all the "did you knows," about them. After all, some days were a bit boring as the juice machine seemed unable to produce a fresh and frothing brew of steaming hot rumors.

Jackson told Peterson to look closely at his police department. He recommended officer Barney Billings after his chief declined. The State Representative then contacted a public relations firm to help with the campaign needed to deliver an election victory to her candidate. It was difficult for a write-in to be successful, but not impossible. It had been done before.

The district had five polling places. Labels for the new candidate would have to be pre-printed and a greeter would be posted at each poll to distribute them with instructions. Jackson said these "volunteers" should be friendly and attractive. Persons from among them, well known and liked, would be best suited for this task. Pretty, young blondes would fill the bill.

The public relations firm jumped at her command and vowed to bring success. Karen Jackson was an important and repeat customer.

Next, she called the director of the election bureau in the county. He was summoned to a meeting, which he had no choice but to attend. Jackson had some insinuating questions for him. He had sway over the judges of election at each polling place and was charged with overseeing their accumulation for the final count. She knew that some manipulation was possible there.

And finally, she yelled for her legislative assistant. A timid girl, she could not have been out of college more than a few weeks, quickly stepped inside her boss's office with a pen and paper in hand. She was instructed to contact the **Herald**. Jackson wanted another interview. What was the name of that reporter she liked? Oh yes, Maggie Johns.

"Get Maggie on the phone," she ordered. The girl was writing on her tablet. "Did you get that? I want to talk to her within the hour. I have Monday's headline for her. Tell her it's an update on the election."

"Yes Ma'am."

"In fact, call the TV stations too. I'm going to give a press conference."

The legislator was confident of success; she easily out-ranked the magistrate. Was he guilty – or had the sex been consensual? Jackson didn't care one way or the other. He was a nobody. At his trial it would be his word against that of his female accuser, and the rape victim willing to testify always prevailed.

With pressure from a State Representative, and the expertise of the state police to establish guilt, Urban's conviction would be a shoe-in.

A short time later, Luke was searching for Father Jacob. He had some questions about the fire. As he crossed through the front lawn, a police cruiser pulled up and stopped at the curb. Luke paused to watch briefly but then decided to run. After all, why should he make himself readily available to the cops? They were his enemy.

"Luke!" the officer called; the demand directed at his back.

He stopped in his tracks. He had been spotted.

Ken Kapish approached in full gear: uniform, holstered pistol, billy club dangling on the other side with handcuffs. The equipment weighed heavy on his belt and pulled his tan trousers down, low on his hips, to be bunched over the tops of his shiny black shoes. The cop reached out and opened his hand to show Luke what he carried there, within his clenched fist.

"A pocketknife?" Luke inquired.

"Yes. Go ahead. Take it."

"Okay."

"It has your name on it."

"So… I'm not the only Luke in existence?"

"Is it yours?"

Luke hesitated. "No, I don't think so. I might have had one like it… sometime before."

"When? Did you lose yours?"

"No, I don't think so. I mean, I'd have to check."

"Well then, you do that," Officer Kapish instructed. "If you find it, show it to me. Will you? It might help clear up some things."

"Yeah, sure, but why?"

"This one was found at the scene of the house fire. It was arson – could have belonged to the person who set the fire. It was already dusted for prints," he noted while watching for Luke's reaction.

"And?"

"Don't know yet. Still checking."

"I'll look for mine. But like I said," Luke was trying to backtrack in the conversation to cover over what might have been an admission, "I'm not sure that I even owned one like this. Mine wasn't this color," he lied.

Ken held out his hand as Luke took a step back. The officer snapped his fingers and returned his hand, open palm facing up. "Give it back to me, Luke," he instructed.

Reluctantly, the suspect did so, his sneaky plan foiled.

"Okay," the officer concluded. "Let me know."

"Yeah, sure." Luke stood in silence as he watched the cop return to the cruiser. Its turning signal blinked once before entering the roadway. Slowly, it pulled away.

Father Jacob was watching from the upstairs window of the rectory, adjacent to the church. Within minutes he met Luke in the vestibule.

"What did the cops want this time?" Jacob inquired.

"Found a knife. They think it's mine, but I don't see how it could be…"

"Where did they find it?"

"At the house fire. Strange though, I…"

"I'll vouch for you," Jacob interrupted. "We were up late that night watching TV together in the basement," he suggested as he looked for confirmation.

Luke nodded slowly. "Oh, yea. Sure, that's right… Thanks, I guess."

"It's an important alibi. We will cover for each other."

Luke returned a blank stare. He was still trying to grasp the full meaning of his boss's suggestion.

"So, what's up with the girlfriend?"

"Who, Faith?"

"No, you imbecile! The girlfriend of the magistrate."

"She's a tough cookie. I tried to slow her down. You know, did damage to her car. But she keeps going."

"Where did she go?"

"To the courthouse. Believe me, there's no stopping her, unless I put some hurt on her."

"Where is she now?" the priest persisted.

"I followed her to the police station. She is visiting with Urban there."

"Well, what are you doing here then? Don't you think you better get back on her trail, before you lose her?"

"Yeah, well, but I wanted to ask, when Faith is getting out of the hospital. Is it okay?"

"Yes, but then you'll have to watch her too. Are you sure she will behave?"

"I think she'll stay inside her place for a while," Luke reasoned, "especially if she's still taking those pain pills."

"Then keep her well stocked. There's only two more days until the election. She just has to keep her mouth shut." He hesitated. "Let me know if you need more pills."

Luke edged at that, a little uncomfortable with the offer.

"Now get going!" the priest ordered. "You have to stay on top of this." He turned and casually walked back to the sanctuary.

++++

The General Hospital was a fearfully looming structure of six stories, the tallest in town. It had an unusual glass and chrome facade, giving it a modern, even space-age appearance. Visitors entered by driving onto a narrow lane that led to the parking garage. Rarely was anyone able to find street parking within two blocks of that place.

The first level of the garage connected to the third floor of the hospital, a med-surg wing. If parked on one of the upper levels, you had to first descend to the bottom, level one, of the parkade.

After walking through a long corridor without windows, Jodi entered the hospital. Next, she had to use an elevator, and select "L" to descend to the lobby. Why did it all have to be so complicated?

The lift vibrated, dropped, and came to a sudden halt, in a way that did not inspire confidence. Stainless steel doors, smudged with finger prints and smeared by the swift motion of the cleaner's cloth, opened slowly revealing a large open space. People were walking briskly across the lobby. To the left was a small gift shop and to the right a tiny café with coffee and bagels. Straight ahead was a long circular desk. A single person, a middle-aged woman, sat in the center of it, seemingly isolated there. She watched Jodi approach as she obviously had little to do.

++++

"How may I help you?"

"Hi," I answered meekly. "Um, Faith… Faith Culver," I noted matter-of-factly. "I'd like to visit a friend."

"Let's see."

The woman examined a long list of names. "Don't see her… probably was already discharged today."

"Really? You sure?" I pressed. "I was just told that she is still here."

The woman picked up another paper. "Oops!"

She said it with a chuckle, looked up at me, and smiled apologetically.

"She *is* still here. Room 616. Am I bad?"

"616. Got it."

"You have to get to the C elevator."

While offering me instructions, I thought she was trying to compensate for her mistake.

"Take a left past the café, go down the long hallway and through the doors, then turn right, and you'll find the elevator on your left."

She said all this while seeing the confusion on my face.

"It's not far after you go right," she paused, "down the hall, on your left."

"Pass the café, then I turn left," I repeated.

"Right… I mean no! Pass the café, through the doors and then you turn right."

She was talking now with hand gestures, pointing one way, then the other. It was confusing me even more.

"Go ahead, you'll find it, Honey. There are signs."

I wondered who could have designed such a place. It was so disorderly. I'd try to follow the arrows.

This is a place where you see many people worse off than yourself, and your mind shifts, self-pity taking a back seat to an appreciation for health and wellness. Actually, I wasn't sure what I was feeling, or what to expect next. Despite our problems, or should I say Sam's, I had good health, and endless opportunity abounded before me… if I could just see through the fog. So many others were battling debilitating illnesses. I should be grateful.

I reached into my jacket pocket and felt the letter intended for Faith. I dreaded seeing her. Surely, she wouldn't be happy to see me. Was I doing the right thing? I wondered. *Maybe she really is a victim, and I am about to deliver another blow, below the belt.*

Does she deserve to be hurt, and is this the best way to defend Sam? I wasn't sure.

But really, the pressing question involved why. Why would she go after Sam and cry rape; I mean, why would she do it – what was her motivation?

I managed to make it to the sixth floor and quickly looked for room numbers as the elevator C door opened with a bang. I noticed something smeared all over the tiled floor in front of me. I stepped out cautiously, thinking that housekeeping must have just had a mop there. I didn't want to think about what they cleaned up. As I neared a nurse's station the odor of alcohol made my nostrils flare. A young woman clothed in white gave me a side glance as I walked by. I realized that I could never work in a place like this.

I continued down the hallway. Patient's names were hand-printed on narrow pieces of paper and slid into metal holders on the doors. The room numbers were posted above. 630. As I progressed the numbers declined. Even numbers on the left. I got to the end where there was a window with a view of a flat roof and realized that I had to be in the wrong wing. The lowest number there was 618. I was looking for 616.

I returned to the nurses' station and waited at the counter. A couple of them sat at a desk and held telephones. Beyond them, several others were clustered around a handsome young man, perhaps a doctor, or intern, engaged in animated conversation with laughter. He was obviously enjoying all the attention he was getting from the gals, most of them much older than he was.

I cleared my throat loud enough to draw the attention of the nurse nearest me. She sat the phone down.

"Can I help you?"

"I think I might be lost," I admitted with a smile. "I'm looking for room 616."

"Oh, you went the wrong way. It's down there," and she pointed. "Turn right after you pass the elevator. It's the second room on your left, after the day room."

Without waiting for confirmation of her instructions she picked up the phone again.

As I passed the C elevator, I noticed that the floor was still wet at the edges of the hallway. I turned the corner and nearly bumped into a stranger. I mumbled a faint "excuse me," but then turned around abruptly as he dodged and darted past me. He looked familiar. Baseball cap, black shirt, denim jeans.

"Hey! Hey you!"

++++

Luke was already sprinting down the hall and made the turn to the elevator.

++++

"Wait!" I yelled. "I need to talk to you." I began running after him. I rounded the corner and the elevator came into view. Its doors were already closing. I darted for it and through an eight-inch opening gained a better view of the man who was stalking me. He had a smug grin on his stubble face. His goatee was long and unruly. He saluted as the rubber seals of the doors connected and his chuckle quickly faded away.

"And there you go." I looked at the tilting arrow above the double door. He was going down, probably headed to the lobby. "It's no use." I was talking to myself. I waited for the elevator doors to reopen. "He got away again."

Room 616 had the door tightly closed. Most others were open, at least a crack. I stood there, already flustered, as I tried to gather my thoughts. The name on the door caused me even more anxiety. 'Faith Culver'.

I saw her once before, but had never spoken to her. I really never cared to. Now, in the clinical setting I wasn't sure if I felt pity for an abused woman or anger at a false accuser, but it didn't take long for my true feelings to emerge from beneath the cloak of uncertainty.

I fiddled with my purse as I searched for the envelope. It had to be there. Finally, I found it in a side pocket.

Okay. It was time to face the saboteur of my life, the *other* woman, the sadist who construed me to be a fraud. No doubt, she was also taking pleasure in hurting me. This was the person who was threatening my future and caused all that was precious to me to come crashing down. Yes, she was also my accuser, because I was culpable by association, the partner of the alleged rapist. The accusation attacked my integrity and tarnished my reputation. *If she is lying, who the hell does she think she is? Well yes, of course she is lying!*

As I opened the door, I saw a young woman sitting in a high back recliner. Faith was wearing cotton pajamas with an animal print. There were cats, and paw prints everywhere. She was gazing at a small television set that protruded from the wall above her bed on a steel arm. It looked like the elbow of a robot, holding the box with moving pictures, and it was jointed, so the viewer could adjust the TV's height and distance. Faith glanced up and I shuddered, feeling panic. Then, without saying a word, she just looked back to the TV.

She had long, dirty blonde hair pulled back in a tight ponytail. I noticed a light brown blotch on her face, left cheek; it was a healing bruise. Not wearing any makeup, her skin appeared oily and her facial features faint. She slouched in the chair.

"So… What do *you* want?"

I could see that the young woman before me needed a shower and pampering, yet she had potential. Primped and primed, Faith would turn a head. Her body shape was not lost in the baggy covering, as it was proportional, not too large or small in all the right places: legs long, boobs – full and firm.

"What!? What is it?"

She turned her head and placed her eyes squarely on me.

"Who the heck are you?!"

"Hi Faith," I couldn't help but to smirk. "Don't you know me?" I leaned in.

++++

The patient's eyes focused some more but lacked the sparkle of awareness. She had recently been given a pain pill.

++++

"No, I don't know you."

Her speech was slurred. She looked back to the TV. It seemed as though she was already beginning to lose interest in me.

"Why are you here? What do you want?"

"You need to wake up. Now! This is important." I held out the envelope.

"What? What is it?"

She glanced my way and I sweetened the offer with an evil grin.

"I don't want it! I don't care what it is. I don't give a shit about anything anymore."

"Faith… take it, it's important!"

118

"No, I don't care."

"Oh, but you will! You'd be wise to consider this… before you go into court."

++++

The statement seemed to resonate even in a mind that had been numbed. She took the letter from Jodi's hand.

++++

"What are you talking about?"

"Rape!"

Faith dropped the letter as her eyes grew wide.

"I know what you did," Anger was seething out of me. Saliva escaped from the corner of my mouth and ran down my chin. I pounded with a clenched fist against my thigh. "I know everything! Sam told me. And you'll never get away with it… You bitch!"

Faith glared.

"You won't get away with it, you lying bitch! The only thing we don't know is why – why are you hurting someone who has helped you? Who is putting you up to it?"

"Get her out!"

Faith screamed at me but the door was closed and I doubted that anyone would hear her.

"Get out. I'm calling security."

She leaned toward her bed and struggled to find the call button.

"You won't get away with it," I repeated. "You're going down," I growled as my lower jaw protruded, my bottom teeth showing.

"Out! Get out!"

119

Faith grabbed the button at the end of the gray cord and held it up for me to see as she pressed hard. I knew that my allotted time with her was expiring.

"Leave me alone!"

With that I made a quick exit, slamming the door hard enough for a nurse passing nearby to notice. She returned a questioning gaze.

Enter John Paul Rogers (JP)

I darted for the elevator and was relieved to see the doors already open. Inside I looked at the buttons. I had to make a quick decision. *How the heck do I get out of here? What button? What level is the exit at?* I pushed the circle displaying the number 2, hoping that was the floor connected to the parking garage. I wanted to avoid the lobby where security guards loitered.

Exiting the elevator, I took a quick left. I didn't want to appear as if I didn't know where I was going. There was a long line of patients' rooms on each side. Then I noticed a man in a uniform approaching, so I quickly ducked into the nearest room.

As I pushed on the door, I noticed the patient's name. It was Jen Foster. I stepped inside, closed the door softly, and pondered on the name. It had recognition. And then I remembered. *This is the woman whose house burned. It was an arson fire. Yes, an awful shame. I know her. Mrs. Foster is a sweet lady.*

Since I was there, I decided that I better say hello. I approached her bed.

It was then I noticed that she was not alone; she had another visitor, a young man sitting in a high-backed chair in a dark corner.

"Oh, I'm sorry. I… I didn't realize that someone else was here."

He smiled without saying a word in return.

"You're visiting?" Not knowing what else to say, I stumbled for words. He didn't speak or move. "Are you a nurse?" I looked more intently, "do you work here?" It felt like an interrogation, but all I wanted was simple conversation.

"It's okay," he finally spoke.

As I stepped closer, my eyes adjusted to the dim light. He was young, probably in his twenties. His brown hair completely covered his ears and curled at the base of his neck. He had a dark complexion and wore round, wire rimmed glasses. His clothing was a golf shirt and shorts. Tanned legs and sandals. It became obvious that he had to be a visitor.

He was handsome, and I immediately felt an attraction for him. *But really?* I put a check on myself. *Stop! Tired, lonely, needy, vulnerable. So, what. Get a hold of yourself.*

"She's been sleeping," he explained. "I think she might be heavily sedated. Said some words… but really not legible."

"Oh."

"I'll step out. Give you a private moment."

He didn't ask any questions or inquire about my relationship to the woman lying in the hospital bed. He rose, stood for a moment, and walked slowly toward the door.

"Thanks," I shot back at him.

"Sure, no problem."

"I hope she is going to be okay," I said, wanting to interrupt his exit, as I needed to ask more questions. My curiosity had spiked.

He hesitated.

"I'm Jodi. Just a friend... well, a neighbor, guess you could say... but not that close." I was rambling, felt a nervous twitch that was unexpected. "Jodi," I repeated softly and offered my hand in greeting.

He accepted it.

"JP" he introduced himself. "Well, better be going."

"Yeah, okay. Nice to meet you... JP."

He disappeared behind the door as I turned my attention to the patient. Standing bedside, I grasped the rail that was elevated.

The woman moaned, turned toward me and opened her eyes a slit.

"Mrs. Foster? Jen... how are you doing?"

She stiffened and opened her eyes a little wider. There seemed to be recognition.

"It's Jodi, Jodi Culp," I offered my name quickly.

Jen nodded once and closed her eyes again. I reached for her hand and took it in mine. I watched intently and waited for that moment to reconnect. Soon she reopened her eyes and locked them on me.

"Yes, Jodi..." She whispered in acknowledgment of my introduction, but slurred the second word, my name, as she drifted away again.

I saw her body quiver. The woman's hand was icy cold. Her lips moved ever so slowly.

"L...l...let."

Jen's voice was barely legible. I leaned in and positioned my ear close to the woman's lips.

"Let…" she stammered, "ers."

"Letters?" I repeated as a question. Jen nodded ever so slightly and turned away. Her body relaxed and her hand drooped. She was gone, taken into a drug induced slumber, nearly comatose.

++++

Jodi caringly placed Jen's hand on the bed and stood back to observe her. There weren't any bandages, but her hair was nearly gone, the short frizzy ends that remained obviously singed. Her scalp and face were a dark reddish color.

The poor woman.

Jodi gathered herself, promised to visit again, and turned to leave.

After a few wrong turns and retracing her steps, she finally found the elevator to the garage. She had to go up one more level.

When Luke returned to Faith's room, she was dazed, a handwritten note lying on her lap. He noticed an envelope on the floor nearby. On it was Faith's name.

He stood there, taking in the scene, first biting his lower lip, then mumbling something under his breath. He was supposed to keep Urban's girlfriend away. Now, it seemed that he had failed to do so.

"She was here, wasn't she?" he finally asked.

"Who?"

"His girlfriend!" Luke exclaimed. "I tried to chase her away."

Faith didn't answer at first. "I don't know who you're talking about.

"The magistrate's girlfriend… Culp! She was here, to see you, wasn't she?"

Faith nodded in reply.

"What's that?" Luke pointed to the note. "Is that from her?"

She nodded again, her expression blank.

As a result of the 'care' and medication she received in the hospital, Faith was declining more than improving. It was probably the neglect, combined with uncertainty and fear, the emotional trauma she experienced, that wore her down.

"Can I see it?"

Another nod.

Luke picked it up and read aloud, ***"If this is the way it's going to be – why shouldn't I tell them everything?"***

There was no signature, just those words, one hyphenated sentence, written in black ink.

"Is it from him?" Luke inquired.

She made no response.

"What does it mean?" he pressed.

Faith finally spoke, "It means… it means we're screwed." She hesitated. "I told you…"

"What!?"

"That this wouldn't work…"

"What are you saying?" Luke insisted, as his face turned red.

"He's got dirt on me," her words were firm, clear. "Serious dirt. Enough to put me away."

"What do you mean?"

She paused, then spoke without answering his question. She had already come to a conclusion. "I can't testify against him… Not now… I can't do it."

"You have to!" Luke insisted. "Jacob already paid."

"I'm telling you," Faith looked long into his eyes. "Luke, I can't do it."

"But why?" He forced himself to wait for an answer as she looked away.

"I can't talk about it now," she whispered. "I need to rest. Feel… feeling very tired."

Luke took a step away, clenched his fist and punched at the air. He paced for about thirty seconds and returned to face Faith. "We can't tell Jacob about this. This note will be our secret."

But his suggestion didn't register with her.

"We've got to get more. He has it," Luke was working his plan audibly, "he's good for it. After all, another ten 'k' is nothing for him." Luke was pacing again. "We'll just tell him that we hit a roadblock – it's going to mean we have to take a hit – and he will have to pay us more. Then we'll make a break for it – get the hell outa here." He looked to Faith for agreement but her head was turned away, her eyes closed.

Luke left the hospital with anger in his stride.

Thirty minutes later Faith revived somewhat and realized that Luke was right about one thing – getting more money. She picked up the telephone and dialed her mother's number. They seldom spoke and soon she would be leaving for church. The plan was quickly hatched in Faith's mind. She'd ask her mother to put a note addressed to Father Jacob in the offering satchel as it passed along the row her mother sat in. The note would demand the ten thousand dollars Luke said he was good for. She would give her mother five hundred for completing the devious task. The priest would never suspect her mom's involvement.

The note Faith dictated to her mother simply said, *"They know. We need more money. $10,000. Consider it charity for one in need."* It was to be signed, *"Faith and Luke."*

And she wondered how much of the new windfall she would actually let Luke keep.

++++

My day was going by quickly and I was exhausted. I was in overload, my emotions raw. I felt like I was losing control. My stomach growled. I needed a break from it all and I needed food, so I turned my car toward the mall.

At the food court I ordered Chinese and took a distant table. Consumed with my thoughts, I didn't want to talk to anyone. My mind replayed the hurt I saw on Sam's face when I slapped him. *Was I too hard on him? That wasn't fair, not to him, or to me.*

Images of other faces flashed in my head, one with the appearance of a corpse. A chill ran down my spine as I felt a spirit's presence. I looked for a window, wanting to see far away, as if I could flee to another place, escape, anywhere, just to be away from the terror that gripped at me. It was as if the walls were closing in. I shuddered at the thought of Jen convulsing and suddenly dying. Had she?

Then I saw JP smiling at me, expressing kindness, without saying a word.

I know that the mind can play tricks. I needed to be rational, stay in control.

But Jen really was in bad shape.

126

I thought about the guy who was obviously stalking me. I'd gotten a good look at his face, close up. And now, I needed to tell Sam about my encounter with the man who wore a baseball cap and a long goatee.

So many people were getting seriously hurt.

Faith – I almost felt sorry for how mean I was to her. It wasn't like me to act that way, not in any situation. Faith was a victim too; after all, *someone* had abused her.

++++

Jodi had taken some classes in psychology and child development in college, but never finished her schooling, diverted by her mother's sudden illness.

A woman in her fifties and divorced, her mom was suspected of having cancer, had a colon resection, but then fully recovered in about eight months' time. Thankfully, there was no cancer.

Jodi took the job at the newspaper to work part-time while her mother recuperated, spending more time at home; that was five years ago and now she often wondered why she was still at that lousy job.

It's easy to get stuck.

She met Sam and about a year later, rented a townhouse, intending to purchase it as soon as she saved enough for the downpayment. Yes, she would have to work full time. Her boss promised her that position in sales, with a hefty commission, but she hesitated after seeing drama in that department.

There was Kara, a true diva, one of the most narcissistic persons she'd ever met. Kara was constantly yakking about something, demanding attention for herself. If she wasn't bragging about her success with a client, she was modeling a new outfit, or if the switch had flipped, she complained about anything and everything. If you angered Kara, she became one of the most spiteful persons you'd ever know.

She wouldn't be Jodi's boss, but she would be her superior. Jodi saw through the promise of prosperity and decided to wait, wait for Kara to leave, or for a better job to open up. It was enough to have to deal with Kara when the display advertising she sold needed a special design, which was Jodi's job to produce.

Jodi was draining her college fund, having promised her mother that she would replace every penny she borrowed. She knew that she should go back to school. She'd never have a chance in the world without completing her degree.

Now, something had to change.

But how could she think about all of that now, after everything she'd just been through, and with what was happening to Sam?

After meeting Faith, she was having trouble quieting herself. Jodi remembered the lectures she endured in college.

A brain's development is affected by the environmental experiences of the individual. Sure, there is some predisposition to genetics, but more is determined by how the child is treated; or so her professors claimed.

Abuse and neglect, causing insecurities a child cannot understand or process, causes the brain to be re-wired, short-circuited, for certain lobes to be over or underdeveloped. It changes a person's feelings and response. Later, as an adult, they will often over-react, often inappropriately.

A kid is overtly shy, but is that okay, or is it a bad thing? Is it something they'll outgrow, or evidence of abuse and pending harm?

It's true that we're not all cut from the same cloth. Everyone is unique. And in that regard, is there a standard for perfection? Superiority, no doubt. But doesn't everyone have their own, individual strengths and weaknesses?

Anti-social. Well, that's a bit harder to explain, and it seemed to be an issue with Faith. Could it have been the result of childhood abuse? What must she have endured?

Disappointments, difficulties and disasters, widespread or individual, continue to affect the person's mental health during adulthood. But does the brain continue to change?

++++

Enough already! I wasn't about to answer questions that plagued generations of scientists. Whatever was Faith's motivation, her reason for accusing Sam, well, he knew her better than I did, and he'd just have to figure it out. Hopefully, the note I delivered would hit the mark, shake her up enough to make Faith reconsider; but that was doubtful.

More than likely, her brain was damaged.

I needed a distraction. Shopping always helped when I hit the skids, so I decided to do just that. Later, after having bought a new outfit and two pair of shoes, I headed for home, feeling a wee bit better.

It was 5 PM as I approached the Orthodox Church pastored by Father Jacob. Both sides of the street were lined with cars. A couple holding hands darted in front of me. Parishioners were driven to get their dose of religion, enough to cover their sins for another week. It all seemed like such a farce, even though I was somewhat of an active participant. Yeah, it was my church, Jacob my pastor. I had the thought just then, that I should go in. I even felt obligated to do so. But it was only for a second that I was tempted to stop and join the throng of the faithful. Then again, maybe it would help me to be better rooted, centered. Perhaps the priest would console me or better yet, use his influence to help Sam. *Naw, I'm not going to church today. But maybe… should I ask him for help?*

++++

Mrs. Culver, Faith's mother, followed a young family closely; it appeared as though she accompanied them as their grandmother. Once inside she held back and looked for a single seat, amongst a large group, needing to be inconspicuous. Candles gave a dim, flickering light in the vestibule.

Despite others sitting nearby, she was alone in the cavernous chapel.

It was a place that hosted contrasting events. Babies were baptized, welcoming new life, and funerals were held for the deceased. The large stained-glass windows that usually filled the sanctuary with bright colors attracting viewers to brilliant scenes eliciting serenity were now dull and lifeless. The gloomy weather hid the sun even as the clouds outside were indicative of the sadness that settled upon the souls that visited there, in that place of religious authority. The priest would proclaim forgiveness, sealed by the regimental sacrament that followed. But in reality, nothing changed for them. Their brief moment of relief, that good feeling, was fleeting.

Forgiveness – are not some incapable of such a noble act? God have mercy!

Mrs. Culver reached into her pocket and felt for the note she was to deliver. Her brow furrowed.

Was Faith getting in too deep?

This sanctuary was usually the place where a needy person would come seeking relief, offering penance for their wrongdoing. It was supposed to be warm and inviting. But today it was dark and cold, presenting gloom.

The gray stones stacked one upon the other loomed in the dim light as the columns they formed reached upward from the black tiled floor, providing a covering for evil spirits that hid, lurking nearby. They came to reside in this fortress of religion, escaped from the many corpses of the dark souls displayed there in open caskets. A cold chill flitted through the open spaces. Mrs. Culver shuddered in their presence.

The six stone pillars on each side of the building supported massive wood trusses that were perched on top of them, reaching upward to form the high ceiling. Behind and between them, five tall, narrow stained-glass windows were mounted on each side of the building. The front and rear of the church was decorated with wood panels, mahogany. The altar was separated from the sanctuary by railings which formed a complete visual as well as physical barrier. Behind it were three large paintings that depicted the life of Jesus: his birth, the Sermon on the Mount, and his crucifixion.

A procession was underway. An altar server, the crucifer, carried a cross at the front of the line. He was followed by a deacon, carrying the Evangelion, the Gospel Book which she held high for everyone to see, before placing it on the altar.

Father Jacob's vestment was a dark green cassock, a full-length robe with button closures and long sleeves, a tight fit. He trailed his deacon swinging the thurible, a metal censer suspended from chains that emitted smoke.

The pungent smell of incense wafted at Mrs. Culver's nostrils. She became woozy. But was it the incense or dread that jabbed at the pit of her stomach?

Mass began with introductory rites. Mrs. Culver subconsciously repeated the words, "Lord, have mercy," barely audible. She startled when the person sitting in front of her suddenly turned around with a greeting. An elderly man extended his hand and offered the words, "Peace be with you." She nodded and briefly touched the stranger's open palm.

"Today's reading is from the Gospel of Matthew, chapter sixteen," the priest began, as the service progressed quickly. The topic of his homilies that month was "Pillars of the Faith." This message was about Saint Peter, posthumously acknowledged as their first pope according to tradition.

Finally, the moment came that Mrs. Culver anxiously awaited. The ushers were called, came forward and passed the collection container; it was an open purse-like bag suspended from two short wooden dowels, shaped with handles and painted in bright colors. Mrs. Culver moved swiftly as she put her hand deep inside and at the bottom deposited the envelope addressed to Father Jacob. It was a second thought, but this concerned mother added the word "Confidential" on the front of the envelope, under the priest's name.

Following the observance of the Eucharist and the singing of songs she rose to make a quick exit. Father Jacob stood near the open doors at the rear of the sanctuary. Some individuals lingered there, talking to him in soft, muffled tones in an effort to display piety as others went by on their left side. Mrs. Culver stepped fast, dodged and passed those who lingered, cut the line and sped past the clergyman without speaking a word to anyone.

Jodi was thinking about chocolate as she opened the door to her home and stepped over the mail. With her foot she scooted it to one side. At that moment she had no interest in it.

Two Days Later: A disagreement, a false accusation, a fit of rage. Two lives hang in the balance. One man lies in a pool of blood, his life essence weeping out of a large wound in the back of his head.

The other man looks at his hands. They are trembling. Now he must decide what to do next. But how did it come to this?

CHAPTER SIX: Religion

Sunday, May 12, 1985 – day five.

HEADLINE: There was no Sunday paper in Walthem.

Bang, Bang, Bang! Jodi's mind was like an obsolete computer rebooting. Her operating system had not yet fully loaded. She was coming back from a deep, alcohol induced slumber. The server was pressing for an update to be installed. She was remembering the events of yesterday, visiting the hospital, and at the same time she was trying to figure out what day of the week it was.

Conscious thoughts were coming into clarity, but very slowly.

Bang, Bang, Bang! And there was a voice, muffled, calling a name. She recognized it, it was her name - someone was calling her. She sat upright on the sofa; the cushion had slid forward and was positioned under her knees, her buttock sunk into the back of the furniture where a void existed between the framework and the springs. ***Bang, Bang!*** Someone was pounding on her door.

++++

"Hold on, I'm coming," I attempted to interrupt the rhythm of the intrusion. A memory of my dream from that night passed through my mind quickly. It was about Jeremy, a flame and a fling that I had at the time of my high school graduation. He was my

134

first sex partner, the time I lost my virginity. But why was I thinking about him – was that even allowed?

++++

The operating system in her brain stalled.

Bang! Like pressing F1 on the keyboard, the mind began to churn again.

++++

"For god's sake stop the banging. I said, I'm coming!"

++++

As Jodi stood, her foot went into an empty box of chocolates. She recalled her binge. Yuck – they were stale anyway. She lifted her foot and the plastic lining of the candy box stuck to the bottom of her sock-slipper. She shook her foot but it persisted to stick. Sitting on the arm of the sofa she reached down and pried it off. A pink truffle was stuck there acting as an adhesive.

Bang! Jodi jumped forward, smearing the crushed candy into her carpet as she stepped away from the site of her night's fitful slumber.

Without considering the risk of a stranger being there and not knowing who was rapping on her door, she threw it open, a reaction to the incessant *banging*! But now it was her head that was throbbing.

++++

"Susan! It's you." I stepped aside, "Well you might as well come in. What are you doing here?" I yawned and mumbled, "What time is it anyway?"

"And a top of the morning to you, my dear," Susan greeted me.

I looked at her with dreary eyes, her enthusiasm more than I could take. "Cut it out." My mind, the sluggish computer, was finally humming as it waited for input, commands from the operator.

I turned and walked back to my living room.

"It's eleven twenty," Susan announced.

She paused to pick up the mail and placed it on the hall table. It was then that she noticed a letter addressed to Sam and thought it might be important.

"Hey, did you see this letter for Sam?" she inquired as she followed and held up the envelope for me to see.

I pushed the cushion back into place and dropped into the sofa with a dull thud. "My head is banging… and so is my butt." I reached under the edge of the cushion and retrieved an empty wine bottle and dropped it on the coffee table.

Susan was picking up, like a true friend without condemnation. She placed the empty box of chocolates on the table and lowered herself next to me. "Why didn't you invite me over to your little party? You should never drink alone."

"It wasn't planned."

"Oh, pity, pity."

"No, don't feel sorry for me."

"I don't. Jodi, I'd trade places with you any day," Susan stated firmly and then suggested, "How about today?" She looked directly into my eyes expecting a quick response.

"Oh, just shut up. Please…"

"Here, I found this letter on your foyer floor addressed to Sam.

"Yeah… yeah, so what?"

"You better take it to him. It might be important."

I examined the letter still in Susan's hand. "No… no," I rubbed my eyes. "It's one of those notes from his secret admirer, or whatever the hell he, or she is… I don't really understand them and don't care nothin' 'bout 'em." I looked at my friend needing understanding for the confession I was about to make. "I really don't want to see him today."

Susan focused as she examined me more closely. Bloodshot, my eyes burned as veins erupted in the whites.

"Why don't you give it to him," I paused, "bet he'd rather see you anyway." I dropped my head in despair, not caring to see her response.

"Okay…" She placed the letter into her jacket pocket. "I was thinking about visiting him today… I have an idea I want to talk to him about…"

But I wasn't really listening.

"So, what's up between you two?" she pressed. "The other night you said you were having second thoughts… that we needed to talk."

A beam of sunlight hit the mirror located behind Susan and it suddenly appeared as though she was wearing a hallo. I squinted against the bright light. I needed to answer her. I rubbed my eyes some more and realized that my contact lenses were dirty, very dirty.

"Well, here I am" Susan announced, "just as ordered… in the flesh… because I care about you…"

I smiled. She had a way of making me laugh. "Thanks," I said, feeling a sincerity for her, "You *are* a good friend." I paused as I noticed Susan waiting for an explanation, but more than that, a revealing of my deepest thoughts and feelings. "I had a couple of real bad days. Really, Susan, I've been taking a beating."

"Looks like you're being hard on yourself," she frowned. "I know that you guys are going through a tough time. But is it really *his* fault?"

"Damn right, it is! I mean, why not?"

"No, I don't know what you mean."

"Well," I said while straightening my back for emphasis, "If he was really committed to me, then why was he going to *her* apartment in the middle of the night?"

++++

Anger flashed in Jodi's eyes, giving them the appearance of a flame erupting from a propane lighter.

Susan was thinking. She noted that it wasn't very late when Sam first arrived at Faith's apartment, but still searching for a better answer and finding none, she took Jodi's hand and held it gently. It was understanding that she needed most and another woman, a good friend could quickly discern that.

++++

"I know that he is committed to you," Susan nodded for emphasis, "He loves you."

She got me. I choked back a sob, evidence of an emotional surge I did not want to express just then. "But why, why did he go there?"

"It's his job. He was just doing his job."

"What do you mean? Does his job include private, passionate consultations?"

"Well, no… but I'm sure that wasn't his intention. Jodi, he is a lawyer; she is an old friend who asked for help… it was after

138

work hours, but it was just one person helping another. Don't you still care about old friends?"

I remembered my dream about Jeremy, my first lover, and began to soften a little. "But what if he really did it? I mean, maybe it wasn't his original intent, but maybe things got crazy. Maybe he lost control of himself... Or, did he plan it, to fulfill a sexual fantasy, and relive a past thrill? I think she was his first... you know what I mean." Susan's eyes widened as I continued, "And did you know that the date rape drug was found on him...?"

"No! I don't believe that. That's not Sam," Susan blurted, obviously shaken. "Didn't the girl that was supposedly raped take the drug to the police?"

I looked away. I already made my point. I wasn't yet ready to consider hers.

"So, you're believing *her* now? And besides, Sam didn't push his way into her place. He was invited. I'm sure he had his guard up too."

++++

Susan continued to comfort her friend as she addressed Jodi's fears, finally sensing some calm settle upon her. Then she began talking about her infatuation with Jared, repeatedly thanking her for setting them up. She was waiting for his call. She expected a formal date. Finally, Susan asked if it was okay for her to see Sam, and Jodi gave her full permission.

++++

"Tell him I'm a little under the weather today," I instructed. "Oh yes, and tell him that I delivered his note to Faith."

"Really?!" Susan probed. "Sounds interesting..."

"It's for another day. But really, thanks."

We stood and held each other in a long embrace. "You truly are a good friend," I whispered into her ear. "I mean it." A tear escaped from the corner of my right eye.

"Thanks," Susan replied.

She squared off and looked into my tear-filled eyes.

"I love you…"

Her expression of sincere affection caused a slight smile that quivered momentarily on my face.

"It's going to be okay. You'll see, everything's going to fall into place."

I nodded in agreement and we hugged again.

++++

In Room 616 Faith was sitting on the edge of her bed, fully dressed, waiting for her doctor to make his morning rounds. She was expecting and hoping for him to sign her release papers.

Holding the note she received the day before, she was thinking about Sam. Would he really betray their trust, a secret held for so long that it was nearly forgotten? If he did spill the beans, could she still face criminal charges? What did they call it when a crime was too old to prosecute? Normally she would ask him, as he was her "go to" for legal advice, always respectful and polite. Their history meant something to her, but no longer, for now he would surely keep his distance. Their long-term friendship was over. She was burning bridges.

Faith decided to make a couple of quick phone calls before leaving the hospital. The first one, to her mother, would verify that she delivered the message to Father Jacob. Then, she felt that she better inform Luke about it, and she needed a ride home.

Surprised, he wasn't happy with her news. "You did what?" Luke shouted.

"I sent a note asking for another ten thousand, just like you said I should."

"I didn't tell you to send a note," Luke nearly dropped the phone he cradled between his shoulder and ear. He was making himself a sandwich. "And how did you deliver it?" he asked, needing to verify what she just said. "Your mother took it to church?"

"Yeah, I already told you. She put it in the collection basket."

"Faith, that was dumb, really dumb." Luke dropped the sandwich to catch the phone that slipped away. "I needed time… time to figure out the right way. You don't put something like that in writing!" He paused in thought. "And how do you know no one else read it?"

"Guess I didn't think about that…"

"Oh my god, I have to get it back, before everyone knows." Luke raked his dirty hair with his fingers. "This is bad, really bad."

It was after the third message she left on a recording device that Jodi finally got a return call from the church secretary, Mrs. Thomas. The woman appeared disinterested and was somewhat apologetic for not returning her call sooner, noting that she did not know Father Jacob's schedule but he was likely in a meeting. Jodi explained that her boyfriend was in prison and that she urgently needed counsel and prayer, that she was very discouraged. What was his name? "Oh my," Mrs. Thomas seemed alarmed after Sam was identified as the inmate. "I must check with Father first. I will get back to you."

The switchboard was busy that morning as Jen Foster also received an important call as she continued to recover in the hospital. She was sitting up in bed, feeling much better and nibbling on a piece of white toast with orange marmalade. She did not yet know that her brother and sister, Jacob and Karen, were plotting together against Sam, but after that last conversation with her sister, Jen suspected that Karen would not want to help the troubled judge.

The phone at her bedside began to ring.

"Hello?" she answered.

"Jen, it's Karen," came the swift reply.

"Oh, Karen, it's you."

The patient was on a reduced prescription of pain relievers and still a bit groggy.

"How are you? Are you okay?" Her questions came in rapid fire. "I tried to call yesterday, but you didn't answer and when I called the front desk to connect with the nurses' station, they told me that you weren't able to take any calls."

"Oh," was all Jen said in response to the unnecessary explanation.

"Jen, I'm so sorry… Sorry about the fire. Thank God you got out alive! I'm sure you can rebuild. You have good insurance, right? All that matters is that you're still alive." Karen hesitated. "A life cannot be replaced."

"Well, yes, I'm still here. Haven't kicked the bucket yet, although…" she paused, "I'm not feeling my best."

"Sure, Jen… That's to be expected. You have to take it easy for a while. But your doctor says you will make a complete recovery?" Karen listened for a response and then continued, "And that's great news, right?"

"Yes, of course. You talked to my doctor? I thought that was confidential…"

"Oh, don't worry, it is! He didn't give me any particulars, just a general prognosis. I wouldn't pry, you know, into your private affairs."

"No, of course not."

"But hey, we're sisters and I'm concerned. Don't I have the right to be?"

Jen doubted her sincerity.

The two women talked for a while, mostly small talk, news and gossip about the townsfolk. Finally, the conversation came around to the topic Karen was most interested in – Samuel Urban.

Jen was surprised to hear about Sam's prolonged incarceration. "He's still in jail?"

"Yes, most certainly. They will probably set bail tomorrow. At least that's what I'm told."

"But the letters, the letters from Darcy, didn't they help him?" she persisted. Jen's voice trembling slightly as she became upset with the news about Urban.

"The letters?!" Karen posed the question to pursue her interest in the subject. They were the reason for her call. "Oh yes, I remember," she directed, "you mentioned them the last time we talked."

"That's right."

"Well, unfortunately, they were destroyed in the fire. Jen, I'm sorry to say that just about everything had damage, smoke and water. Most of it won't be salvageable."

Karen waited for a reply as her sister processed the devastating news. No one had yet reported to her how bad the fire was or how much damage there was to her home and belongings.

It was her entire life, everything she owned, and all her photographs. A widow's memorial: all that remained of her beloved husband, Fred, killed in a tragic accident involving the heavy equipment he operated, many years ago. He perished much too early, and she never really moved on.

The sound of a sob reached Karen at the other end of the line.

"I'm sorry. I thought you knew."

"Please, I just need a moment." Jen struggled to regain composure. "The letters," she continued, "I mailed them to Jodi before the fire."

"Really, that's strange… Well, I hope you're right. I hope they help Urban," Karen lied.

"Oh, I'm sure they will. It sheds light on what is really going on," Jen concluded.

An awkward silence prevailed just then as both were consumed with their thoughts. Adversaries more than confidants, each were processing the information they had just learned, while trying to decide what it meant and what was required of them next.

"Sorry, Sis, have to go. Duty calls. Lots for a legislator to do…" intimidation intended.

"Thanks for the call."

"Goodbye."

The dial hummed in Jen's ear before she could respond. She returned the receiver to its cradle.

Karen was fuming and wasted no time in calling their brother, the man who was supposedly guarding their culpability.

She dialed Jacob's personal number and the phone that rang in the rectory. After nearly twenty rings there was no answer and she almost threw the phone at her desk, an angry, animated hang-up.

Something was amiss. Why hadn't she heard about this sooner? Panicked, she decided to call the church secretary after attempting to calm herself with a swig from a whiskey flask kept in her left, bottom desk drawer.

Mrs. Thomas answered on the third ring.

"This is Karen Jackson." She was flat and firm but demanding, as she tried to hide her anxiety.

"Ms. Jackson, how are we today?"

"I'm fine. Thank you. Is Jacob in his office?"

"Sorry, I'm not sure where he is. But I think he is on the grounds somewhere. Is it urgent?"

"Yes, it is urgent! Can you have him call me back, as soon as possible?"

"Yes, of course. And I have other messages for him. A woman wants to meet with him tonight."

Knowing it was none of her business, Karen pressed for more information. She hoped her brother wasn't straying again into an illicit affair. A private meeting? He seldom gave parishioners such personal attention.

"It was a Miss Culp," Mrs. Thomas volunteered, "she said something about needing prayer. She seemed to be very upset."

"You don't know any more… what her concern is?"

"No."

"What was her first name?"

"Wait, I wrote it down. It's here somewhere. Oh, here it is. Jodi. Jodi Culp was her name."

In that moment Karen knew that their adversary was closer to finding her than she had realized. She reasoned that it was probably because of the letters.

"Thanks for your help, Mrs. Thomas," Karen concluded. "But please, I need to talk to him within the hour."

"I'll do what I can."

And the phone call ended abruptly.

Enter Dennis Canton

Across the way, on the western edge of town, Grants University was located in a hilly section with stately old buildings, large trees, and sprawling lawns. Some of the natural beauty of the place was sacrificed when the college launched an expansion project which included a new gymnasium and recreation center, new dormitories, and the required parking lots.

JP came to Walthem with baggage. He chose Grants U because he wanted to discover his origins. He needed answers.

When the college freshman got a ticket for running a traffic light he quickly appealed. He contended that the light was still yellow. But for this driver, it was about more than just avoiding the fine; he had an unusual interest in meeting the judge.

During his first year at Walthem he focused on learning everything he could about Samuel Urban, observed his relationship with Jodi and then followed her. He knew where each of them lived, what they did in their free time, and where they liked to eat. Yes, he was stalking them.

Before coming to Walthem, he had been told about Jen Foster. She was also in the cross-hairs, a target of his investigation. He had many questions for her.

Distracted as he was, JP's grades began to fall, mostly due to late and uncompleted assignments. One professor seemed to care. Dennis Canton took an interest in this student, the young man who always sat in the back of Psychology I. The boy seemed to be a loner.

One day Dennis asked JP to stay after class; he just wanted to break the ice. Conversation was casual and Dennis knew that he had to keep it comfortable, or the student would become suspicious and clam up, probably bolt. He did learn that JP was an orphan, raised in a foster home, and that he stepped out on his own as soon as he turned eighteen. The kid was also working his way through school, paying as he went and struggling to meet deadlines for tuition. When asked where he was living, JP withdrew. This was more information than he was willing to share.

In the following months Dennis and JP spoke often, shared an occasional lunch together, and soon became more casual with each other. With fewer topics off limits, conversations became longer in duration. Eventually JP disclosed that he was renting a bedroom from a family in town. It was just a place to sleep.

Dennis hosted a meeting at his home called "Friends," its purpose was to discuss a book, or movie, or whatever they were drawn to, sometimes religious writings. He invited JP, who fit like a glove and quickly expanded his contact list. The loner was making new friends.

Now, classes at Grants U were concluded for the year and student conferences officially ended the day before. JP was on campus early this day to loiter there, talk to classmates, say goodbyes to those leaving town, and scope out prospects for the fall semester. He would be working as a landscaper's helper during the summer months.

"Mr. Canton," he greeted his professor who was packing books in a pasteboard box. "You're moving?"

"Hi JP, most likely. With the new hall they are completing I expect they will juggle us around." He looked at JP to see if he was listening. "I've learned the hard way – not to leave anything behind. Things seem to disappear."

"Hey, did you hear that they got the judge?" JP picked up a book and handed it to his friend. "You think he did it?"

Samuel Urban was already a frequent topic with them, when they weren't discussing something more significant.

JP had eventually unfolded the tapestry of his life, exposing its patterns, woven by events considered unorthodox by most people. Slowly, bit by bit, he told his story: what he knew about his birth and upbringing, his interest in Walthem and his reasons for returning. He never really knew his birth parents. His mother was identified, and he had a vague childhood memory of her, but his father remained a mystery. Unknown. It was a burden he had always carried.

The professor was forthcoming with details from the town's past, but JP still had questions about particular incidents and relationships. Due to a void of answers, as most townsfolk were guarded about certain subjects, his inquiries about the magistrate mostly remained unanswered. JP was a stranger, and others didn't know if he could be trusted with their insights. He decided to ask Dennis, his new friend, about the charges against Sam.

Dennis Canton, on the other hand, was a third-generation resident of Walthem and well informed. A bachelor, he inherited his father's good looks and was well regarded in town, especially by the lady folk. But for the time being, he preferred to stay single.

Dennis and Sam had a long history together. They started kindergarten in the same class, played Little League with the same team, and remained buddies all through high school. So, Dennis was very opinionated on the subject just raised by JP.

He firmly respected Urban, even had high regard for the way the judge dealt with the problems he encountered during their teenage years. Actually, he was rooting for him all along.

And, Dennis was now suspicious of the rape charge, knowing how the locals could act out because of the jealously they harbored toward another person's success.

But what was JP's agenda – evidence of his bearing a grudge was sometimes discernible in his remarks about Urban. This was one of those times.

JP was weaving a web, apparently a trap more than a safety net. He was like the spider intent on capturing and devouring the fly. But how could he remain untainted by the rumors he consumed?

As a mentor, Dennis tried to direct JP through his process of discovery to realize acceptance. He attempted to lead him away from revenge and hatred, promoting instead a soul that would achieve peaceful resolutions.

"Actually, no, I don't think Sam would do that." Dennis looked at JP. "Such a crime is easier to prove, then to disprove." He sounded like the teacher he was. "People like to believe the accusation that condemns another person. In this case the odds are stacked against Sam. Seems to me, the way this town works, he is guilty until proven innocent."

"Hmm… Aren't you concerned for justice?" the student prodded.

"Well, yes, of course… But you know me, JP. I believe in a higher power, an arm of justice, beyond the control of even those who hold the power here."

"Yes, I know," JP answered. "Actually, I think you're a little sick that way."

"Maybe, but I believe you will come around."

Dennis moved a couple of books to make room for more in the box. "Look at you. You're here, when you probably shouldn't be, after having such a difficult childhood. You've already been through a lot – I mean, in a way, survived against the odds." He looked at his friend and smiled. "I mean, I think you turned out pretty good. Was it just luck and good fortune? Or, did you get some help along the way?"

"I see your point," JP admitted. "Maybe you're right, who knows?" He gestured toward the heavens and proclaimed, "Maybe there is a God, after all."

"You mean despite all," Dennis corrected and they both laughed.

Then, a pause in their conversation ushered in a change of topic.

"But there is one thing I've been thinking on – can't quite figure it out," he challenged, "why did Judge Williams leave Urban off the hook so easily, after that young woman died in the crash?"

"Oh, you mean Uncle Willie?" Dennis replied. "Yes, he was my uncle, on my mother's side. If you go back far enough, you'll discover that just about everyone in Walthem is related. Sometimes, in more ways than one."

"So, Williams was your relative... Did he ever tell you anything, about Urban, about his case, I mean..."

"No, not really," Dennis was reluctant to share more. "Nothing factual, but I heard some rumors back then and some whispers since."

"Tell me! Please, I need to know!"

"Sorry buddy, can't. It wouldn't be right... Just gossip anyway." He paused. "Maybe you should go and meet him, have a talk with Sam... get some answers for the things that are still bugging you. Get it straight from the horse's mouth..."

JP considered the challenge.

Dennis continued, "I will vouch for him. Sam isn't an evil force. I always liked him just fine, and we always got along."

"Sure, but that was then. This is now." JP brightened. "How many years ago are we talking, fifteen to twenty? Ancient history! People can change, you know?"

"Yes, but I believe that Sam is solid. You should go and talk to him. What's the harm in it?"

"Okay, I'll think about it." JP lifted another book, looked at the title, then put it back on top of a higher stack. He turned to go. "You're probably right, you always are. Well, most of the time."

"See you around. Don't be a stranger this summer," Dennis urged.

"Yep!"

Jacob was dreading this call. From what his secretary related, the witch in the state capital was on her broom again. Delaying it would only increase her rage, so the priest went to his library and dialed her number. He knew that a verbal beating was imminent, as he was negligent and had to face his master. Much like the puppy holding its tail between its haunches after being scolded for peeing on the living room carpet, Jacob had failed to meet her demand, and now discipline was unavoidable.

She answered with, "You incompetent fool!"

"Nice to talk to you too," Jacob sneered.

"You have our sister's house burned down, nearly kill her, and still those incriminating letters are out there?!"

"Apparently so. Don't worry, I'll take care of it." Jacob was bluffing, pretending he already knew that the letters survived the fire. But he didn't know. This was news for him.

"Why did you tell your janitor to torch her house? Didn't he try to find them first?"

"No, I didn't, and, apparently not."

"What's wrong with you?" Karen demanded. "Once they make a connection back to you, this is going to be a high-profile case."

"Then we'll just let Luke take the fall. They already have evidence against him." Jacob explained.

"You sadistic maniac! You think he'll go down without a fight?"

The insult should have shamed a man of the cloth, but Father Jacob wasn't really bothered by it.

"He's still on parole. It should be a slam dunk."

"And Jen won't say anything when she finds out it was your man?"

"I don't know. She should be scared by now," the priest revealed his intentions.

"I'm not so sure…" Karen paused in thought. "And I already know about the pocketknife. The chief told me it had Luke's prints on it. Also prints from someone else – unidentified, probably not in the system," she explained. "I told him to sit on the evidence for a couple of days. I hope to convince him that it is only coincidental, well, certainly circumstantial evidence at best. Without a witness they will not be able to prosecute," she paused again. "At least I don't think so. We need to hide Luke right now. Keep him off of the radar, a low profile. We don't need any additional charges or investigations going our way."

"You worry too much," Jacob suggested. "We're on top. We call the shots."

"Jacob!" she shouted, "I don't trust you… and… I won't be part of your schemes!"

"I've got everything under control," he noted saucily, in an attempt to calm is bossy sister.

"Jacob, you have to get those letters! And don't do anything else rash."

"I'm taking care of it." He raised his voice, his prideful impertinence evident in his tone.

"Don't you shout at me. Oh, no you don't…" she fired back, even louder. "You! Who do you think you are: yelling at me?"

Jacob, knowing his place, withdrew in submissive silence.

"Get them, without drawing any more attention to us!" Karen ordered.

"As I said…" Dial tone. He was cut off.

Down below – Luke was looking for his pocketknife. He opened his cabinet's top drawer and rooted through the host of small items stored there. He knew without a doubt that that was where he put it. But it wasn't there. He sorted through all his stuff a second time. Now frustrated, he pulled the drawer all the way out and dumped everything on the table. A small jar of lip balm rolled away, hit the floor, and continued until it disappeared under the dilapidated sofa.

"Damn, it's not here," he nearly shouted to himself. "I know of only one person who could have taken it."

It would be a busy day for Sam, the last he hoped to spend in the lockup. Surely Monday would force action on a bail decision.

Sam heard the bolt on the outer door bang as it slid backward into the massive lock. He stood, expecting and hoping to greet Jodi. They parted the day before on bad terms. He needed reconciliation. But his elder brother, Joseph, greeted him with a quick step and a flashy smile.

"Joey?" Sam acknowledged. "What the heck are you doing here?"

"Well, Mom was asking a lot of questions," he began. "Trish and I decided to come north for a weekend respite, with the kids of course."

"Still, you went out of your way to come here. Is everything okay?"

Joseph nodded and looked around. "We're staying at the lake, at the cottage," he explained casually and stepped back as Ken opened the cell door.

"Make yourself comfortable," the cop said.

Sam's guest paused, took a couple of steps to enter the cubical and stiffened, the accommodations obviously disagreeable to him. He spoke with sarcasm as he eyed Sam's chair, the only one in the place. "Nice digs."

Sam quickly sat on the inmate's (his) disheveled bed and felt humiliation in owning it. Reality poked like a pin in the collar. "Take a seat," he instructed his brother, motioning to the vacant chair.

Joseph, the firstborn in the Urban family, was a stockbroker and financial advisor in Philadelphia. His lifestyle consisted of client meetings in swanky restaurants or on the golf course if the weather was agreeable, evenings at the club, and frequent trips to exotic places. His two young daughters were enrolled in an expensive private school and often stayed with friends as their parents traveled.

"Mom's been a little off tilt since Dad died," Joseph began. "I just wanted to put her mind at ease."

"Well, I guess that's your job... to check on the prodigal..." Sam's mood darkened as he contemplated his brother's purpose. "You always were their favorite."

"Sammy, Sammy," his brother wooed. "Let's not go there."

"Well, look at me." He gestured with a sweeping motion of his hand. "This place reeks of luxury!" His statement was offensive.

"You had your chance," Joseph noted. "Dad gave you an education, but he always said you would blow it."

"Well, bless his peace-loving heart! His negativity reigns on," Sam was obviously agitated. "Why can't you let it rest? I say, let the cynic rest in peace!"

Sam grew up in a religious family. His parents required regular church attendance; he seldom missed the weekly worship service, that is, until his father's passing, at which time he fell away despite his mother's objection, and that is most likely the reason why she wasn't speaking to him now.

But as he thought back on all those gatherings, and all those required greetings – the service was paused after the reading of lengthy announcements and everyone was asked to greet their fellow brothers and sisters and especially acknowledge anyone who might be new, as surely, they must be made to feel welcome – he realized now that not one of them became a friend, not even in the least. He could still see their faces and fake smiles, and feel their loose hugs, but couldn't remember any of their names.

Everyone wore a mask, their true selves guarded and unknown. What was their struggles, their hurts, their pain? Why didn't anyone care enough to ask – to connect on a deeper level?

He knew what Jesus called the Pharisees. He was taught that in church. Fools, blind guides, hypocrites! Serpents and vipers. Whitewashed tombs! They were the defenders of their religion.

Sam thought about his religious cousins. He hadn't talked to Tracey in years, but they were close during their teens, the times of self-seeking in troubled puberty. They stayed in touch after high school when Tracey, a Catholic, quickly married a Protestant named Todd, and started a family. Sam was a groomsman in their wedding.

Tracey called often, but then they drifted apart, her calls fewer and further apart, and finally, the occasional messages she left on his answering machine; it seemed that she called when she knew Sam was at work, but he couldn't be critical. His attempts at contacting her were even less. He didn't want to interfere with her fragile marriage.

When Tracey birthed a baby boy, she and her husband decided against infant baptism. The church of her upbringing claimed that it saved the soul, but her husband didn't believe that, and in reality, neither did Tracey, despite her religious training.

Henceforth, they were shunned by her parents and siblings. At first it was their breakfast club, their meeting each Sunday morning after Mass. Tracey didn't even know that her family was gathering, because she and Todd weren't invited.

When her UTI became a kidney infection, Tracey spiked a fever on a Tuesday morning of 104. Todd panicked. He couldn't reach her doctor so he called his neighbor who was a RN. Tracey was nearly delirious. He was urgently, and firmly instructed to get her to the hospital, even call 911 for an ambulance. He was warned of his wife going into septic shock.

As he watched from the nursery window, the ambulance made a quick exit, lights blinking red and yellow. He looked at his newborn son. What should he do next? He called his in-laws and both of Tracey's parents got on the phone, anxious to learn the details of their daughter's illness. Todd was generous in conversation, answering all their questions, to the best of his ability.

Then he asked if they would come to his home and babysit their grandson, the only infant in the family not baptized, as by then they had many other grandchildren. They answered with a quick and firm "No!"

One word, it said it all. There was no explanation, no counter offer of assistance.

It became obvious to Todd just then that the decision had been previously made. But why would his son be so rejected? He was stunned.

For years he had been observing Tracey's parents as they went out of their way to do everything for their other grandchildren.

No, they didn't go to visit their daughter, Tracey, in the hospital.

A neighbor was willing to call off from work and babysit so that Todd could visit his wife in the ER. Time had been crucial. The IV dose of powerful antibiotics was lifesaving. He had not realized how serious their situation was.

Many years later, Sam heard of Tracey being rejected by her parents. The reason, obvious. And still, she had never abandoned them, or even rejected them in any way. She was faithful to attend every family gathering and event, even the ceremonies for her nieces and nephews: their baptisms, confirmations, and first communions. These events were always celebrated with elaborate luncheons and parties.

Now, Tracey's husband was becoming distant toward his in-laws. The cracks in their marriage became wider. Tracey and Todd's relationship was crumbling.

The couple had made a prenuptial agreement not to tolerate religious bias, but then, she stood idly by and simply watched as her family shunned her husband, and to some degree, her son too.

She was conflicted, her devotion divided. Todd had tried to bridge the gap, but really, he didn't have a chance.

In Sam's view, it was all because of religious prejudice. Despite his family's Protestant tradition, he didn't consider himself to be a religious person. Although Jodi was Catholic, he hadn't considered that to be problematic in their relationship, yet truthfully, the seeds of doubt were planted.

"Sammy, take a chill pill," Sam's brother Joseph said with challenge. "Come on, I didn't come here to fight with you, or rehash your absurd allegations about the inequities *you* believe that *you* have endured." He paused and with a glare forced his younger brother of two years to shut up. "Enough now."

"Sorry," Sam relented. He looked at the floor of his holding cell. "If she really cared, she would… well, let's just drop it."

"Yes," Joseph agreed.

"How long has Dad been gone? Isn't it more than two years now?"

"Yes."

"And Mom's still having a hard time with it?" Sam was prying for information. Seldom was he informed about any of the family's business.

"Sam, she's okay. Okay… But you, well you're another story… apparently!"

Sam couldn't refute the obvious, so he allowed Joseph to continue. "I know you're innocent," he offered as a peace treaty. "But are you going to beat this thing?"

"I don't know who is framing me, or why, so it's very difficult to fight back against an invisible foe. But yea. I know my accuser and I think she's way out there, on a limb."

"Isn't that the girl you dated in high school?" his brother suggested. "The same one that was with you in the accident?"

Sam sighed at the mention of the unfortunate event. "Yes, that *is* her."

The security door clanged again and both men turned their heads to see who would come in. Susan arrived with a skip in her step.

"Hi Sam," she smiled and lingered on his name before acknowledging the brother, "Hope I'm not interrupting anything. I can come back another time."

"Oh no!" Joseph stood quickly. "That's not necessary." He looked at Sam and continued, "I was just leaving."

Sam nodded in agreement.

Joseph offered his hand to his brother, confirming the conclusion of their short talk, much the same way he would have done at a business meeting with a stranger. It was limp. He straightened his sweater vest and turned to take in some details of the female visitor. Looking back, he gave Sam a questioning gaze.

"She's Jodi's friend," Sam explained quickly. "Just a friend."

"Take care."

Joseph's words were insincere and stated quickly as he turned and sauntered away with an air of distinction.

Sam watched, and shook his head as he pondered on the purpose of his brother's visit. Was it just to get more dirt on him? There was an inheritance, one Sam was unlikely to receive if he disgraced the family. It would be a windfall for his brother, Mom's incomparable delight, her firstborn, "Joey!" Sam grimaced at rejection revived and turned his attention to Susan, whom he hoped would be better company.

The Interview

Susan ran in without hesitation and held her arms out, offering a hug. Sam quickly accepted the warm embrace, one he sorely needed at that time. They settled in and Sam spoke first.

"How is Jodi, is she okay?"

"Yeah, but she's kind of messed up right now," Susan answered. "I just talked with her, a little while ago."

Sam appeared as a pleading puppy.

"I don't think it's really your fault," Susan conceded. "She's been really getting ripped by everyone, you know?"

"Yeah, especially the DA," Sam remembered.

"And Faith too." Susan suggested

"She went there?"

"Said so."

"What else?" Sam was desperate for more information. He looked pleadingly into Susan's eyes. She was Jodi's closest friend, she had to know more and he needed it, reassurance.

"Oh, don't worry," she waved her hand. "Let it go... you just need to give her some space. And then..."

"And then..." Sam repeated.

"And then you will know how to win her back. Don't worry so much," she counseled him, "She's still in love with you. She can't deny it for long."

"Thank God," he nearly said with a rejoicing amen.

"Sam," she said firmly and tapped his knee to demand his full attention. "I came here this afternoon to talk to you about something else." She paused as she watched his reaction, "An idea I had."

"Okay..." he drew out the last syllable as he exhaled, expecting a surprise and fearing the worse.

"Let's do an article."

"What?"

She was cheerful, her smile a distraction from the agony he felt. A welcome relief. Susan brought friendship into a place of hostility, and it had a calming effect on him.

"Sam," she suddenly became serious, "you've got to tell your side of the story. Fight back," she urged. "They're using the press against you. And the election is in just two short days. You've only got one more chance. Tomorrow."

"Really? That's your idea?" he paused and then continued, Well, believe it or not, I was just thinking this morning about the same thing!" he proclaimed with newfound enthusiasm. "Will they print it, my side of things?"

"Well, they might edit it down. There won't be time for the opposing side to respond, or for a retraction, so they won't let you make any punches. You understand." She was appealing to his role as a negotiator and public official.

"Yes, of course. I do. I won't do any name calling or make any accusations. I understand." Sam reached for the notebook on the edge of his tiny dining table. "Here," he handed it to her. "I started working on an outline."

"Oh, wow. Good." Susan accepted the pad and began reading his notes.

Four headings were jotted there: **second chances, police brutality, victim's rights, and mercy**.

"Second chances?" she questioned.

"Everybody deserves one, I have always believed that."

Susan asked for a pencil and began taking notes.

Sam continued, "I took that philosophy into my courtroom and to the best of my ability, as much as the law would allow, I gave everyone that deserved it a second chance."

"And now you deserve one too?" she asked.

"Well, yes, but I'm innocent, so that really doesn't apply to me right now. I didn't assault anyone. I love and respect all of my friends, and I especially respect my *female* friends. You know, most of us go back a long way, some of us even to preschool."

"Why did you go to the apartment of your accuser?"

"I was invited!" Sam nearly shouted. "She begged me to come. It was the only way she could show me the papers which contained his testimony – her brother's," he noted, "he was arrested in another county. The lawyer for the prosecution has already deposed him. I saw the affidavits."

"So, it was all business?" Susan suggested.

"Yes, but getting back to second chances," Sam redirected. "I had my second chance. Anyone that has lived in this town very long knows all about it," he reflected in deeper thought. "I don't want to belabor that point, rehash it all, but I want to say that I will never forget the mercy that was shown to me. Judge Williams gave me *my* second chance. That changed my life and it changed me. I live every day grateful, yes, so very thankful for the second chance a kind judge afforded me."

"So that's your angle on mercy?" Susan clarified. "What about police brutality, what's that all about."

"I would never tolerate it," Sam proclaimed. "But it doesn't happen here. We have good cops, police with conviction and caring."

Susan raised her eyebrows. They indicated doubt.

"Let me explain. Every arrest results in a stressful situation. No one is really happy about a citation, not even the cop that issued it, but... he had a responsibility to do so. It all comes into my courtroom. I try to finesse them through it. I let them blow off a little steam – that's understandable. But no one holds a grudge, especially the cop. Every person walks out of my courtroom, after the citation is addressed, with a clean slate, like it never even happened. No grudges," he emphasized, "You see… second, and third, even fourth chances."

"Oh yes, I think I'm getting it. Your application of the law," Susan noted.

Sam hit the table with his palm, "That's it! And don't forget," he continued, "we all make mistakes. And… always remember, the next time you see that police officer, he, or she, might be saving your life."

"But they have to pay a fine? The accused, I mean."

"Sometimes. Most of the time, but that isn't the point."

"And victim's rights?" Susan queried.

"Okay, the issue of rights is a little bit more complicated, but essentially, it will boil down to respect, primarily. See if you can get this… When a person is wrongfully harmed by another, the victim has been compromised, but he still has his rights according to the law, and he may be due restitution. But… the accused," the judge continued, "also has important rights. I firmly believe that a person is innocent until proven guilty, not the other way around. Let due process of the law take its course."

Sam continued, "If the accused is not a threat to anyone, including himself, let him go home and live as much a normal life as possible, until the day of his trial and sentencing, if it comes to that. Remember," he concluded, "I only interpret the law for minor charges and disputes. If, for example, the person is charged with a serious crime, a felony, my role is only *and simply* to determine if there's enough evidence for the case to continue, in other words… was it a good arrest? I listen to the cops who investigated and consider the explanation offered in the defense of the accused. Their guilt is determined by a higher court, as well as the penalty."

"But you set their bail?"

"Initially, yes, and that's hard. There are guidelines, and bail can be reduced, but most people are not a flight risk."

"So, everyone has rights," Susan reviewed. "It's a bit much. Can you simplify?"

"Respect. If we would all truly respect each other's rights, the law wouldn't have to be applied harshly. But when push comes to shove, a judge who is truly impartial and respects all parties involved, is crucial in resolving the dispute. That's me," Sam concluded with a smile. "And, I love mercy."

"What about yourself, have *your* rights been respected?" Susan asked.

"Good question. I don't understand why I have been held here for several days."

"Is the charge against you legit, I mean should it have been pushed through to the next level?"

"No, I don't believe so."

"Why not?"

"Because my case is being influenced by someone with power."

"Who?"

"I don't know. Let your readers figure that one out. They're perceptive."

"Are you being framed?"

"Yes."

"By whom?"

"Again, I'll let your readers decide."

"Thanks, Sam," Susan suddenly seemed excited. "This is good stuff. I've got tomorrow's headline."

"I need to thank *you*," he said with emphasis. "Thanks for believing in me, and caring."

"Oh, before I go," Susan remembered, "I have this letter for you." She reached into her pocket and handed the crumpled envelope to Sam.

Jodi was about to give up on the idea of seeing her pastor when a return call came some hours later. Father was available that evening. He reluctantly agreed to meet with her after having that unpleasant conversation with his sister, Karen. He instructed Mrs. Thomas to pass a message on to Ms. Culp. She would be asked to bring the letters to their meeting. What letters? She would understand.

++++

The vacant church seemed different when I pulled on the iron handle attached to the heavy wooden door and stepped inside. An uneasy feeling quickly came over me. In the vestibule I noticed several candles in front of a portrait, a Station of the Cross. I considered lighting one: for my soul was remorseful; and for Sam, for surely, he must be in great distress.

All was dark except for a light coming from an open doorway near the front of the sanctuary. I paused, felt the rejection of loneliness, and stepped forward. "Father?" No response. Regret taunted me next. It acted with authority, unrelenting and hard as stone, grinding away the little hope that remained. "Father, are you there?" and I took several more steps toward the light. At last, condemnation crept over me, icy cold, chilling my heart. "Father! Father, where are you?" I screamed as fright overcame me.

166

A figure crossed into the lighted doorway and its shadow extended from the man silhouetted there. The apparition was large, the scene intimidating. Unnerving.

"Father, is that you?"

"Yes. Come to me, my child."

I nearly ran up the aisle, past the empty pews to reach the dark form. As I neared, my eyes adjusted. His face became dimly visible. I recognized the expression of contempt, the same one I often observed as Father Jacob gave the homily during Saturday mass.

He was unwelcoming. No embrace, no handshake, not even a polite inquiry as to my well-being. Just as well. I didn't feel any warm and fuzzies toward him either.

He stepped away and I followed him down a stone hallway to another planked door. He jaunted inside, looped around the end of a big desk, and sat in a buttoned high-back leather chair. A candle flickered on a console table located at the side of the room under a stained-glass window. The large crucifix displayed there by the interior light was lifeless before my eyes. It portrayed so much pain. I began to have doubts about this meeting, but knew I had to push through it.

"I'm sorry to bother you," I stammered. "I didn't mean to interrupt your work." I looked around the room and wondered what duties he had to fulfill.

"Did you bring the letters?"

I puzzled at his sudden inquiry and really didn't know how to answer. *What is he talking about?* "Excuse me?"

"The letters. My secretary was supposed to instruct you to bring them."

"But I don't know what you are referring to."

"Really!?" He paused. "What do you want then? Why have you come here?"

The large man pushed his chair back from his desk. Away from it he fell into dimmer light. His face darkened. He cleared his throat. "My dear child!" he proclaimed, "Do you have an emergency?"

"Yes, I… I mean *we*, need your help."

"What can I do for such an attractive, young woman as yourself?"

I didn't hear a question, but a suggestive assertion, one cloaked in lust as he wet his lips with his tongue. Had I misread him?

"Have we spoken before?"

Uncomfortable with his insinuations, I cleared my throat to speak a little louder, more distinctly. "My boyfriend, Samuel Urban, is in prison. He was arrested a few days ago."

"And what is the charge?"

Now covered in shame, I looked away and swallowed hard. "Rape."

"That is a very serious offense."

"But he didn't do it!"

"How are you so sure?"

"He is innocent!" But my declaration seemed hollow as I shifted in my chair. It was firm and uncomfortable. And in that terribly awkward moment I needed understanding and sympathy, more than ever before.

"What can *I* do?"

"I don't know. You must be able to help us, somehow…" I blurted. "Don't you have some influence you can use?"

"Is Mr. Urban a congregant here?" the priest asked and then answered himself, "I don't believe so." He looked to me for confirmation and continued, "I am a minister of the gospel of the Holy Church. I lead faithful congregants to be purified in union with Christ as they partake in the sacraments. My ordination serves them well as I provide the Eucharist. This truly is the source of the Christian life."

"Yes…of course." What else could I say… but secretly I wondered, *is that all there is to it? Just a religious ceremony - a frequent ritual? If so, why doesn't it work for me?*

"Sin not confessed interrupts such religious communion. Truly you must know that those who are not confirmed are objectively sinful. There is no means for them to receive a blessing, not even the intercession of the Holy Mother. Lost souls, without salvation."

"But Sam…" *Is he hopelessly lost, condemned to hell? Am I?*

"He must confess sincerely for himself," the priest bellowed.

I could feel the heat of his anger. *But why? Are we so unworthy?*

I clenched the forearms of the chair and looked to the ceiling hoping to find God there. Was He willing to intercede, or was this to be my final humiliation?

"I have this month's confession scheduled for tomorrow, beginning at five o'clock. I will look for you then, and I will expect you to attend the Eucharist that follows."

"Thank you!" I was stunned at the arrogance of the man. Feeling an explosion of emotion, my ears felt hot and began to ring. My blood pressure was probably going off the charts. I stood quickly, spun on my heels and darted for the door. *"Thanks, but no thanks,"* I reasoned in rebellious thought. *I'm not buying this lode of crap. Sorry Father, but I'd rather do it my way.* I paused at the exit of the building as rain and sleet began to pound the pavement in front of me. *No way. If this is God, I don't want any part in it!*

++++

The darkened sky rumbled and the building shook above her. There was a flash of brilliant light as it streaked across the parking lot and struck a utility pole where the church property intersected with the street. Sparks, like fireworks, flew everywhere and momentarily illuminated the way to her car. She gave the exit door an extra hard shove, expecting it would slam behind her, and ran into the heavy downpour. She just wanted to get away from that place, and as quickly as possible. A transformer on the pole was smoking as she drove past it. Then a wire lurched upward and dived, jumping and sparking on the ground as it danced on the wet pavement.

Inside the church, Father Jacob leaned back in his chair and grinned sadistically. For him, this was one of those special times, when he cherished his job the most. He reveled in her pain, knowing the great humiliation she was surely experiencing. Truly, in that moment, revenge was sweet for him.

But then he suddenly rose to his feet with the realization of urgency in the situation. If she didn't know about the letters, maybe they remained with unopened mail. If there was still a chance to retrieve them, then the time to do so was now. He had to get Luke and send him out there. Quick! Hopefully Luke would find the letters before she did.

Despondency revisited Sam that night. The day had passed and Jodi hadn't come to see him. It was a long time he waited, watching the minutes slowly pass by. What was the signal she was sending?   The anxiety he felt was enough to make him sick. A bellyache.

In that moment of rejection, Sam's thoughts progressed to consider the plight of couples estranged. In his courtroom he intently and respectfully listened to arguments from both sides of the relationship conflicted. Charges of spousal abuse and requests for restraining orders were almost always related to very nasty divorce proceedings. He felt the terror of their hatred. It was so unfortunate to see a disparaged person stand before the bench and vehemently attack his or her spouse.

He often wondered about their vows and why their religious training was not enough to save them from such despair. But then he remembered a pastor who always advised the complaining wife to leave her husband, even without conferring with him or offering counsel to the couple. Divorce was inevitably the result, and Sam wasn't sure that was the best outcome.

In what they considered extreme cases, Pentecostals sometimes prayed for the husband/father's removal. Yes, it was better, in their view, for God to end his life then to prolong the suffering of his alleged victims. And this was largely because they opposed divorce. They boldly proclaimed his many sins with extreme condemnation. Were they sending him to Hell? Sam just couldn't understand their theology or get his mind wrapped around it. The abuse was alleged, seldom proven.

He knew what Jesus said to the woman caught in adultery. He saved her life, forgave her, and set her free.

And there are the 'unspeakable offenses,' the reports documented by articles that creep into the newspaper and make headlines near the bottom of page three. No one wants to be confronted by the immoral acts of the clergy: the preacher who sexually assaulted a teenager. Such corruption is unthinkable.

How do we process it?

In his legal mind Sam understood the crime and the punishment required. That was clear. Defined.

But it wasn't enough. He remained conflicted. In his heart he felt the pain of the victims' suffering, the shame of religious authorities, but also regarded it as a greater loss for the institution, which should have done so much good, but overall, is still worthy – isn't it?

For many millennia religious institutions ruled with unchallenged authority and clenched the power allotted. The phrase "power corrupts, and absolute power corrupts absolutely" is attributed to Lord Acton, a 19th century British historian and moralist. But as the 21th century arrived, the evil that had infiltrated the ranks of the religious hierarchy was soon exposed.

The Pennsylvania Attorney General began to prosecute priests who abused young boys. Once the veil of silence was torn asunder, a horde of victims came forward. The news was inflammatory. The institution faltered. Thousands of parishioners turned away, disgusted by the offense, and disheartened by the breach of their precious trust and loyalty.

The prosecutor became famous for his aggressive and courageous campaign to bring justice to the victims and their families. He was then elected Governor of the great Commonwealth.

The public had spoken.

Sam was also thinking about the arrogance of his brother and again felt the rejection he had always known from them, his immediate family, especially his father. Joey received the lion's share of their attention, Sam a mere pittance.

Reluctantly, he opened the letter Susan delivered. He hoped to share it with Jodi, but she was a no show. He removed the single sheet of paper, unfolded it and read:

"Religion is sometimes a bad actor, often performing as a thief, and a liar, stealing authority and usurping it."

"Do not concede the belief of yourself to this veiled mask of intimidation, even as the masses do."

"Religion will dilute the TRUTH, minimizing its effect for knowing the purpose of your existence; for God must willingly be granted permission to be involved in your life. He does not use coercion as one who forces obedience."

Compliance to a religious institution is often unproductive, even hurtful, for such an authority does not truly represent God.

"Such religion holds us in bondage to dead works; but in freedom we become complete.

Having a clear conscience is such a relief!"

"Your Advocate"

Three Days Later: A woman is panicked. She slams her hand against the top of her desk. Looking upward toward the heavens, she screams, "How could this have happened?" She raises her fist against God. "Damn you!"

Her world is crashing in around her. Fear charges against her few remaining rational thoughts.

CHAPTER SEVEN: Intrusion

Jacob opened the door to the cellar of the church and called for Luke, who was ordered to come to the priest's office. It was urgent.

"Luke, you know the letters you were supposed to get?"

He was puzzled.

"From my sister's house, you moron."

"Oh yeah." He wanted to fabricate a story about finding and trashing them, but realized it was not the time to answer untruthfully.

"They still exist."

"They survived the fire?"

"No, you fool," Jacob raged, "they weren't there."

Luke sighed long and loud enough for his boss to hear. "Not this again."

"Yes! Again. Until you get it right!"

"No. Like I said before, no!"

"You arrogant fool! You will do as I instruct you to do."

Luke shook his head.

"Okay then, I'll make the call. I'll call your parole officer right now!" The larger man stared with daggers in his eyes. "They've already got evidence against you."

"Yeah, well… how did that get there?"

"What?"

"The pocketknife."

"You tell me."

Knowing that he was beat, like a hostage at gunpoint, Luke relented to his oppressor once again. "What now?"

"You know where Jodi Culp lives?"

"Yeah, I've been there."

"Well, get out there, and I mean right now!" the priest pointed toward the door. "We don't have any time to lose."

"And do what?"

"Get into her house and retrieve those damned letters. Bring them back to me. I want to see them right here," he jammed his forefinger onto the top of his desk. "In front of me, on my desk, within the hour."

"How do I know what I'm looking for?" Luke asked.

"Come on, use your brain, you idiot. Letters! That is letters plural: probably in a large envelope, and from my sister. Check the return address."

"What's that?"

"Church Street. Jen Foster, 64 Church Street."

"Church Street," Luke repeated. "Jen Foster, 64." He committed the address to memory.

"Well, get going, you fool. Didn't you hear me? We don't have any time to lose. Culp just left here a few minutes ago?"

"She already left here? Then how can I beat her?"

"That's for you to figure out. Now go!" the priest thundered.

Their distrust for each other was growing —a confrontation of huge proportions on the horizon.

++++

Needing gas, I pulled into the Seven Eleven on Oak Street. As I filled my tank, I watched lightning in the western sky. The storm was coming my way, a cold breeze picking up. But inside, it was already raging. I felt the chill of death and stiffened against it. My heart hardened. I was icy cold.

Still, to this day, I sometimes feel the rejection and struggle with the doubts that stirred in me then.

Father Jacob was not a kind or caring person. Yeah, that was obvious.

The suggestion that he would only help a person in his church, one in good standing, well, that sickened me. And what about *me*? I was a member. After all, by helping Sam, he would be helping me, and I was the one asking.

Is that Christianity - availing assistance only to those who have jumped through all the hoops and paid their dues?

Where is love in that?

That's the kind of hypocrisy that turns people away from the church.

++++

Piety is a deception when it is shrouded by symbols and pompous ceremonies that a person can easily hide behind.

++++

I don't want to be alone with him, no, never again. He really gave me the creeps. Confession? I would never confide in him, not about anything. I don't trust him.

++++

And in a moment of deeper reflection, Jodi realized that the offense she harbored was much broader than her feelings about the encounter with a single clergyman. She would never forget the rejection she felt in her time of desperation.

++++

Careful… put it in check.

I respect a priest's achievement and authority, but Sam and I were the victims. We didn't and still don't deserve that kind of treatment. Our lives were being ruined by a false accusation, and God's representative couldn't see it, and didn't care?

No, I don't think he represented God, and I won't submit to that kind of judgmental intolerance, not ever again, because I now know in my heart that God is so much more!

He has to be…

God… forgive me if I am rejecting you, and help me to know the truth. I need You now.

Is religious authority true to God?

++++

The questions came with the force of a torrent flooding into her soul. And then, Jodi wondered if they could be temptations from the Evil One.

The church where Father Jacob resided was a fortress, a testament of time for survival and dominance – yet its falsehoods were no less than a tower of deceit.

Jodi's heart had been broken, but her eyes were opened. Still, her soul was troubled.

The fortress of religious authority she had known and trusted since a child was breached by the arrogance of a rude and uncaring clergyman. That assault allowed light to shine through a small crack in the façade of that bastion of false faith to touch her

178

at the place where she had been confined, but finally sought freedom. Truth dispelled the darkness of deception.

But still fogged, full understanding was difficult to perceive. Enlightenment brought many more questions, even as she continued to be held in a dungeon of religious oppression.

++++

I wanted to believe that the Lord truly cared about the pain I felt, but where was He then, when I needed Him most? I was obviously looking for help in the wrong place.

++++

As she continued with her story, Jodi felt the remnant of the anger that consumed her after meeting with Father Jacob.

Thunder roared and shook her car.

++++

Although lacking an appetite, I went inside for milk, bread, and eggs, the basics. But I needed comfort. Food or alcohol? *Could this be an addiction?* Probably, because I *needed* it.

I wanted to binge again, but I knew that I had to eat something nutritious. My clothes were getting tight.

A line formed at the checkout counter as a customer requested lottery tickets, several types. The clerk, a large brutish woman with black circles around her eyes, wore a man's haircut shaved several inches above her ears. She was tugging at a large roll of colorful foiled tickets, counting, then recounting, and finally tore off a row of seven.

I had my arms full and shifted on my feet as I overheard a woman behind me scolding her little boy for grabbing a candy bar from a display rack within his reach. Other customers joined the line. *God help me.* I was growing impatient. I had a short fuse. I bit my lower lip hard enough to taste blood.

Finally, the customer in front of me cleared away and I dropped my groceries on the countertop. "You got everything you need?" the clerk prodded.

But I was focused on the rack of cigarettes prominently displayed on the back wall. My appetites were ravenous. My eyes searched for the brand I once enjoyed, many years ago. The clerk followed my gaze to the rows of cigarette packs.

"What can I get you, honey?" she urged.

My mind was reeling with temptation. I could almost feel the warm air gushing through my nostrils once again. It helped keep my sinuses clear and my mind focused. I was stressed to the max and a cigarette would help me relax. I needed it, even just one. Just one!

I remembered the calming effect of nicotine, the dopamine that rushed into the receptors of my brain. The faint smell of tobacco summoned me. The ciggies were calling my name. The Gold Shorts, that was my brand. I needed the comfort they would give.

"Come on, we don't have all day," the brute flexed muscles in her forehead as she gave me that disgusted, demanding look that has become so prevalent among convenience store clerks.

"Next!" she called to the person behind me and pushed my groceries toward the other end of the counter.

"No… no, I have to get going," I corrected her, still in a daze. "This is everything." I sighed and held my breath. I wanted to fight, have a scuffle. I needed to vent, but my eyes remained fixated on the cigarette display. Temptation was making its final call. Just one, to relax; no one would have to know.

"You sure?" Without waiting for an answer, the register began to chatter. Quickly my order was complete.

I paid and pulled myself away, my nerves shot, my brain still pleading for the fix. I picked up my bag and looked at the clerk as I forced myself away from the counter. She was a nasty one. Probably the distraction was a good thing for me. If I raged, she would have bashed my head in.

++++

In the meantime, JP Rogers sat on a bench as he watched youngsters run after each other in the playground at the town park. They were likely playing tag: the opposite sexes beginning to exercise their attraction for each other. It was the great chase, demonstrated at an early age. Just to the right of the ruckus, the sun offered a magnificent display of colors spread across the western horizon. But reminders of his past left him unappreciative of nature's beauty. His childhood was different, one of strained relationships in unfortunate circumstances, rejection that he couldn't overcome. Even then, he knew something was terribly wrong.

Earlier, JP had the conversation with Dennis Canton, the professor, who told him to take his questions directly to Samuel Urban, and then even vouched for the disgraced magistrate's credibility. But JP was reluctant to do so. And it was then that the idea occurred to him to visit Jodi instead. After all, they recently met informally at the hospital. Surely, she would remember him and be quicker than Sam to welcome a stranger with such an unexpected intrusion.

He returned his bike to his apartment and then drove to her townhouse. He was sitting in his car in the visitor parking lot, waiting for her to return home, when a vehicle unknown to him, a K-Car, screeched to a halt and pulled into a space nearby. There were two other cars between them and by instinct, JP ducked low.

A man jumped out and ran toward Jodi's housing unit, pushed through a hedge row, and went to the rear of the building. JP saw it all. Just then the headlights of another car fell upon him and Jodi pulled into her usual parking spot.

JP watched as Jodi casually walked to her house, unlocked the front door, and disappeared inside. She was carrying a bag of groceries. He saw a light come on in her front room. Struck by the mystery of the stranger headed her way, he decided to follow at a distance.

Jodi took two steps into the foyer and froze when she heard a noise coming from the kitchen. She wanted to deny it, but told herself that the sound was certainly very real. It was distinctive, undeniable. She gazed into the darkened rooms ahead. Then she heard the noise again. Someone, an intruder, was in her home.

Arriving just before Jodi did, Luke gained entry by using a pry bar as he easily forced the sliding door open in her dining room.

++++

"Who's there?!" I shouted as I dropped my bag onto the floor. But silence prevailed.

++++

The hunter and the hunted: each were distinctly aware of the other's presence. Each waited for the right moment to make his or her move, but neither were sure of when or which way to go.

Paralyzed by uncertainty, the intruder listened for several moments, hoping for a clue.

Luke seemed to have the advantage over Jodi. He was the bolder of the two, and more reckless. He would move first, as fear immobilized her.

JP saw the house lights go out.

++++

After flipping the light switch, I dropped to my knees. I was trembling. Darkness enshrouded me except for a soft glow from the rear kitchen window. It reflected on the ceramic floor in the hallway and offered a pathway that was unencumbered. I wondered if I should follow the light? Or should I turn and run?

Despite the scare drum pounding in my ears, part of me wanted to identify the intruder, even catch him. I was gripped by fear, but that strong determined spirit, the same power that drove me into the lions' dens: the D.A.'s office and the creepy room inhabited by the priest, it lingered and fed on a pool of adrenalin that had not yet fully expired. I crawled forward to gain a view into the living room. No one was there.

++++

She saw movement, blurred in her peripheral vision as Luke ducked behind a recliner chair.

Jodi slithered some more, on her elbows and knees, and gazed into the kitchen. She heard the footfalls of the intruder as he ran through an adjoining room. The sound was paralyzing.

++++

183

Then I felt a breeze, it brought comfort, coming from the dining room and realized that the slider was open there. Had he made his exit?

It was then that I noticed knives standing in their usual spot, in their holder, on the kitchen island. A large butcher knife sparkled in a sudden flash of light. Like the spotlight highlighting the main performer on a theatrical stage, the beam came from somewhere above, perhaps the rear window. What did it mean? The knife was summoning me. It would be my defense.

The spotlight moved. Then another came through the sliding door. Were there more intruders? I had to get that knife. I suddenly believed that it was my only chance for survival.

I half stood and scrambled for the kitchen. Simultaneously, I heard a shuffle in the living room, now behind me. Making the required destination, I reached just high enough to take the knife. I gripped it with all my might, white knuckled.

As I ducked down, a figure appeared at the sliding door. Again, I listened intently. I heard a noise coming from the front of the house. Pressure in my ears increased with a sudden pain in my head. I felt woozy. I had to choose: fear or determination, surrender or attack? I had to take control of myself – this was no time for a panic attack. I was better than that.

++++

She peeked over the top of the island. A man stood there, his back toward her. This was her chance. She pounced like a wild animal, the knife raised, a high-pitched scream her war cry. But as the blade, thirsty for blood, came down, the man spun around and caught her wrist with his left hand. It was an instinctive move. He squeezed hard. She pushed against him and looked directly into his uncovered face.

"Jodi, stop!" he screamed as he held her hand. His trembled under the pressure she exerted.

++++

I felt his hot breath on my face as my mind reeled. Did I know this person?

"Jodi, it's me, JP."

I relaxed my arm.

"From the hospital."

I recognized his face and allowed him to move my hand, still gripping the weapon, off to the side. I dropped the blade and it fell to the floor with a crash, banging on the ceramic tile. "You...?!" My eyes filled with tears. My entire body began to shake. I ranted about the intruder, regained some composure, and looked intently at JP. "What the hell...?"

Suddenly I let go of determination, that which had sustained me. I dropped to the floor, slumped in a pile on my knees, put my face in my hands, and sobbed. JP lowered himself, knelt in front of me and waited, without saying a word.

I gulped, wiped at my eyes with my wrists and started crying again, this time more softly. "Why are you here?" I managed between sobs.

"I came to see you," he paused, "to talk."

But my mind was blank. What did he say?

"I have some questions about Sam."

"Well, don't we all," my shoulders shook as I tried to hold back more sobs. But I needed to cry. I was still shaking with terror. "I thought you might kill me."

185

"No!... oh no…. Don't think that. I'm here to help."

He looked for my eyes with a convincing gaze, but I still couldn't fully understand what was happening. "Help? How can you help me?"

"I saw the intruder and came to see if you were okay. Your front door was locked, so I followed him to the back of your house."

I tried desperately to comprehend all that he said, my thoughts trailing behind. And, he just kept talking, adding more details to his report.

"I saw you come in here, and then I saw the man run through your living room."

I noticed the flashlight which he still held in his right hand. "Oh, thank you… I think."

"Jodi, I think you should call the cops."

"Damn right!" I suddenly turned and looked to the front of the house. "Where is he?"

"It's okay. He's gone… I think."

JP looked questioningly at me. "Gone? Are you sure?" I needed to be absolutely sure.

He rose first and shone his flashlight toward the front hall. I stumbled as I reached for a light switch. Together, cautiously, we walked forward. The front door was hanging open. Groceries were strewn across the floor. Eggs were broken and milk was still lapping out of its container.

"I better get a towel," I said instinctively. I took a step toward the kitchen and stopped, turned back to look at the hall table and realized that the large manila envelope was missing. I remembered that Susan placed it there that morning.

++++

It was the one sent by Jen Foster.

Luke was successful.

JP was focused on the woman he secretly adored. He didn't move as he studied her and waited silently. Finally, she seemed to be calming down.

++++

"911, what's your emergency?" The voice answering my call for help was flat, robotic, uncaring.

"There was an intruder in my house," I blurted.

"Are you sure?"

"I saw him! He scared the hell out of me!"

"Were you attacked? Are you injured?" The operator was reading from a script.

"No, he got away. But I saw him!"

"Okay, now let's relax. Do you need medical attention?"

"I'm pretty shook up, but I'm okay… I think."

"Good. Secure your house and stay inside. An officer is on the way."

"Thank you."

Forty minutes later a person pounded on my front door. I faintly heard the words, "Walthem Police Department. Is anyone home?"

I opened the door to see Officer Barney Billings. His approach was very formal, nonchalant, as he asked questions for the basic information and wrote on a clipboard, frequently flipping between the first and second pages.

After inspecting the sliding door in the dining room, he noted, "Yep, easily forced open, probably with a simple pry bar."

187

I was a little taken aback by his description. *Is it that easy to get into my house?*

"You really should get a better lock."

His advice sounded a bit cocky.

"Get the kind that puts a bar across the stationary door and pins the slider to the other side. That way it won't open, and no one can get in from the outside."

"Really!?" The cop looked at me to check for sarcasm, but I didn't mean any. I was simply acknowledging his advice. Of course, I was now interested in better security. "I didn't know," I said as I pushed my emotions back a notch.

"You said you saw him, the intruder?"

"Yes, but I didn't get a good look."

"Can you describe him? Was it a man?"

"Well, like I said…"

"I can!" JP interrupted. He was standing off to one side, quietly observing.

"Who are you?" the cop asked.

"Oh, he's a friend," I interjected quickly. "He was arriving just as the burglar fled the scene."

"So, you saw him leave?" Billings redirected to JP.

"No, I saw him come in. I was in the parking lot, waiting for Jodi to come home. I saw a man park near me, go to her house, Jodi's," he clarified, "and then he pushed through the hedges and ran around back."

"But you didn't actually see him in the house?"

"Well, yes… I did," JP corrected. "I went to the front door and it was locked. Jodi had just entered, and apparently, relocked it as she went in."

He looked at me for confirmation and I nodded.

JP continued. "So I went to the back, where I saw the intruder go. I looked inside and saw him right there," he pointed, "in the dining room."

"Well, this is getting a little bit more complicated," the officer complained. "Now I have to get your information as well. You're a witness."

"Sure," JP agreed and quickly answered the basic questions.

"Can you identify him?" Billings asked.

He directed the question to both of us. I shook my head. "He was wearing something over his head."

"I can!" JP interrupted again. "He was wearing a hoodie, but I saw him before he pulled it up over his head."

"Okay…" the police officer waited for more information.

"Medium height, medium weight," JP offered. "Brown hair."

"Great! You just described ninety percent of the males in this county, probably in the entire country."

"There was a beard," JP remembered. "A goatee. It was… long and untrimmed."

"Hey!" I blurted. "That's the man I saw in the hospital."

"Okay, okay," Billings flipped some papers over. "You want to give me more details on that?"

"Sure," I was determined to sort it out. "Yesterday, it was yesterday. First, right there in my front yard, hiding behind a tree. It was the morning. He was stalking me."

"You got a good look?"

"Good enough."

Billings paused, lowered his clipboard and looked hard at me. "I know you. I've seen you at the police station… visiting our prisoner." He raised his eyebrows and cleared his throat. "You're associated with *him*… aren't you?"

I really didn't want to talk about Sam. Too late. He raised the subject.

"Oh… indirectly, I guess you could say. I'm just his girlfriend," I felt a little embarrassed in admitting so. "You know. Steady. About four years now."

"I'm really not interested in your personal life," the cop shot back.

"Yeah, right."

The cop seemed a bit frustrated at that point. "I saw him at the hospital that afternoon," I continued. "I chased him down the hall, and yes, I got a real good look at him as the elevator door closed between us."

"And why were you in the hospital," Billings prodded. "What business did you have there?"

I hesitated, again unsure of how much information to disclose. The interview was supposed to be about the break-in at my house, not about the visit I had with Faith. There was much I didn't want him to know. I quickly decided not to mention Faith and the note I delivered to her. Yeah, that information was surely off limits. "I was there to visit Jen Foster." It wasn't a total lie, but maybe a half-truth by omission.

The officer was taking notes.

"She was badly burned when her house got torched," I informed.

"Yes, I'm aware of that case. So, you think this guy was following you?"

"Isn't that obvious?"

"And can you describe him?"

I was sensing that the cop was getting impatient with me. "Just like JP said. He was wearing a baseball cap, black shirt and jeans. But I saw the goatee," I emphasized. "Very clearly, I saw his beard."

"I saw him there too," JP jumped in once more, surprising Billings again.

A bit astonished at JP's admission, I was relieved to have the cop's attention redirected, away from me. He was prying, getting too close to the secrets we had to keep for Sam's defense.

"Yeah, I was with Jodi in the room with Mrs. Foster," JP continued. "I left so that she, I mean Jodi," he corrected, "could have a little private time with her. I passed that guy in the hall. Yeah," he concluded. "I can verify that he was there."

"Okay, okay, this is all a little bit much," the policeman returned his pen to a shirt pocket holder. "I'm not sure what it all means anyway, or if it means anything. Probably irrelevant."

He looked at me directly.

"Seems like a lot of trouble comes your way."

I was disturbed by the remark. "And what does that mean?" I retorted.

As he stood before us, he spoke with calm, confident of his superior position of power. "Nothing. Just an observation… I think I have everything I need for now. Call us, if anything else happens. It wouldn't be surprised if it did."

I cocked my head at the remark but abstained, whispering instead to JP, so the cop wouldn't hear. "Sure… thanks, I think,"

Billings took a few steps toward the front door and stopped. "One more thing. Is there anything missing? I almost forgot to ask."

"Yes!" I noted with concern. "My mail was over there on the table in the foyer. He took a large manila envelope."

"Do you know why he'd take that?"

"No. I didn't have a chance to open it. I don't even know what was inside."

"Sure." The officer took two more steps. "Again, one more thing," he stopped. "Could you pick this guy out of a lineup?"

"Yes, I'm sure I could identify him positively," I said with confidence that was meant to be displayed.

"And you?" he directed to JP.

"Yeah, I got a good look at him. He caught my attention." JP offered an explanation that was unwanted. "Because he was acting suspicious."

"Right. Okay."

And Officer Barney Billings made his way out of my house without further delay.

I went to the refrigerator and came back with two bottles of beer. "You want one?" I held it high enough for JP to see.

"Thanks."

He watched as I sat on a stool at the island in the kitchen.

"So, what do you think?" he asked.

I was deep in thought. "Well, there is something I'm still not clear about. So… why are you here?" JP stiffened at the question and I felt a bit guilty for challenging him so abruptly. "Sorry," I redirected, "I don't mean to be blunt." I looked toward the sliding door, still partially opened. "You were asking about the break-in, or the cop?"

"Yeah, right. Both, I guess. Guess you decided not to tell him about the knife attack?"

His comment caught me off guard. I choked and coughed on my drink, spitting out what was misdirected as I laughed and swallowed at the same time. "Guess you decided not to disclose the fact that I almost took you down?" I hacked some more.

"Almost stiffed me… is that what you mean!" JP grinned. "Well, after all, I was an intruder, too. Guess it was best not to tell him that?"

++++

They laughed together as the ice between them melted. JP took a few swigs of beer and sat in a comfortable chair as Jodi eyed him suspiciously, then moved to the seat next to him.

Both could identify the man: to Jodi he was a stalker and to JP the intruder. It seemed that he was one and the same, but neither yet knew that he worked at the church or of his connection to Father Jacob.

Yes, Jodi was getting closer to discovering the identity of Sam's nemesis. But why was Jacob so passionate these many years afterward, still intent on destroying Sam?

Although the clock hadn't yet stopped for Sam and Jodi, they only had a few precious hours remaining before everyone would vote, and they were running out of time.

++++

We talked at length. He explained himself and his reason for coming to my home. He noted that Jen Foster was his unofficial aunt: his birth mother had never actually married because his father refused, or so he was told.

I knew that Jen had been married. Was JP's connection through her late husband; or was she his father's sister – at least I thought that was what he implied.

193

I prodded some more. "So that's why you were at the hospital. Because you're related?" Although I wanted to, I did not ask for the names of his parents. Somehow, he seemed guarded about them. "I'm sorry about what happened to Jen. It must be hard for you."

"A little. Actually, this whole trip to Walthem has been pretty crazy for me."

"But you came here to study…" it was a statement more than a question. "Right?"

"True. That, and I wanted to learn more about my origins."

"How are you feeling about it all now?" I regretted the question as soon as the words left my mouth. It was too personal. JP was attractive, energetic, and certainly a very interesting young man. We were making a personal connection, and I felt my guard was compromised just then. I was still feeling neglected and vulnerable.

"Lonely. Very much alone," he said.

++++

Their eyes met and locked. His were dark brown, her's hazel blue.

JP needed a friend. He wanted to have confidence with someone, but desired more than friendship with Jodi. Intimacy, perhaps romance. He held her gaze, searching her heart for an invitation.

++++

I felt like I was falling into a trance. Was he putting a spell on me?

"Another drink?" he interrupted.

I nodded. He went into the kitchen and returned with the bottle of vodka I had placed alongside the refrigerator for my next bender into remorse and self-pity. *Yeah, this is a better use for it. Share it with a friend... What? But he is so young - just a kid... but so handsome.* It was what I felt just then that caught me off guard. I recoiled. *No, no you don't. Absolutely not!*

"So..." I looked away quickly to hide the feeling that was surging. I also wanted to squelch it. "What did you want to ask me about?" JP said he came with questions about Sam. "Is it my boyfriend's accident?" I decided to get right to the point. "So... how do you feel about that?" I hoped the conversation derailed by lust was back on track with my correction.

"You know, it was a long time ago," JP offered. "But the question that is haunting me is about the judge in the original case. William Williams was his name, I believe."

"Yes, I think that's right."

"Well, why did he let Sam off so easily?"

JP took a swig of the liquor, smiled, and handed the bottle to me. I did the thing that would be courteous to do. I took a sip and felt the heat of the alcohol as I swallowed hard. I took another mouth full. The liquid therapy was beginning to work its magic.

JP elaborated. "I mean, he dropped all the charges, let him go free, and then gave Sam the remainder of his term when he got sick."

"When you put it that way..." I was thinking hard, now distracted from my first instincts about JP, "it does seem a little odd. But honestly, I really do not know the answers to your questions." I sorted through my memory bank. "I don't think Sam ever really talked about it." In that moment, I wondered what else he was hiding from me.

JP saw my concern and gave me his serious look, his eyebrows raised, his brow wrinkled.

"Oh, stop it!" I began flirting with him. He smiled broadly. Now we were teasing each other.

"Well, doesn't that seem strange to you, at least a little? I mean, what are they concealing? Does he have some secrets that we don't know about?"

"Humph! I don't know." After a quiet moment, I noted, "Well, Williams is gone, but Sam's still here." I wanted to change the tone of the conversation.

"I know… I know! I should go and talk to him. Everyone keeps telling me that," he admitted, "and I will, maybe after he's released from the jail."

"Should be tomorrow."

"Really?!"

"Sure," I chuckled at the thought of JP confronting Sam. Another swig. I held up the bottle spontaneously and proposed a toast. "To freedom! May the innocent be free!"

"Free indeed!"

JP became enthusiastic and reached for the vodka again.

"You know, there is one more thing," he interjected. "I'm wondering what Jen Foster knows too. I heard that she and my birth mother were close at the end."

"Then let's go see her. She should be getting better by now. She was really groggy, but she recognized me, I believe, and she was trying to tell me something." *Letters!* "That's it: the word she said was 'letters.'" I sat erect with the revelation. "But I don't know what it means."

"Let's go and find out."

JP was getting excited and I didn't see any harm in it. "Sure, tomorrow morning? About ten?"

"Thanks! I'll meet you in the lobby, unless you want to go out for coffee first."

++++

He couldn't deny it. JP was attracted to the beautiful, intriguing young woman that sat next to him. He had to hit on her.

++++

"No…" I was remembering the temptation I felt just moments earlier. "How about we meet in the hall, outside her room." But somehow, I didn't think it would happen that way.

"Got it."

There was a long pause, and JP spoke next. "You like sushi?"

"What?"

"Sushi. You know, raw fish." he paused, "how about seafood?"

"Well, yes, but not always raw."

"Well, the one that took me to the ER was still alive. I swear it."

"What are you talking about?"

"Oh, I guess you haven't heard that story?"

"No… guess not…"

"Well, it's a sad, even scary tale of torment and woe. Actually, I think it was part of a crab shell that got caught in my throat." He grabbed his neck, as if he was about to strangle himself.

"Torment… really?"

197

He squeezed his neck and wrestled with himself. He coughed, wheezed, banged on his chest, then became straight and began shaking. It looked like he was having a seizure and I began to laugh.

Finally, he asked, "Want to hear it?"

"Think I'm gonna."

++++

The strong drink took over. The couple talked, laughed together, and shared embarrassing stories until long into the night, each trying to outdo the other with the revelation of a shocking experience. Reasoning was hushed and impulses became bolder.

Hours earlier:

Luke ripped the large envelope open as soon as he got back into his car. Sure enough, it was full of smaller envelopes – letters. His tires screeched as he accelerated on the sharp turn that led from the townhouse parking lot to the street. He wanted to know what was so important about those letters – and why Father Jacob wanted them so badly. He decided to go to Faith's apartment, to do some investigating. He would return to his place in the church basement late at night, to avoid his boss. Depending on what he learned from reading Darcy's letters, he would then decide on his next move.

Faith had made a mistake by sending her note to Jacob, the one demanding more money; perhaps this would give Luke the opportunity he needed to even the score.

At about the same time, Father Jacob was in Luke's lair complaining and rooting through the janitor's things, looking for those very same letters, the ones he had been sent to get. "Why the hell isn't he here," he mumbled to himself and tossed a magazine onto the floor. His face turned bright red as his blood pressure spiked. "I've got to get my hands on those damned letters!" he shouted to no one.

CHAPTER EIGHT: Indiscretion

Monday, May 13, 1985 – day six.

HEADLINE: **"Urban Breaks Silence, Claims He Was Framed"**

It was a sensuous dream about JP and I wanted to stay in it. I held my eyes tightly closed but could sense daylight pressing on the outer lids. I turned onto my back and my legs fell open. My head began to throb. I remembered the vodka. *No, please no. Not a hangover today...* I smiled to myself as an image of JP flashed through my mind. He was leaning back in the recliner and laughing, laughing so hard that tears streamed down his face. *It is a very handsome face.* I remembered more. *JP. He rescued me.* I recalled the break-in and the interview with the police. *But when did JP leave? He went home right after the cop left. Didn't he?*

I reached for my vulva and covered it with my hand. I felt something tacky. With my forefinger, I gently felt for my clitoris. It was enlarged. I was already aroused, at a six or seven, not far from the explosive number ten. I had the urge, but just then a disturbing image came into view. I tried to focus for clarity. I saw JP, kissing my inner thighs. *No, it did not happen. I would not have allowed it... or did I?* I quickly looked around the room. No sign of him. I was alone.

I threw the sheet to the side of the bed and swung my feet to the floor. This was not my usual place for exiting my bed. I was on the opposite side. My bra and tong lay on the floor there in front of me. Anger surged. I jolted for the bathroom, nearly tripping over an empty bottle. Vodka – all gone. *No, NO… NO, NO, NO!!!* I turned on the shower, my left hand still covering and guarding my genitalia, and then dropped onto the commode. *What now? Oh God, what now!?*

++++

"All rise for the Honorable Benjamin Jones," shouted the bailiff. It was an unusual 8:30 AM hearing before the county judge. Jones, upon hearing of Urban's continued incarceration, called the district attorney's office and demanded the early morning meeting.

Jared McCabe startled Sam at the police station holding cell at 8 AM. Another novelty: for the attorney to be visiting with a client that early in the day. Sam was given no time to prepare for his appearance before the judge.

"The State is prosecuting this case," the judge noted. "Who is representing the Commonwealth?"

A young man stood. "Sir, Andrew Stonewall, for the District Attorney's Office. I am an Assistant District Attorney," he paused, "and co-counsel this morning is Betsy Hartford."

"What is the charge against the accused?" the judge bellowed, his voice echoing in the empty chamber.

"It's rape, your honor, rape in the second degree."

"And who is representing the accused?" The judge was working through the preliminary details.

Sam's attorney quickly rose to his feet. "Jared McCabe for the defense." Sam sat at a table next to him, wearing a five-day beard and casual clothing: overall unkempt in his appearance. The judge ignored it.

201

"Are we ready to proceed?" Heads nodded on both sides of the aisle. The judge shuffled some papers, held one up to read for details and asked, "When was Mr. Urban first incarcerated?"

No answer.

"I'm directing to the prosecution," Jones clarified as he raised his voice. "Are you informed about this case?"

"Yes…" Stonewall stood again. "Yes, Your Honor."

"Well?"

"It was on Wednesday, May 8."

"That was five days ago!" the judge howled. "Why?" He raised his eyebrows and stared long and hard at the assistant district attorney who was looking to his colleague for support.

Again, no answer.

"Speak up, man," the judge scolded. "Why was this man imprisoned for four days without a bail hearing?"

Stonewall and Hartford whispered to each other.

"If you please, I don't have all day."

"Yes, sorry, Your Honor," Stonewall stammered. "I was not involved in the preliminary hearing, but we, that is, my co-counsel and I believe that a request was made to our office for more time."

"Time!? Time for what? A request made by who?"

The prosecutors whispered to each other again.

The judge cleared his throat close to the microphone.

"I apologize," Stonewall began, "I believe that the request was made by the Pennsylvania State Police who are investigating the incident. They expected to bring forth additional documentary and testimonial evidence to establish the severity of the crime," he paused, "and then possibly charge with first degree."

"This isn't a trial… we are only discussing bail," the judge frowned. "I am directing the district attorney's office to submit a brief before 4 PM today documenting the explicit reasons for delaying this bail hearing."

"Yes, Your Honor."

"Now, what is your recommendation for bail?"

"One hundred and fifty thousand dollars," Stonewall answered quickly with authority in his voice.

"That's excessive," Judge Jones countered immediately. He redirected to the defense. "How much bail is your client prepared to post today?"

Jared looked to Sam and spoke without conferring, "Twenty thousand." He continued, "Mr. Urban is a distinguished citizen of Walthem and certainly not a flight risk."

The judge paused and looked at both sides of the aisle with eyes like lasers, burning through their expectations jotted as notes on paper. The atmosphere was more than flammable, it was explosive.

"This man has been held for a long time without due process and it seems to be unjustified… in my opinion," Jones began. "I want him released immediately on his own recognizance, with a bail bond to be filed before 4 PM this day, in the amount of twenty-five thousand dollars." He slammed the gavel down. "Stonewall…"

The duo from the district attorney's office was already packing their briefcases, anxious to make a quick exit and hoping to avoid any further humiliation.

"Yes, Your Honor?"

"I will be looking for that brief this afternoon."

"Yes, Your Honor."

Sam shared a smile and hearty handshake with Jared, then turned for a quick exit as his attorney picked up his documents.

"Hey, where are you off to in such a hurry?" McCabe fired the question at his client. "Don't you need a ride?"

"A shave and a hot shower, for starters," Sam paused and turned back toward him.

"I'll take care of the bail," Jared said.

"Thanks for the ride, but I'll manage. I have a few urgent matters to attend to. Thanks again, Jared."

++++

I nearly tripped on the newspaper at my front door as I started out for the hospital. I was supposed to meet JP, to interview Jen Foster.

My emotions were raw. Right or wrong, love or lust, friend or foe? The contradictions were like a boomerang throwing explanations and accusations back in forth, between the thin walls that guarded my sanity. *I'm a slut.*

But mostly, I felt anger. Like a blacksmith's bellows fanning the forged flame of reformation, I was heating up. Red hot. Iron in the fire. *What am I to become?*

I had waited a long time for Sam. I was enduring much for him this past week. I wasn't going to throw it all away, not for a fling, with a boy, a college jock more than ten years my younger. And, what will Sam do when he finds out?

I still could barely believe it happened. It was not my intention to have sex with JP. *Only a slut would act like that. I'm not a slut – or am I?*

++++

A substitute for anxiety, self-condemnation was to some degree effective for Jodi in that moment. Salve on the wound. But, the offense to Sam, and herself, it was reprehensible! Healing, if even possible, would take time. And how could she continue to condemn Sam for what she thought he might have done with Faith?

Isn't it interesting, how we judge others harshly but expect leniency for ourselves, seeing the speck of sawdust in our brother's eye but unable to acknowledge the plank in our own?

++++

Walking briskly to my car, I pulled off the rubber band and shook the paper to straighten it. There, on the front page, was Sam, wearing the judge's gown, smiling at me. The photo plucked at a chord in my heart. *Sorry, I didn't mean to do it… maybe… maybe you didn't mean to either?* I felt like the mouse caught in a spring trap, injured, but still alive and struggling to get free.

I noticed the byline, the writer's name: **by Susan Kasper, staff reporter.** *She's such a good friend,* I reminded myself. *Thanks Susan.*

With the other hand I yanked on my car's door, tossed the paper onto the front seat and plopped inside. I dug in my purse for the car keys. They always seemed to be hiding from me. Found them. The Cutlass started promptly with a roar of the engine.

I looked at my watch. There was no time to spare if I was to meet JP on time. Thoughts were forming in my mind, words that would declare the statements I needed to make to him. *Maybe I should take the role of the victim.*

++++

Jodi paused to quickly read beyond the headline. Sam had made a statement; finally, he became proactive. As she did, a smile spread across her face. "Wow," she whispered to herself, "he really told them." Then she sighed, oohed and awed, and felt appreciation - the first positive feeling she experienced for Sam in several days.

But the haunt of implications from the night before, the illicit affair, continued to seize her mind, and her mental dissertation, a debate, expressing confusion in response to conflict, began.

++++

Hands on the wheel, I remembered my meeting with Father Jacob the day before, and my rant about him. *God, are you going to punish me now? Surely, I deserve it.*

An emotion surged; my breath quivered. I felt dirty, evil. I wondered how my punishment would affect Sam? *Will he also become a victim of my indiscretions? Who am I kidding? I am downright sinful! If Sam's convicted, it's all my fault!* I wanted to ask for forgiveness but the words were blocked by insincerity. Doubt.

I desired and needed justification: was it wrong to allow some love for myself? They say that outside of marriage, sex is not love, but lust. But can love be known without some heat in that moment?

Then I wondered about commitment… true devotion. I mean, that requires maturity.

Love or lust – both are surely fueled by passion. Can't be all that bad… It was invigorating. Gratifying. So why is self-love so wrong? But it is momentary, not lasting, and in that sense, insignificant. Yes, I did feel guilty, but if Sam truly cared for me, he would be forgiving, even understanding.

I would have to tell him… Sometime… *Sooner or later?*

Afterall, we were separated. I had been threatened and scared to death. He wasn't protecting me. I slipped on diminished security and literally scrambled for survival. I felt insecure.

It doesn't change my desire for Sam or my willingness to commit to him, if and when he ever asks me to marry him. I can rationalize and make it all okay, can't I?

And what if JP was not there to scare off the intruder?

Yes, it was a mistake, perhaps even more like an accident.

I'm going to have to tell Sam someday… if I'm going to give him another chance.

And God, well, He already knows. Obviously, that is another broken relationship. But is it all *my* fault? Really?

I know that I must be better, stronger to resist temptation. But how can I? I am just me… still, I am sorry.

On the way to the hospital, I passed through the town square where the courthouse was located and I recognized a woman standing in front of the portico on the steps. It was the state representative. Officer Barney Billings was standing alongside her in his dress blues. Something was going down.

I quickly tucked my car into a diagonal parking space and stopped in front of a reserved sign, within hearing range. That was when I noticed the press. A large video camera was on a tripod and news reporters were standing alongside with microphones in their hands, waiting for their chance to field their best question, hoping to earn notoriety for themselves.

Karen Jackson introduced the patrolman. He stepped up to the mic.

I scanned the area and after deciding that no one had noticed me, turned the window crank, opening it all the way, wanting and needing to hear their every word.

++++

"Folks, you know me," Barney stated with a stern look directed at the camera. "I gave you my best years, my career in law enforcement, working hard every day for the past thirty plus years to keep you and your children safe. I know the law."

"And now we have a crisis in our town. When a man uses his hand to strike a woman, well, that is an intolerable offense." He raised his own fist to emphasize the point. "And sexual assault – from one who is supposed to defend and interpret the law for us, well, this situation that we find ourselves in *is* just reprehensible."

"Today, with the full support of Representative Jackson, I am announcing my candidacy for the seat of magistrate, District Justice, 12." He smiled broadly, his eyes glistening with enthusiasm. "Let's fix what is wrong. This is the only way to make it right again!"

Barney stepped back, animated by the excitement that was palpable. Appearing as the Energizer Bunny with a hop of enthusiasm, the thrill of the moment surged through him. He was supercharged by the limelight experience and his expectation of coming glory. The few people assembled there applauded.

Jackson came to the microphone next and began to read a long list of credentials and achievements for her candidate. Then, she held up a poster that illustrated the ballot. Barney stepped forward with a large sticker. He stuck it on top of Urban's name, as it appeared on the rendering of the ballot voters would soon encounter at their polling places. It was too late to reprint the ballot, to add Billing's name. He would challenge the incumbent as a write-in candidate.

"That's all you have to do," Jackson instructed. "It's easy, so don't be confused. You will get a sticker from a poll worker. They can help if you still have any questions." She paused and looked steely into the glistening lens of the camera. "We have to save our system of justice. We have to remove Urban from office… Remove him, remove him!" she shouted as a victory chant. "He will soon be convicted in a court of law, but first," she paused for effect, "first… he must be convicted in the court of public opinion… Remove him! Remove him!" she punched at the air with synchromatic movements.

It was obvious that the press conference had climaxed and the intended excitement was achieved. "Thank you, thank you dear voters," Jackson concluded, "and May God bless America, with justice for all!!"

She came forward and a horde of reporters, like flies on road kill, swarmed her as many shouted questions simultaneously.

++++

Unbelievable. Just unbelievable. I started my car and yanked the shifter to reverse. I needed to make a quick exit before someone recognized me. But someone already had!

As I looked for traffic in my rear-view mirror, I saw a man, in a Plymouth K-Car, a dilapidated four-door sedan, who was obviously watching me. He was across the street. I quickly threw my arm over the back of the seat and turned around for a better look.

209

He was wearing a baseball cap pulled low on his face. I saw the goatee. A black shirt. He immediately turned away and yanked the car's sun visor down to block my view.

His car lurched forward as I gunned mine, the Oldsmobile still in reverse. We nearly collided. I hit the brakes and he stomped on the accelerator.

++++

Luke swerved to avoid colliding with Jodi's car and sped down the street.

JP arrived at the entrance to Jen's hospital room five minutes before the appointed time and was pacing in the hallway. It was four minutes after the ten o'clock hour when he finally peeked inside. The bed was ruffled and empty. JP hadn't seen a nurse, or anyone else for that matter, during the time he waited there. Ten minutes. He looked at his watch again. His new girlfriend was late, and the patient was gone. He began to fidget with his car keys.

A few longer, agonizing moments passed by. JP was about to leave when he heard footfalls behind him. He turned and saw Jodi approaching. Overall, she looked great, still hot, but her facial expression was one of disgust. Their eyes met and he smiled. She didn't.

++++

"Sorry to keep you waiting," I said to him. I knew that I had to be civil and was feeling a bit stronger after reading Sam's newspaper article and talking to God. But now I had to confront JP. I had to be accountable for what happened the night before.

"Oh, it's okay."

210

It was the first time he saw me with my makeup on. He stood there, frozen like an ice sculpture, gawking. I sensed his preoccupation with my appearance and frowned to show disapproval. I had seen the opposite sex immobilized this way many times before and usually enjoyed the attention, their unspoken compliment, but not today, not now. These circumstances were very different. Conflicted.

"JP," I nearly whispered, "we need to talk."

++++

Desire lingered. What Jodi felt just then was a tingle, like an electrical impulse, a sexual urge, hormonal craving, heightened physical sensations. Because she had been there, done that. Now it was temptation that she had to overcome, as well as guilt.

JP shuddered and tried desperately to regain composure, hoping to hide his feelings. To display them so, was unmanly. But it was too late; she already knew. Her reaction indicated that his desire had been fully exposed.

++++

"I passed a waiting room, just down the hallway. It was empty. Now! We have to talk now."

"Okay."

A housekeeper suddenly appeared, pushing a cart full of cleaning supplies. A mop stuck out of the top of it and swayed with the motion of her gait. I waited for her to pass.

"Not here. In private." I stepped away but he hesitated. "Now. This way." I pulled on his shirt sleeve.

We came upon the room and JP quickly sat down. I chose a seat, leaving an empty chair between us.

"What's up?" he asked.

"Last night," I began. "I don't know what happened. No, I do know. I think I know what happened."

"You mean you don't remember?"

"No. Yes. Yes, I do." I clenched my fists. "It was wrong. What we did. I didn't want to…"

"Sorry. But I didn't force you. I was following your lead."

"No. Maybe. But I was drunk. I didn't know what I was doing. You took advantage of me."

"No… that's not true. No, I did not take advantage. You knew what you were doing. You wanted it."

"I'm not accusing you of anything, at least not yet." As I stumbled in my scolding, I paused for reflection. "Nothing happened!! Got it? If you ever tell anyone, I will deny it. I swear…"

"I won't."

"If I am forced to, I will threaten you with sexual harassment… or was it assault? Do you get my drift?! Last night never happened. No one is to ever know about it."

"Okay!"

"Don't press me. I mean it. I was intoxicated."

His face contorted. He was obviously surprised by my anger and threat. "You did not have me last night. You had the vodka."

He was clearly becoming forlorn.

"Okay, it never happened. Backoff. Really. I can handle myself."

I wondered if I said enough. My anger was beginning to subside. "You know when it's rape?"

"What? What the hell are you talking about."

"All it takes is an accusation. The woman only has to say the word. She is always the victim."

JP had no answer. He must have been stunned by the insinuation.

"I had a break-in at my house. Why were you there? I can always change my story."

"No, you wouldn't do that. You wouldn't…"

"I have to protect my reputation. Don't make me do it." I was stern with him, but was it enough? A thought came to me. "You could end up just like Sam. That's exactly what happened to him… you know… why he's in a world of shit."

"Okay, okay!"

We sat in silence for several minutes. I felt exhausted. Confused. Conflicted. Empty.

"What now?" JP finally asked in a whimper.

"We came to ask Jen Foster some questions."

"We're still on?"

"It never happened," I reminded. "Nothing has changed. I am still with Sam, and intend to get the charges against him dropped… Now, I do need to talk to Jen. Are you coming?"

He paused before expressing compliance. "Yeah, sure. It never happened. Nothing has changed. I got it."

"Okay then. Let's go. We've got business to attend to." I stood abruptly and turned toward the hallway. JP followed to the patient's room.

"She's gone. Not there."

He interrupted before I opened the door, finally finding his full and firm voice again.

"No one has been here," he explained.

"Oh, well, let's find out where she has gone," I said in command. "There," I pointed. "We'll ask at the nurses' station."

Together we approached the counter. The office area was vacant. Phones were ringing and lights were blinking on an intercom panel; their patients were calling for help. "Where do you think they are?" I asked.

JP shrugged. "Hello… Is anyone here?"

A door at the far end of the workstation opened as the sound of laughter and loud voices drifted to our ears. A middle-aged woman wearing a white uniform, blouse and skirt, came toward us as she wiped icing off her mouth with a napkin. Apparently, it was somebody's birthday and a party was already underway.

"Can I help you?" Her tone indicated annoyance with our intrusion.

"Mrs. Foster?" I quickly responded. "She's not in her room."

"Went for respiratory testing."

"Oh, well…" I wondered what was appropriate to say next, "do you know when she'll be back?"

"Can't say. Depends on how busy they are down there."

"Okay, thanks, guess we'll come back later."

The nurse was already headed back to the party room. She looked back, "Visiting hours end at eight. Don't wait too long." She ignored the calls, still unanswered.

JP and I took a few steps toward the elevator. "What do you think?" he asked.

I felt unsure. "Damn, I really wanted to talk to Jen. How about after lunch… about one? Hopefully we'll have better luck then." And without waiting for confirmation, I turned to leave.

"Okay, but… where are you going?"

JP fielded the question that showed his disappointment at my leaving abruptly without him.

"Got to check on Sam," I shot back. "See you later."

++++

Wondering about Faith and remembering that Susan said Jodi delivered his note, Sam considered an attempt at convincing her to drop the charges. He stopped his car across the street from her apartment. But what was she still capable of? Would she call the cops? He had to think it through… be very careful.

Livin' the lie – but aren't we all?

Lies about relationships. Lies shrouded in justification.

Sam knew what his intentions were, the night he went to Faith's apartment, despite the way the evening ended; details were still fuzzy about those hours that went into the morning of the next day. Sam had intended to give Faith some advice, that's all… well, maybe also feed his ego, just a little.

Sam's previous time with Faith as a couple had been complicated by lies. He was relieved to end that relationship and wanted to be free of everything it represented.

She was disappointed, maybe even scorned to some degree. Perhaps she thought that the lies, the secrets they shared, were something she could use to coerce and keep him. If she was able to please him in other ways, make him content, she could hold onto him.

A woman wants to manage her man. Keep him within her grasp.

Live the lie.

But it wasn't enough for Sam. She wasn't enough.

Now it was a legal matter. He wondered if she would lie in court. She would be required to say the oath, "I swear by Almighty God that the evidence I shall give will be the truth, the whole truth, and nothing but the truth."

Was she capable of lying after reciting the pledge? Sure, why not? It's not perjury unless it's prosecuted, and surely that wouldn't happen.

Her accusation about him – it was 'bearing false witness', further disobedience to God, in violation of the ninth commandment. But she cared little about religious requirement.

Yes, untruth would prevail. Her testimony was the basis of the lawsuit. She had already committed to it, to proclaim the lie before a courtroom filled with townsfolk, before the lawyers, before the judge and jury, before God.

So, how could Sam persuade her to do otherwise? It was unlikely.

He thought about his brother, Joseph, and his wife, Trish. Theirs was another relationship conflicted by lies. Only days before their wedding, Joseph confided in his younger brother. "Well, she's not a virgin, but neither am I."

Sam seemed unfazed by the confession. He already knew that.

"But at least there isn't any baggage," Joe continued.

Sam raised an eyebrow.

"You know, kids. That would be a real drag. Another father, visits, shared custody, compromised allegiances."

Joe's best friend had married a divorced woman with three children. He complained frequently about the demands of her ex.

"Oh yeah," Sam answered. "I see what you mean."

"I want to have a family. And I expect to have her undivided, uncompromised affection for our kids... she will be a great mom!"

Trish was to be his trophy wife.

"Yes, of course." Sam was a bit startled by the assertion, but it was Joseph he was talking to, his brother's narcissism on full display. "I wish you and Trish all the best."

The newlyweds did have a family, and Sam's nieces were great, but years later, it seemed that his sister-in-law became distant toward her husband and her children.

It was a former friend of Trish that later told Sam about the abortion. It was about a year before their wedding and Trish was already dating Joseph. Had she cheated on him, or was the baby his? Didn't matter. He didn't know about it.

Sam wondered if he should have a conversation with Jodi... about former flings. No, he rejected the thought. She would never cheat.

Joe's girls were baptized, the promise of eternal life granted. But they hadn't sought affirmation before God. They really didn't care. It was nothing more than a ritualistic ceremony.

Live the lie. Ultimately, we choose to believe what we want, probably what we need. And life goes on. Eventually, the lies we live become established as fact, and even believed as 'truth'.

Sam looked through the windshield toward her apartment building. Faith resided on the second floor. Her bedroom window faced the street.

It was closed and the blind was drawn.

He hoped that being closer to the location of the alleged crime would jog his memory for the time unaccounted for. Despite how hard he tried, Sam couldn't remember anything beyond looking at the papers from her brother's deposition. And now, he needed discernment for the right thing to do. It was his last visit here that changed his life.

He wrestled with the pros and cons and was losing the battle for his desire to challenge his accuser when he noticed a man walk out of the building. He strained for a closer look. He had to be sure. Yes, it was Luke. He was carrying a shoebox tucked under his arm.

++++

I raced to the police station wanting to compliment Sam on his article in the newspaper.

"Gone." Officer Barney was short and obviously not happy to see me again.

"But where? Is he released?"

"I don't know, left with his lawyer… didn't come back. That's all I know."

"Was it a bail hearing?"

"Like I said…"

"Never mind," I interrupted. "I'll find out for myself." I wasn't liking the man who always treated me so rudely, yet I knew the reason why - he was our adversary.

"He should still be behind bars."

Sam's election opponent smirked. So rude! My eyes narrowed; my back stiffened. *Jodi, remember, he is a cop. You're in his turf.* Daggers were in my eyes – thankfully, not in my hands. "Just never you mind."

I hadn't talked to Sam since Saturday morning, it was a stressful meeting, and now I didn't know of his whereabouts. I was concerned, wanting to approach my boyfriend with a reconciliatory tone, needing to know if he was still wanting me. After the night before, I knew I didn't deserve him.

++++

As always, Jodi needed to be in complete control. She decided to go to Sam's apartment next.

Jodi ran up the steps and pounded on the rear door. No answer. She knocked again, a little harder. The single pane window vibrated in its frame. She peered inside. There were a few papers and some envelopes, probably the mail from the last few days, strewn across his kitchen table, but no sign of Sam.

Not knowing where to look next, she decided to visit the cafe, where she often met Susan for lunch. She wanted to ask about her article and offer congratulations on achieving the front page. It just might be the ice breaker Susan desperately needed for her tottering career.

Heavy traffic on Main Street forced Jodi to slow her car to a crawl. As she rounded a corner, she saw the blinking lights of a police cruiser parked up ahead, in the driving lane. She wondered if there was an accident and then thought about Sam. Fear came to taunt as she considered the possibility. Did he find even more trouble?   After all, the cops were surely out gunning for him.

Officer Ken was standing on the left side of the road directing traffic. A stack of posters was tucked under his arm. He stopped oncoming traffic and motioned for Jodi to pass by. She slowly and cautiously proceeded around the cruiser, turning quickly to glance that way, wanting to know what was happening.

Was it a street arrest? No, there wasn't anyone in the back of the police car. There were no smashed cars, evidence of an accident. Then she saw a municipal worker as he placed a cardboard sign on a utility pole and struggled to squeeze the handle of a staple gun. They were tacking up election posters for Billings. Unbelievable! She knew that it was illegal to attach them to a utility pole.

As the bell above jingled, the door to the restaurant closed. She scanned the place for Susan, but saw no sign of her. Jodi decided to have a coffee and went to a booth at the rear of the dining room. She picked up a newspaper from the counter near the cash register and sat down to calm herself. She had time to kill.

Counting the hours, JP had two to burn as he drove away from the hospital. Considering the places and persons he still intended to visit, he proceeded to the next item on his bucket list: his mother's grave. It was something he had been putting off for a long time. His nerves were raw. In his present mood, conflict was almost welcome. He had to be tough.

The Maple Grove Cemetery was located on the far western edge of town, on a hilltop overlooking train tracks that paralleled the river below. The place offered a serene view as the sun set over the distant mountain ranges on the horizon.

JP drove past the last of the brick ranch houses that lined the street before coming to a dead-end where a gravel parking area was large enough to accommodate four or five cars. At the front of the cemetery, a tall rod iron fence ran the length of a well-manicured lawn, about the distance of four city blocks, overhung by large sugar maple trees. Their leaves had recently sprouted in a bright color of unblemished lime-green. The ground was littered with browned blossom shells, the dried refuse of their budding.

A large ornate gate centered in the fence presented itself in an opened position, each side angled inward as a gesture of welcome for new tenants. The swinging gate was anchored there, pinned to pipes driven deep into the ground.

JP could see a narrow macadam road that turned sharply and zigzagged around large trees as it cut a pathway into the hillside and disappeared over the top of the ridge. Part of it appeared as switchbacks and he was unsure of its navigability. He had been instructed by his foster mother that the family plot was at the top of the hill near an outcropping of a rock ledge. He sighed at the uncertainty of his quest, wiped fresh sweat from his brow, and began the strenuous trek up the hill.

He stayed on the roadway until nearing the ridge. It would have been irreverent to take a shortcut and walk over the graves, the places where they rested in peace, wanting to be undisturbed as they waited for the resurrection, but also needing to be remembered until then.

Some had fresh cut flowers laid at the base of their tombstones that memorialized their short existence on earth; some had recently planted blooms, the disturbed soil neatly packed around their stems. Others had weeds already sprouted close to the edges of their markers, these deceased seemingly forlorn and forgotten.

JP looked at the small bundle of grocery store flowers he held in his left hand; their stems were wrapped in translucent paper. They suddenly seemed inadequate.

Once near the top, he walked along a narrow footpath, a trail that meandered below the graves, nearer to the backs of the headstones in the row below. Many unfamiliar names appeared there. They represented lives that surely were relevant in times past, undoubtedly important to someone back then and perhaps to someone still.

One must ponder the insignificance of their own life and feel unworthy among the deceased.

JP had no one. The gloom of death came upon him disrespectfully, demanding that he evaluate his own contribution to humanity. And there it was: he had nothing to report, nothing worth acknowledging, no tender mercies.

Fearful we are of accountability, the place of final reckoning. Still, we strive, pressing onward, hopeful of the chance to redeem ourselves, yet most of the time, lacking the sincerity to do so. That is human nature.

And God will be our judge.

Looking down the row of headstones he recognized some familiar names: Jackson, Williams, Canton. Then, farther down, the name barely visible on a light gray headstone, the engraving nearly worn away: Rogers. Etched there was the name of Theodore Rogers, 1901 – 1978, and his wife, Leona Rogers, 1912 – 1969. Could these be the grandparents he never knew, never even heard their names spoken?

Anxiety increased as JP did a visual sweep of other engraved names. No other Rogers. Miffed, he looked over the family plot and noticed a faux rose, an artificial flower, lying in some high grass nearby. He picked it up. Its color was faded, its texture brittle, its appearance dirtied by the frequent strike of the weed trimmer. Garbage. He let it drop back to the ground. And it was then that he saw a narrow rectangular stone that laid flat upon the earth's surface, covered with dried leaves. He knelt there and brushed away the debris. A name appeared:

"Darcy Jane Rogers, Beloved Daughter, 1940 – 1968."

JP discovered the modest burial place of his birthmother, known by some as "Janie." Yes, Darcy and Janie were one and the same.

He placed flowers there, below her name. Kneeling, he pulled at some weeds and felt the prick of a long reaching root from a brier bush. He pulled back and saw a thorn stuck in his flesh. Fresh blood appeared as he brushed it away with his thumb. He wiped his bleeding hand on a dry leaf.

This was the closest he had been to his mother since being a young child. He looked upward to the sky. A puffy white cumulus cloud raced by, but he did not see any form in it. She wasn't there.

Leaves rustled and he turned to see a sparrow as it lighted on the small branch of a tree nearby. Its head spun back and forth, chirping in loud warning, and then the bird took flight for refuge.

No, she wasn't there.

JP looked at the engraving, calculating her age. She was only twenty-eight years old when her life was snuffed away. The injustice of it all was on full display. It struck at him, like a slap on the face.

"Well, Mom, I'm finally here," he spoke to the unknown, needing to hear his thoughts audibly as a reinforcement of his mortality, an existence in a place where only reminders of past humanity remained. "All grown up… I guess. Sorry I never got to know you," he paused and swallowed hard. "I hope to make you proud… to be worthy of your memory."

The cemetery grew dark, the sun's illumination blocked by a thick cloud. It seemed as if it might rain soon.

"How did I happen? Was I meant to be? Who was my father?"

The inquiry was difficult, one that came from a troubled soul, mournful as it was.

"But I'm sure that you loved me."

It was an assertion needed by an orphan, a bleeding heart. But there was much more to ask.

"What happened to you?" Tears edged at the corners of his eyes. "I'm here to find out. It was just a terrible accident, I know, but did you get the justice you deserved?"

Unbeknownst to JP, his question echoed in the chambers of a stone church in the valley below, where it had been reverberating for many years, torturing the soul of a wayward clergyman. JP shivered as chills ran down his spine. Was his suspicion the counterpart of curiosity or the directive of evil for revenge? Was he in the presence of something more? A ghost, a spirit, a demon? He shook it off before it could take hold of him.

"Mom, I'll let you know." It was his promise.

JP pulled at some more weeds and repositioned the flowers. He waited a long moment. All was quiet, except for the sounds of silence.

"Rest in peace." He rose to his feet and looked away, back toward the road, his mission renewed.

Now, he needed to clearly define the inquiry intended for Jen Foster. But the planning of that imminent interview was interrupted by lingering questions for the person he believed to be responsible for his mother's premature death: Samuel Urban. That was a matter he still needed to resolve.

++++

Realizing that I was again late for my meeting at the hospital, I ran toward the elevator door in the parking garage. It was about to close when a hand came out and pushed on its edge. It jerked, hesitated, and then reversed direction. As the doors came open, I saw JP standing there, a big grin on his face.

"Saw you running in this direction," he explained.

"Thanks for holding the elevator."

"Considered racing you up there, just to make you feel guilty for being late again."

It seemed like he was flirting. "I have enough guilt already."

"Guess so."

"You don't?"

"No."

"Come on JP, you know better than that."

"Guess so, but I can always hope… Can't I?"

I returned a stern look, the kind you'd get from your mother, just before she scolded you for disobeying. "No, no you can't. Nothing happened. Nothing is ever going to happen between us again."

++++

At the surface, it was unrequited love. But with more analysis, it might have just been infatuation - lust aroused. Case in point: they hardly knew each other. It was merely a one-night stand.

++++

Jen was sitting in a recliner holding a plate in one hand as she nibbled on a piece of lemon angel food cake.

Not wanting to startle, I approached slowly. "Mrs. Foster," I called gently as I stopped half the distance to her. The woman, her forehead now wrapped in a bandage, smiled and nodded.

225

"Please, come in."

"Are you up for a little company?"

I watched as Jen stretched for the portable table and managed to place the edge of the plate there. Expecting a spill, I stepped quickly to offer assistance, but without waiting, she gave it a shove. I heard a clatter as it slid onto the table, and the remaining food spilled there.

Her eyes grew wide. "I know you, don't I?"

"Yes, I was here…"

"Don't tell me," Jen interrupted. "Let my mind do the work. I'm still pretty sharp you know. Now sit down here next to me and let me have a better look at you."

I pulled at an upholstered chair. It screeched on the floor as I slid it closer to the patient. Then JP came forward and caught her eye.

"Now wait a minute," Jen said. He froze in place. "Who's this nice-looking young man?"

He stepped closer and offered his hand in greeting. "Hi, I'm John Paul, her friend."

He intentionally withheld his last name and I noticed the omission. Actually, I still didn't know it.

"My friends call me JP."

"Then we'll be friends too," Jen smiled and took his hand. "But this one," she returned to me, I still have to remember… I've got it! You're the magistrate's friend. Jill, no… Judy… no, it's Jodi… Jodi Culp!" and she clapped her hands together, obviously pleased with herself. "Told you I would remember!"

"That's me," I smiled and settled into my chair as JP carried another one closer to us.

++++

Jen paused and puzzled on the reason for their visit. Confusion was evident on her face. But still, neglected patients are always glad to have some company.

++++

"I was sorry to hear about your injury," I began, choosing my words carefully. "I hope you're feeling much better." I leaned back to take in a full view. "But you look really good today!"

"Thanks," Jen accepted the compliment. "They're taking good care of me here… and I am getting a little better each day."

Her eyes got dim as her lips pursed. Waiting for her next words, I wondered what she was thinking. She looked away, toward the window.

"I don't know where I'll go next. I lost just about everything; you know…"

A deep frown carved into her face and I feared she might begin to cry. I reached over, took her hand, and squeezed it gently. "Don't worry. It will all work out. You'll find a lovely house, or maybe an apartment."

"I guess so…"

"We wanted to visit you today," I redirected, "and if you are up for it, we have a couple of questions."

"Yes, I thought so. It's about the letters… right?"

"Well, no… but yes, I guess. I don't know about the letters. Why don't you tell us about them?"

"You didn't get them?"

I shook my head.

"I mailed them to you the day of the fire, in a large manila envelope?"

"Something like that arrived, a couple of days ago, but I lost it, well actually, I think it was stolen. But I didn't get a chance to read them…"

Jen frowned as I wondered why they were so important.

"Can you tell us who they were from?" JP interjected.

"Yes, of course. They were from Darcy. She wrote to me frequently during the year of her pregnancy. She had a sweet little baby boy."

"He is the reason we came," I noted as JP nodded once in quick affirmation. "We wanted to ask you about him."

"Well, I don't know much about the child," Jen confessed. "At first, I thought he perished in the accident. There was a fire. Her car burst into flames. It was a terrible thing…"

We leaned in closer, anxious to hear more. But just then, the woman's demeanor changed and she clenched her jaw firmly.

"I heard rumors that he was rescued and placed in a foster home. Somewhere, but not here. But I never knew what happened to him," she explained.

"I heard about the accident." I wanted more information.

Jen's eyes narrowed as she recalled a conversation that was difficult for her.

"I called Jacob, my brother, the priest," she explained and continued, "Darcy, the poor girl lingered for more than a day in the hospital before she died from her injuries. I begged my brother to go and see her, but he wouldn't." She squeezed the arms of her chair as her body shook slightly. "I'll never forgive him for that… and he completely denied the child."

"Denied the child?" I repeated. "What do you mean?"

Suddenly aggravated, she shouted, "He was the father! It was their big secret. Even Darcy didn't tell anyone, except me, in her letters. She continued working for him as his housekeeper and lived as a single mom with her parents, her baby's father unidentified. It was a hard life for Darcy. She did everything for him. Cooked, cleaned, laundry… everything! Darcy's mother watched the baby at first, but she was already sick. Deathly ill, with cancer. And Jacob, after their first trip together, refused to take Darcy anywhere, the woman who should have been dignified by him in marriage as his wife. But he still wanted his privileges."

Jen paused after the rant and looked to me for understanding, but it was a lot of information, and I was still processing.

"You know what I mean: marital relations," she clarified. "But he wouldn't give up the priesthood, despite breaking his vow to chastity. Darcy told me all about it in her letters. She needed someone to talk to. I would have been her sister-in-law, you know."

I felt slightly numb as I struggled to comprehend all that she said. At first miffed, I nodded slowly, to show her confirmation. She had my full attention.

Then it hit me, like a lightning bolt, a shock to my nervous system. Jen – this is JP's aunt, 'unofficial.' That's what he told me.

"So… the little boy," I asked, "Darcy's baby, would have been your nephew." I had to be absolutely sure.

"That's right."

I finally understood about JP. *So, he is their son: Darcy his mother, and Jacob, the priest, is his father!*

"He is…" I spurted the words, but stopped abruptly and looked to JP who was vigorously shaking his head. His eyes told me not to divulge his identity, unknown to the woman we were interviewing. I paused and swallowed hard. "So, you had a history with Darcy?"

"Yes, of course, and when she was a child, I often babysat her. We were…"

++++

Across town Jacob was lounging in his library at the rectory. He puffed on a stogie like an old steam engine, its smoke swirling in the air above his buttoned wingback recliner. He was contemplating a trip after a quick stop at the travel agency on Main Street the day before. He looked at photos of young women scantily clothed on the beaches of Cancun, Mexico. He lingered on the close-up photos of lean bodies in bikinis. He wanted to get out of town, and told himself that he deserved a vacation.

So much was happening, and soon it would be the right time to leave. The election was tomorrow and he was confident of Billings' victory. The charges against Urban were progressing through the judicial system. His sister, Karen, was on top of it all. He sighed and blew a ring of smoke that floated in front of his face. It was a trick he mastered after much practice.

Glancing at the photo of Darcy on the bookshelf, he finally felt gratified. Luke and the letters were the only loose ends that remained. He peered out the window toward the place where his janitor parked his car. It was still vacant, but surely, he would be arriving soon, with those damned letters.

The sweet memory of the trip to Jamaica with Darcy was on his mind as he indulged his lustful thoughts for another rendezvous with the opposite sex. He had no travel companion this time, but he intended to meet someone nice, or hire an escort, once he arrived in Mexico.

230

Latina women are very beautiful, but Darcy, she was his first, and by far, she was the best…

Jacob remembered seeing the reflection of himself in the mirror at his hotel room. He was much younger then, in his prime. He combed his thick black hair after applying some gel. He smelled the tantalizing aroma of the cologne generously splashed on his clean-shaven neck.

His swim trunks were the latest style, cut several inches above the knees and notched on the sides, designed to display his muscular legs, quadriceps in front and bulky calves in the rear. His tan was already beginning to show.

He was the Italian Stallion. His mother, a very devout and reverent member of the church, always bragged about Jacob's good looks. It seemed a waste to devote them to religion, she joked, but who was she to question God's calling?

He applied sun tanning lotion on his chest and contemplated the pleasure of having his companion, the charming young woman who was his housekeeper and travel mate, to rub it on his back.

He stepped into the hallway of the hotel and locked the door to his room with the key provided by the front desk clerk. Darcy was nowhere to be seen, so he draped a towel over his bare shoulders and trotted toward the pool. Apparently, she would meet him there. He decided that he would arrange two lounge chairs in a private spot and order some drinks.

Darcy was shy about showing any affection to him. Obviously, he was pushing the boundaries and she was notably uncomfortable with it all. A couple of frozen margaritas would loosen her up, he reasoned. But he preferred a long island iced tea laced with extra vodka.

Jacob remembered being a little disappointed and aroused at the same time, when Darcy approached the pool's deck. She was wearing a single piece swimsuit that generously concealed her figure, topped off with a large terry cloth shawl that served as a cover-up.

He watched with intense interest as she strolled toward him. Her gait was distinctive, her legs long and shapely as the sun shined on them. In one hand she held a paperback book, in the other her room key. Her long hair, light brown with blonde streaks, was pinned on top of her head in a bun. Wearing sunglasses, she would have resembled a movie star, except for the overly modest attire.

Finally, his housekeeper fantasy was coming true. But when Jacob asked her to apply tanning lotion to his back, she looked over the top of her glasses as if to suggest that his request was inappropriate. She hesitated, then complied. Quick to return to her novel, she rarely gave him another glance.

The tension between them was palpable, so Jacob waited for the lotion to dry and went for a quick swim in the pool. On his return he stood erect, puffed out his chest, and sauntered, water dripping off of his body, hoping she would notice his masculine physique. But she didn't look beyond the pages of her book. Teasingly, he leaned over her, allowing water to drip onto her chest. "Jacob, know your place," was all she said as she pushed him back with the open palm of one hand against his forehead.

A bit deflated, but not defeated, Jacob lay on his chest to tan his back and quickly fell asleep. It was sometime later that he aroused and realized that Darcy was gone. He scanned the pool and deck, but she wasn't there. On a small glass table, next to her lounge chair, her drink glass was empty, sitting in a puddle of condensation. Next to it was her room key, apparently forgotten.

Jacob reached for the key and turned it over in his hand, while contemplating what he should do next. What was required, or offered: appropriate, or allowed? Surely it was not meant as an invitation, yet she might not have another and could be locked out of her room. He decided on the chivalrous thing to do. He would return it to her promptly.

Jacob approached her room, number 38, directly across the hall from his. Her door was locked. He knocked lightly, to not disturb others or draw attention to himself, and then quietly called her name. No answer.

He placed the key in the slot and slowly, gently opened the door, peeking inside and calling again. He decided to leave it on the desk, located at the other side of her bed.

And to his defense, that was all he intended to do in that crucial moment.

As he turned to leave, he saw her standing there, in front of the bathroom door, wrapped in a towel, water still running down her legs. She had just come out of the shower.

Something exploded in his mind. He rushed to her and wrapped his arms around her waist. She yelled for him to stop and tried to pull away. Her towel dropped to the floor. It was too late for Jacob to regain control. He was a race horse leaped out of the starting gate; a rodeo bull fully stimulated as it jumped out of its pen.

Darcy struggled, screamed, and then wept as she was overcome by the strong man.

It is still unexplained how she got into her room without a key. Most likely, a maid opened the door for her.

++++

"...we were friends. When I was growing up, we lived three doors down from the Rogers," Jen continued. "I was eleven years older than Darcy, but we became close back then."

"But why," I decided to field the obvious but difficult question that nagged at my gut as I was determined to dig deeper for the answers I still needed. "Why would Darcy sleep with a priest?"

As he listened, JP sat in silence, seemingly dazed, a look of bewilderment on his face. It was his birth parents that we were discussing so blatantly, even his conception! It felt like dirty laundry being aired for all to see. I felt bad for him.

"She didn't!"

Jen was yelling now.

"Don't you see? He raped her!" She paused and continued, "When they went on that trip together. Poor thing. He was an arrogant brute. He ruined her life and then decided to blame it all on someone else."

"Blame?" Confusion gripped me. "What do you mean?"

"Urban! He shifted the blame to Urban, but that was just a terrible accident. It was my brother who robbed her of the life she deserved. And he got away with it!"

Jen began to tremble as she clutched the arms of her chair again. Her face contorted; she allowed a few tears to fall onto her lap.

As I watched it seemed that time stalled, the drama of that sensational moment unfolding in slow motion. I saw the drip: it

234

descended from her chin as it went downward, through space undocumented, to splash on the blanket that was wrapped around her legs. The dark spot quickly disappeared as the liquid was absorbed.

"She was going home from the rectory, and just picked up the baby." Jen swallowed hard. "Shouldn't have, wouldn't have been there if he wasn't using her like he was. It's all his fault!" She raised a clenched fist into the air and struck at the heavens. "Jacob should pay!!"

I was dumbfounded, and it had to be much worse for poor JP. We watched as Jen attempted to regain composure.

She continued, "Like I said, he refused her in the end. He wouldn't even administer last rites. No wonder he has been consumed with guilt all these years."

I shook my head in disbelief. "Oh, that's just terrible. Such a louse…"

Jen whimpered. It was obvious that she had become very upset. As I became concerned for her health, I wondered if we should stop the interrogation. Cease and desist. But I needed to at least show my gratitude for her blatant honesty.

"Once she was carrying his child, Darcy had no choice but to stay with him," Jen explained. "She put it all in her letters. She needed money, and, she never stopped hoping that he would one day leave the church and be united with her and their son. When she was hospitalized, after a truck crashed into her car," she concluded, "I went to see her. But she was unconscious. I told Jacob that she was dying. Still, he refused. There was nothing more I could do, but I tell you, I will never forget that day."

++++

Miffed. Stunned at the revelation of rape, they had few parting words after thanking Mrs. Foster for the information she provided.

JP mumbled something undiscernible and turned away from Jodi. He was embarrassed. Surely, it had to be more than he could handle. Confused, his reactions stalled as he operated on autopilot. It would sustain him: prevent a crash. Regardless, JP was okay, because he had to be, but inside, his guts were churning.

Jodi, nearly as overwhelmed, also needed time to process the implications of all that Jen revealed. After the two parted ways, she quickly decided to return to the **Morning Herald**. She was beginning to be concerned about her standing with the boss. It had been nearly a week since she reported for work.

The advertising department was buried with orders for ad designs. The sales department had been offering ad space that would be available in special editions within a couple of weeks: an annual Vacation Guide for Warren County, and another Outdoor - Recreation Guide for the summer months.

Jodi dug in and the hours flew quickly by. She worked long into the night. But it was good for her, because she needed a diversion.

The Attack

That night, as Jacob sat in his office reviewing correspondence from the diocese, a severe electrical storm struck again at Walthem. A letter from the bishop demanding an explanation for the decline in revenues was the most annoying to the priest. As he considered a response, the lights blinked and then suddenly, everything went dark. The power was out.

Jacob lit several candles used for vespers, evening prayers. Such accolades were performed during a ceremony observed with acolytes on the second Monday of each month when confessions were heard. These candles were kept in the vestibule near a portrait of the Station of the Cross and also lighted during certain holy days.

Luke was traipsing through the hallway when he noticed the dim, flickering light coming from the doorway at Father Jacob's office. In one hand he held a flashlight and in the other he gripped the handle of a five gallon can of gasoline.

He was taking a shortcut, going to the generator that failed to start. It was his job to get it running, as quickly as possible. Walking through the church provided dry passage for the janitor who was already soaking wet.

Rain and hail were pounding on the slate roof with a thunderous sound.

"Luke, I trust that is you?" Jacob shouted toward the sound of footfalls in the hallway. Luke lowered the fuel can to the floor and shined his battery-operated flashlight into the office. Jacob was sitting there, his facial features shadowed from the light of a single candle placed on his desk below his chin. His appearance resembled that of a werewolf, more than a man.

Thunder roared and within seconds a crack of lightning shook the entire building. As the light burst inside, Luke saw an evil grin on Jacob's face.

"Stop shining that flashlight in my eyes. Come in. We need to talk," the priest said.

Cautiously, Luke approached the clergyman's desk and stopped several feet away, standing erect like a soldier before his commanding officer.

"Things were disturbed in my office." Jacob alleged. "Were you in here?"

"No, not me."

"Well then, who else could it be?"

"I don't know." Anxiety rising in his throat, Luke nearly choked.

"Is this what you were looking for?" Jacob held up an envelope. "It came to me through the offertory."

Luke squinted in the dim light and shook his head.

"It's from Faith, and has your name on it too. I'm sure you know all about it."

"I told her not to do it." Luke was expecting trouble. "That was all her, not me."

"I see," Jacob noted while rubbing his chin. He scratched some more at the base of his neck and tugged on an ear lobe.

Luke stood in silence, like the traitor before the firing squad.

"Well, what are you going to do about it?" Jacob yelled. "What do you have to say for yourself?" His eyes glowed in the dark like those of a lion caught in an illuminating beam of light.

"And, where are the letters that you were supposed to get for me last night? Did you get them? You've been avoiding me all day."

Perhaps Luke should have dropped to his knees and pleaded for mercy, but it wasn't like Jacob to go easy on him. He shifted on his feet and confessed, "I don't know what to do now."

"One more day!" Jacob roared. "You only needed to keep her under wraps for one more day." With an open hand he slammed the envelope down onto the top of his desk. The sound of his outburst echoed in the hallway behind them. "Tomorrow is the election. After Urban loses, a jury will gladly convict him."

"Faith isn't so sure. She got a message from him. He has some dirt on her. She is running scared." Luke spilled his guts with a series of short statements, simple facts without feeling or dissertation.

"Then I'll have you both arrested," Jacob thundered! "This is blackmail. It's enough evidence to have you both put away." It was a cheap shot, enough to anger anyone, to cause their adrenalin to surge.

"Hold on... Hold on there, Mr. Clean... I know all about you." Luke pointed a finger at his opponent, "I know what you did!"

"What are you talking about," the priest was cocky in his response.

"I know that you raped that girl. The one who was killed in the auto accident."

"You're crazy!"

"Oh yeah, you want to talk dirt. Well, you're the guilty one."

"Bull shit!!"

"Oh yeah, well guess what? I got those letters," Luke informed. "Yeah man, I got them last night when I broke into her house. And I've been reading them. You're the pervert!"

"So, you were successful," Jacob responded in calm, the wheels of reasoning spinning in his head. "Why didn't you bring them to me?"

Lightning cracked. It seemed as though a cannon was fired in the room.

"And that's not all… I didn't set that house fire. You! You did it! I'm sure of it now."

"The ravings of a crazed lunatic," Jacob assessed, "a convicted drug dealer and ex-con! You're the one with the criminal record.   And they already have evidence against you. The pocketknife proves that you were there. Besides, who do you think they will believe - you or me?"

Luke flushed and began to tremble.

"And why have you been stealing money from the church?" Jacob accused falsely. "Oh no, it's not me in hot water. But you're in it up to your neck."

Luke's face turned bright red, as if he was in a pot of boiling broth. You could almost see steam coming out of his ears.

"What the hell are you talking about?"

"Go… and get me... those damned letters!" Jacob huffed with the rhythm of a broken record, stalling on its turntable. "No more money. Settle down, or you're going back to prison."

"No!" Luke yelled and advanced toward his opponent, leaning over his desk. "I'm not taking the fall for you. I've got all the proof I need to take you down."

"Then it's time for me to make the call," Jacob said with a smirk and unearthly calm. "This," he picked up the envelope, "This is blackmail."

And those were the fighting words that ignited the fuse, an explosion of desperate actions.

Luke lunged for the letter, grabbed it out of the priest's hand, but lost his balance and fell onto his desk. Jacob, sitting in a chair with rollers was pushed backwards and rammed against a table where a large, solid brass crucifix wobbled, off balance. It was nearly two feet tall and weighed more than ten pounds. The priest pushed away from the table as the crucifix fell; with a loud bang it crashed onto the floor. Then Jacob managed to stand, rising to face his challenger.

Luke was fuming. This was his time, the moment long awaited, and without hesitation he acted, to set the order of things right.

He jumped over the desk and threw a right jab punch, catching the lower jaw of Jacob's face.

The priest moaned and grabbed Luke's shirt at his chest with both hands. "You fool!" he screamed as he shoved with all his might. Luke hit the desk and tumbled downward.

Before Jacob could regain composure, Luke sprung up and charged again, ramming his head into Jacob's gut, forcing him against the front edge of the table. The priest grimaced at the sharp pain he felt in his spinal column and slumped to the floor.

But Luke wasn't done. He grabbed the priest's throat with a stranglehold. "You will pay, and I will stay!" he commanded, "say it! Tell me that you will pay!"

There was a throaty noise as Jacob expelled air from his lungs. He gasped for more. He was beginning to feel light-headed. He threw his head to the right, then to the left, and felt the crucifix poking into his thigh. He reached and grasped it with his left hand.

Luke was squeezing even harder now, lost in the exhilaration of the moment and already feeling the win in his wit. Then it happened. Out of nowhere the crucifix came high in the air and then down with a deadly force that crashed into Luke's skull. The janitor never saw it coming.

His eyes rolled back; blood gushed out of his head and trickled down, over his face. Jacob saw Luke's realization of defeat. His choking hold relaxed and he slumped backward. His head made a thud as it hit the floor. Blood pooled there.

Jacob rose to his knees and stared in disbelief. He waited for awareness to register with confirmation of what had just happened.

His first thought: he wanted the body of the degenerate man out of his office.

The priest stood, arched his back to straighten it, and paused in the dark room to consider his options. He relit the candle.

Next, Jacob went to the janitor's closet and returned with towels and a bottle of cleaner. He placed one towel under Luke's head and tied it into a knot at his forehead, covering the wound. Then, he grabbed his victim's feet and began to drag the body. It was an arduous task and the fifteen feet to the cellarway seemed like a mile.

He needed to have the traitor back into his own place, his basement lair. This was the priest's first and only determination in those initial, pressing seconds, after surviving the assault.

Jacob forced Luke through the opening and watched his body tumble down the stairs to the concrete floor below. He stared at Luke lying there and wondered how to make it look like an accident. His mind was racing, but he couldn't yet see the finish line.

Fact and fantasy swirled together. Jacob pressed for clarity. Then it dawned on him.

Luke was already suspected as an arsonist. The cops believed he set the fire at Jen's house. His pocketknife, the one found there, was evidence.

Also relevant was the 'fact' that Luke stole money from the church, even though he didn't. This would be proved with evidence easily fabricated.

When confronted, Luke attacked. But how did he end up downstairs? He went there to set another fire – maybe. But then something happened, and he never made it out.

Then it all became a bit confusing as Jacob pondered on the real reason they struggled, the note from Faith. What should he do with it?

To charge Luke with bribery and reveal Faith's note as evidence could expose his plot against Urban. Luke should have known that Jacob was calling his bluff. But he was a dimwit.

And there was the evidence damming to the priest, the letters, their whereabouts still unknown. What if they were found?

Could Jacob somehow use Faith's note to implicate Luke as the mastermind of the rape charge? Sure. First, they framed the judge so they could bribe him, but then, they discovered the letters and decided to also go after the priest. That just might work. It accounted for the letters.

So, Jacob would have to face the disgrace of a past indiscretion, probably be a little shamed, but the church and its parishioners would be forgiving. They had to be.

Luke was right about one thing: Faith's note was their big mistake. And it cost him his life.

Then Jacob had another idea, a second way to explain Luke's demise. Again, he'd have to use the accusation of Luke stealing money for the reason they fought. Or did they?

It might have happened this way: once confronted, the janitor pleaded for mercy. The priest granted it, contingent on the return of the stolen money.

Such forgiveness would be appropriate for a clergyman of his stature – sounds good.

Luke was remorseful. Jacob went to comfort him.

It was then that he stumbled in the dark, fell, and hit his head on the desk, the injury rendering him unconscious.

See... it was an accident.

Luke urgently wanted to administer first aid, but first, he still needed to start the generator, to get the lights back on, before rooting for a bandage that was difficult to find.

Unfortunately, a stair tread broke under the extra weight of the gasoline Luke carried as he hurried into the basement. He stumbled and fell. And then, there was a fire.

Yes, another fire. It would finish the job.

That seemed to make a little more sense, so he would go with it. It was all just a terrible accident.

But why was Luke carrying a can of gasoline and a candle at the same time? He had to illuminate the way. There was no flashlight. Jacob would dispose of it, or render it unusable. The candle was in the office when they talked, so Luke grabbed it without thinking of the apparent danger.

So how does one get away with murder? Jacob knew that the answer was in the details, and he was paying close attention to them now.

Luke had not.

But why did Luke go into the basement to begin with? Jacob would explain that the janitor intended to reach the generator after getting tools he needed from his workbench, and then exit through the steel exterior doors that covered the outside steps.

It was certainly foolish of the janitor to carry gasoline and a candle at the same time. But hey, hindsight is always 20-20.

The fire. There needed to be a fire to finish the job, and silence Luke forever.

Jacob remembered the can of gasoline sitting in the hallway near his office. He retrieved it, loosened its lid, and tossed it into the cellar stairway. He watched as it bounced down the steps and spilled on the floor near Luke's body.

The priest stood there looking at his former employee and friend of sorts. At the least, he was a cohort in crime. But how did it come to this? His shadow reached through the opening and stretched over the stairs, flattening on the treads to form a zigzag pattern. Somehow, the apparition was calling, like a demon from the hordes of hell. It was influential.

The lights were back on, so Jacob moved quickly. He meticulously cleaned his office, not just the place where the struggle occurred, but with a mop and diluted floor cleaner, he wiped down the entire room and hallway.

Evidence of the crime was covered over by housekeeping activity. Nothing unusual about that. The church was cleaned every Monday.

Next, he grabbed one of the candles that initially lighted his office. It was cool to the touch, so he placed it in his jacket pocket. Then carefully, he climbed down the stairs. He removed the towel from Luke's head, watchful to avoid contact with the gasoline that pooled there. It was still lapping at the nozzle where the dented cap fell off.

Jacob was heedful to return without stepping in the blood spilled on the steps. Near the top he stomped on a stair tread. It was the third one down from the top. It broke in half and its pieces fell to the floor below.

It would appear as though the stairs failed and Luke fell.

Jacob stood at the cellarway and looked again upon the crumpled body of his janitor, lying motionless below. A strong smell of gasoline was evident as its vapor rose to the first-floor landing. Jacob reached into his pockets.

From his jacket's outer pocket, he retrieved the candle and from the inner vest pocket where he always kept his cigars, he felt for his lighter. It belonged to his father and was an heirloom which he treasured, a vintage Colibri triple jet torch lighter and cigar punch forged in sterling silver and monogrammed with his father's initials, "JRP."

It was the same one he used to ignite the Molotov cocktail at his sister's house.

He flicked a switch with his thumb, the lighter clicked, and a small blue flame burst out of its elongated tube. Jacob touched the wick of the candle and saw it become completely engulfed. There was an eerie, quiet and discomforting calm as he paused to watch the flame grow. It began to melt the wax. The light of the small fire shimmered in his black eyes; his pupils dilated. His mind whirled with the impressions it brought, a candle lit for special occasions: a birthday cake, holiday celebrations, and special dinners. Happy times.

Perhaps in that moment he reconsidered, but then realized that there was no other way; he had to be rid of Luke.

Dead or alive? Could the man that lay on the basement floor still be alive – who knew? But Jacob didn't care.

With a gentle swing of his arm, the priest tossed the burning candle to the gasoline below. He nodded, a gesture irreverent, a silent proclamation of his final farewell.

And then, as time stalled, it seemed to have defied gravity. The candle lingered there, mid-air, as if it had a conscience of its own and refused to complete the dastardly deed. It hit the floor and with a 'woof' and a 'pop' the tiny flame erupted into a blaze that grew rapidly.

Jacob removed the batteries from Luke's flashlight before returning it to the utility cabinet in the supply room. It was useless, that's why he didn't have it.

The priest wiped his fingerprints off the crucifix and returned it to its rightful place. He sat at his desk and waited for the appropriate time to dial 911.

Jacob wondered how he would explain that he just woke up. Well, apparently it happened when smoke wafted at his nose. His story would be that he called for help and then grabbed a fire extinguisher, but it was too late to contain the blaze.

He would be the victim of a terrible accident, surviving a near escape with death; perhaps he'd even be a hero who risked his own life to rescue another. Too bad, that man wasn't saved. Good, he wasn't talking.

In the basement the fire spread rapidly. It licked at the edges of a shoebox that was on the floor near Luke, and then began to burn the thin cardboard it was constructed of. Once inside, it ignited a large manila envelope addressed to Jodi Culp, containing the letters written by Darcy Jane Rogers and originally sent to Jen Foster. They were the only copies, and within minutes, they were consumed. It was a lucky break for Jacob as he forgot to look for them before igniting the blaze.

Jodi arrived home late, unaware of the turmoil in the heavens. A letter was waiting for her, the block printing of her address all too familiar. But the advocate would have to wait for another day. She was headed straight to bed.

CHAPTER NINE: Realization

Tuesday, May 14, 1985, Election Day – day seven.

HEADLINE: **"Church Fire Is Fatal to One; Victim Still Unidentified"**

Sam was awake at dawn Tuesday morning after having his best sleep in a week. He made himself a coffee and went onto his rear porch deck. The sky was dull as fog clung to the trees. They swayed in a brisk breeze as a fine mist sprayed against his face. The weather promoted a feeling of dismay, but this day, Sam was hopeful.

His mind was a race of scattered thoughts, each competing for his attention, as one would pass the other to claim the leading position. He wondered if his newspaper interview would have an impact on the election now underway. He decided not to show himself at the polls; after all, he really did not have a sense for the pulse of public opinion. So much had happened while he was in the lock-up, isolated from his constituents.

He doubted he would have his job much longer and began to think about what he might do next, but that was too difficult to consider.

Sam thought briefly about Faith. Susan had reported on Sunday that Jodi delivered his note. He hoped it would have an impact on her actions, yet in that regard, uncertainty prevailed.

He recalled the surprise visit from his brother Joseph, and his pulse quickened. What his brother inferred stirred anger and poked at old wounds that distance and time failed to heal. He felt his father's rejection most acutely, but his mother's and brother's haunted too. Sam managed to distance himself from them, but not from the complicated issues and feelings associated with his childhood, his dysfunctional family experience.

Finally, thoughts of Jodi raced forward. Why hadn't she visited him since Saturday? Two days with no contact from her – what could that mean? To Sam's thinking, it couldn't be good.

++++

I slept a couple hours longer, still exhausted from the emotional roller coaster ride of the last six days. Once awake, I sat on the edge of my bed and felt the plush carpet under my bare feet. It tickled with unexpected pleasure. I knew from childhood lessons to stay connected to the simple things, those that are unchangeable, even little comforts, such as the feeling of that rug.

The image of Jen, distressed at the memory of Darcy's death, seized my mind. The conversation began to replay like a recording. "He raped her!" she declared.

And now Sam is accused of rape? Really!? And Jacob, my pastor, a priest, is JP's father? The revelation was shattering, even earth shaking.

As I stood to walk to the bathroom, the floor shifted. Unbalanced, and nearly falling, I reached for the nightstand to steady myself. I felt dizzy and sat to wait for my head to clear.

Was it a tremor from an earthquake?

No, I quickly realized the symptoms were due to my physical condition. My personal disaster.

Poor JP. His world must have been turned upside down by the facts Jen dosed out like a doctor's explanation of test results. She was a pill, but her medication wasn't for healing.

She called Jacob an "arrogant brute." I had to agree, feeling again the insult of my visit with him Sunday night. That was awful!

Sam! I needed to contact him. I recalled a visual memory: the hurt on his face, the last time I saw him, as I stormed out of the police station Saturday morning; but so much had happened since then. I reached for the telephone on the nightstand. I needed to speak with him before he left his apartment.

What is he doing? I wondered. *Would he do some campaigning? Should he?*

++++

Both Sam and Jodi had not yet seen the newspaper that day when she reached him just after eight o'clock. They were also unaware of the caravan going through town, causing bystanders to freeze as they gawked in amazement. Several state police cruisers, lights flashing, raced past local businesses as their owners raised shades, flipped signs to the 'open' side, took merchandise to the sidewalk, and otherwise prepared for their customers who would visit them that day. The police cars were followed by a van from the crime lab.

++++

I dialed Sam's number and the phone began to ring. Once, twice… five times, six. *"Come on Sam… You should still be home. Sam… where are you?"* Eight, nine, ten rings and I began to consider hanging up. *"Sam, please answer! We have so much to talk about. Where should I begin? Faith, Jen, Jacob… the intruder!"*

"Hello?"

"Sam! I finally got you!"

"Jodi? Oh Jodi, it's good to hear from you. Are you still mad at me?"

"No… What are you talking about?"

"Saturday. When you stormed out."

"Well, yes, I'm still upset about some things. But we need to talk. Sam… so much has happened since then. I went looking for you yesterday, at the police station and then at your apartment. But you weren't there. I didn't know what was going on, or if they moved you to the county jail."

"I got bail, and… I went to Faith's apartment."

The admission surprised me. Her apartment - not again! Why would he go there?

"Thought about confronting her," he explained, "but then decided against it. She said you gave her my note?"

"Who said? You talked to Faith?"

"Oh sorry, I meant to ask you about Susan. She said that you gave Faith my note…"

"Susan, right. By the way, her article was really great!"

"You think so?"

"Well, I meant to say that you gave a great interview. It was well stated, and very timely."

"Thanks."

"Today is the election and I think your article will impact voters." I paused in thought. "Are you going to the polls to ask for their support?"

"No, I… I'm not sure that's the best thing to do right now. I don't know what they're believing about me. What if someone starts yelling with insults or accusations… even if someone starts asking questions about the charges, or… well, I don't want to cause a ruckus, or make a scene."

"I guess so, but I think the voters will be reassured to see you. They need to know that you haven't given up, that you still want to be their judge in this town."

"Maybe… I don't know. Is it too late?"

"Sam! Don't give up. This isn't over yet. I've been really busy, you know?" I wanted recognition but continued before he spoke. "Yes, I gave your note to Faith, and she was really rattled by it. Although I still do not know what it said."

"Okay, good. I'll…"

"And I stopped in to see Jen Foster, met JP there, went to see Father Jacob, and then an intruder broke into my house and stole her letters…" I couldn't wait any longer. I talked over Sam as I finally downloaded the summary of my adventures, all at once.

"Now wait just a minute," he cut in. "You had an intruder?"

"Yes, and he scared the hell out of me. It was a good thing that JP was there for me."

"JP? Who is that?"

Sam was beginning to sound agitated and was having trouble concealing it. Did he somehow know about JP and me? But he couldn't have.

"This guy, he was stalking me. At my house. And I think he flattened my car tire. It was almost like he was trying to keep me away from Faith, like he knew that I would upset her, or something."

"Slow down, I need to understand. Now tell me, why was this JP stalking you?

"No! It wasn't JP, it was the other guy."

"Well, who was that?"

"I don't know. I saw him at the courthouse and the hospital."

I tried to recall the events in proper sequence. "And he was the intruder. JP came to talk to me, and he saw him at my house. When he described him, I realized that the stalker, the man in the hospital, and the intruder were all the same person."

"But you don't know who it is?"

"No, I don't know him. JP doesn't either. I described him to Officer Billings, but he wasn't any help."

I hesitated as I recalled my impression of the shoddy investigation. At best, the cop was very insincere. "You know… that jerk who is running against you… today!"

I needed to vent my frustration with the election. "I don't think that crooked cop will help us find the intruder… in fact, I wonder whose side he is on."

"What do you mean?"

"You're being framed Sam… remember?!" My anger flared. "And I think the cops are in on it."

"Well, yeah, that's obvious, but you don't have to be rude about it!"

Maybe I hurt his feelings just then, but did he have to become defensive? We both had a short fuse. "Sorry… you're right. But I have been through a lot these last few days. And I'm still unsettled, still riled up about it all, you know?"

"Sure… and you have the right to be upset," Sam conceded. "I'm sorry. I only wish that I could have been there, for you."

"It's okay… I feel safe now, and eventually, I know, it will all settle down."

"Really, Jodi, I feel bad about what you have been going through… and I know that you did it all for me."

"Okay… I'm okay now," I choked back a sob, "thanks for caring."

++++

And in the brief silence that followed their tender expressions, each felt reconnected to the other, their apologies acknowledged and adequate for that time.

++++

Sam spoke first.

"This intruder, you said JP saw him, but I still don't understand who JP is, or how he's involved."

"Yes, JP saw the intruder before he broke into my house."

"Jodi, can you tell me what the intruder looked like?"

"Well, he was average, height and weight, brown hair. But had a goatee, long, ungroomed."

"What was he wearing?"

"A baseball cap, black shirt, blue jeans. He looked dingy when I saw him. But he wore a hoodie when he came into my house."

"I can't be sure," Sam noted, "but the person you are describing sounds like Luke."

"Luke!? Who is that?"

"Faith's current boyfriend. Luke works for Father Jacob, a janitor and grounds keeper. The priest helped him get paroled early. Most of the time he lives at the church."

"Strange, I never saw him there, but I haven't been going to church much lately…"

"I don't think Luke would show his face during the services. But I saw him yesterday, when I went to Faith's apartment. Luke came out and he was carrying a shoebox."

"So, this guy works for Father Jacob?" I asked to verify my suspicion.

Buzz. Buzz.

I heard the noise. Apparently, someone was at the entry door to Sam's apartment building and pushing on his intercom button.

"Sorry, someone is at the front door. I have to go," he said.

"But I need to tell you about Father Jacob…"

I sensed movement at the other end of our connection. Then it sounded like Sam dropped the receiver.

"Sam, the priest is connected to Darcy."

Buzz. Buzz. Buzz.

"Some people called her 'Janie', Darcy Jane Rogers."

There was the sound of a shuffle.

Did he hear me?

"I have to go, sorry. But let's get together so we can talk more."

"I have to go to work, or I'll probably lose my job," I quickly interjected into the distraction.

"After work then."

"Sam…" but the line went dead. The annoying sound of the dial tone hummed in my ear. He hadn't responded to my statement about the priest and Darcy. I didn't know if he heard me.

He needed to know.

++++

If Luke, the church janitor, was the stalker and the intruder, Jodi was becoming increasingly suspicious of the Reverend, the priest who raped Darcy and fathered a child… JP.

It was a lot to process, but what could they prove, and what recourse did they have?

Enter Emmanuel Gulyas

Sam opened the door to a tall man with thick dark hair and black framed glasses. He was stocky, well built, and wore pressed cargo pants and a polo shirt, both charcoal in color.

"Samuel Urban?" He didn't wait for a response. "I'm Detective Emmanuel Gulyas." He pulled a small leather wallet from his pants pocket, flipped it open, and held it up for Sam to see. It contained his badge and identification card.

Sam looked at the photo on his ID and then back to the stranger's face. He appeared to be legit.

"May I come in? I have a couple of questions."

"Sure," Sam stepped aside. "But we don't have any detectives in Walthem, just a small three-man police force."

"I came in from the Harrisburg Bureau. Special assignment. Requested by Chief Sabol."

"Really?" Sam couldn't hide his astonishment at the news, "For what?"

"Guess you didn't see today's headlines," the detective surmised. "There was a fire, appears to be arson… and a fatality," he paused for acknowledgement. "I can't divulge much more than that. The next of kin must be notified first. You know."

"You mean someone was killed in the fire?" Sam asked the obvious, stupefied.

"The paper identified the location. So, I'll tell you that it was Saint Patrick Church. But that's about all I can say."

"And it was arson… really?"

"Uh-huh, it appears to be suspicious. The crime lab is out there right now. We'll know more soon, including the identity of the victim."

"Oh man... I didn't know," Sam responded with unintentional honesty. "I hadn't heard, and like you said, I haven't seen today's paper. I haven't even been out of my apartment yet."

It was Sam's first day of freedom and already a detective was questioning him about another crime, and a fatality, one that was potentially caused by foul play! God forbid that more trouble was coming his way.

The unwanted guest seemed arrogant, uncaring. He was guarded, a man of few words. Coy was his calm.

As far as great sleuths go, Gulyas was no Sherlock Holmes, however, he was highly regarded by his colleagues, law enforcement officials that worked at the state's capital. His stats for the year boasted of twelve cases solved, three unsolved and still open. But the unsolved cases involved missing persons that were not yet found. No corpse, no crime. And Gulyas hadn't given up on them yet.

The detective questioning Sam was not conversational. The people he interviewed were suspects and he didn't care about being nice to them. His insinuations were meant to be intimidating, his peering eyes - unnerving, his pause demanding an explanation - unexpected. It was important to catch the suspect off guard, and Gulyas found that fearful spontaneity often loosened the tongue.

So, he got right to the point with Sam.

"Well, it's your whereabouts that I need to question."

Sam returned a surprised look, his mouth gaping. Were they suspicious of him?

"For starters, where were you last night, about 9 PM?"

"I was here, in my apartment." Sam was uncomfortable with the inquiry. He knew that a suspect had to be very careful, in fact, should not even talk to a cop without legal representation. Could this be another trap?

"Can anyone verify it?" the detective pressed.

"No, I was alone," Sam's countenance dropped with the realization of his vulnerability. He needed an alibi. "But why are you asking me about the church fire? I don't have any connection to St. Pat's."

"Don't you...?" The words hung in the air, at the place where the uncomfortable awaits acknowledgement.

The detective's eyes narrowed as if he was able to perceive his suspect's secret thoughts.

"No," Sam stated flatly. "It's not my church."

Gulyas shifted on his feet and changed his line of questioning. "Do you know Father Jacob?"

"By association yes, but I never really talked to the man. I don't have any reason to." Sam's defenses were heightened now. He thought he should ask the cop to leave.

"And what about Luke Stolarick?" Gulyas fired the question quickly, catching Sam off guard.

"Luke? Well yes, of course. For a long time. We went to high school together." Sam's pulse quickened as his thoughts raced ahead of his words and warned him not to speak of Luke's court case, the one he ruled on.

This interview was inappropriate. It was going too far. Sam was vulnerable, and overly sensitive. He needed to say as little as possible.

"And do you know of Luke's associations?"

"Well, yeah, I know that Luke works at the church."

"And other associations?"

Sam shook his head slowly.

"Do you know who Luke's girlfriend is?" Gulyas pried further.

"Yes, of course. Anyone who has lived here very long knows that." He sounded a bit sassy as he began to lose his patience with the detective's persistent and insinuating line of questioning.

Waiting for an answer, Gulyas narrowed his eyes again.

"He's going with Faith," Sam answered reluctantly.

"And is that a problem for you?"

"No… of course not!" Sam nearly yelled. "And I don't know what you're getting at." Unconsciously he clenched his fists as a bead of sweat broke out on his brow. "What are you fishing for?"

"Motive," the cop answered with a single word. "I'm wondering if you have any reason to want to hurt Luke, or Father Jacob, for that matter."

"No! Why would I?"

"Faith." Gulyas stated, like it was a fact. "Like you said, you know of her association with Luke."

"I'm not getting you. If you're referring to the charges against me, Faith is my accuser, not Luke… he's not involved."

Sam was not yet aware of the confessions of the deceased, those that Darcy expressed in her letters, and he still did not know of her intimate relationship to Father Jacob, so he was not perceiving the next link in the chain, or the connection to Luke.

The detective gave no merit to Sam's suggestion that distanced him from the church janitor. He had already been briefed on the charges against Sam by Chief Sabol, and still had questions.

No one had said that Luke was involved, but as a detective, Gulyas was insightful, trained to put himself into the mindset of the person of interest. Urban was in serious trouble and needed to do something to help himself. Henceforth, the question was obvious to a top cop such as himself.

"What does Luke have to do with the charge against me?" Sam knew he was talking too much, but now he had a few questions of his own. He was tired of being slapped in the face by the cop's implied accusations. This was just too much. "I don't believe he had anything to do with it. So, what are you driving at?"

"I'm just wondering about the connections. You insist that you are falsely accused. What was the way you put it in your newspaper article? Oh yes, 'framed'. So just who do you think is framing you? Certainly, you must be angry at that person. That would give you motive, to want to hurt, or maybe even eliminate him."

Good cop? No, he was being the bad cop. Gulyas was showing his true colors. Suddenly Sam was going from being a rapist to a murderer. Gulyas saw the opportunity and took it. Rattled, his suspect might make a mistake, and admit something.

"You mean the fire? You've got to be kidding me! Me?! Set a fire to eliminate someone?"

Gulyas was successful. Sam's temper flared, but the judge didn't have anything to hide. Incarcerated for five days, how could he be suspect? Did they really think he ran from his cell directly to a church, intending to silence someone?

"That doesn't make any sense. Faith is the one who will testify against me. You didn't say that anything happened to her." Sam looked at the detective directly. He was blank, a poker face. He wasn't revealing anything about either case by expression or body language.

"I don't know," Sam continued, "I really don't know who is framing me. You must believe me. Why would Luke have anything to do with it?" He paused. "He's not capable. And if I did know who it was, I wouldn't take matters into my own hands. It would be for the police to handle."

"Really? And you think *they* would help you?"

"Yes! Why wouldn't they?"

"Okay, that's all I have for now," Gulyas concluded abruptly. "But don't leave town for a few days, until I have this matter sorted."

"I can't, I already have a bail bond and court order that says I have to stay right here."

"Yeah, that's right." The detective grinned slyly. Gulyas turned and took a step toward the door.

It was then that a lightning bolt struck in Sam's brain. "Hey, I just remembered," he shouted at the man's back, a feeling of relief bursting inside. "I called my lawyer last night."

"And what time was that?"

"About eight."

"And his name – the name of your attorney?" the detective demanded.

"Jared… Jared McCabe."

The investigator pulled out a small notebook and wrote it down.

"I'm just wondering, isn't that a little late to call legal counsel?"

"I called Jared at home."

"And he gave you such privilege?"

"Jared and I go way back," Sam explained. "We were college buddies. We've kept in touch." He saw disbelief on Gulya's face. "That's why I chose him to defend me."

"And how long did you talk?"

"I'd say about forty minutes."

"That long?"

"Yes, we talked about different things."

"Can you tell me what you talked about?" Gulyas pried some more.

"My case, what to expect, legal questions."

"Can you be more specific?"

"I asked him about the statute of limitations." But then Sam suddenly felt uncomfortable with his answer. He said too much. He needed to guard his secret. Was he exposed?

"And why would you ask about that?"

"No reason… just brushing up." Sam swallowed hard, not wanting to elaborate, needing to end that line of questioning. "It's easier to ask a friend, then it is to look it up."

"And your friend, he'll corroborate?"

"Yes, of course."

"Well, I'll see about that." The detective poked his forefinger at Sam's face. "You're not going anywhere. And I'll be back…"

Not knowing what more to say, Sam watched in disbelief as Detective Emmanuel Gulyas exited abruptly, slamming the door behind him.

Sam was stunned. Pacing across the living room floor, he tried to make sense of it all. Why would he target Luke, or the priest? In his mind, Luke was clearly incapable of such a plot... recruiting the police, initiating his removal, launching a write-in candidate to run against him. Whoever was behind this intense effort to ruin him was much more influential, even powerful. Besides, there wasn't any bad blood between him and Luke, and regarding Faith, present and past relationships were of no concern to either one of them.

And why would a priest be involved? Answers to these crucial questions evaded him.

He decided to call Jodi back. She had said something about Father Jacob. Perhaps clarification from her would help. He dialed her number and waited. Consumed with his thoughts, he didn't count the rings. Five minutes quickly passed as his mind worked into overload. No answer.

It was then that Sam decided to attempt to locate Luke. Just seeing him would answer his first question: did he die in the fire? Perhaps Sam could get some answers from Luke, that is, if he was willing to talk.

Several pedestrians were crossing the street in front of his car as Sam turned the corner on Oak Street. He jammed the brakes to quickly slow down. Signs crowded the edge of the roadway. They encouraged residents to vote for Barney Billings, candidate for district justice.

Sam proceeded past the polling place. A long line formed at its door and continued for almost the length of the block. He hoped no one would recognize him. Then he saw a young woman turning her head in sync with the movement of his car. She smiled broadly and waved enthusiastically. He was spotted. Sam didn't stop but continued to the church.

The coroner was already there, waiting for the victim's body to be removed from the burned building. Sam pulled up just as a corpse, covered by a white sheet, was loaded into the back of a station wagon, its rear windows blackened out.

The church doors hung open. He smelled a pungent odor, like that of burned rubbish. A fire engine was parked in the rear of the parking lot. He saw a hose stretched across the side lawn. It disappeared into the basement.

Not visible to Sam, a team of crime scene specialists were combing through the basement in an orderly, concentrated effort to collect evidence. A photographer's flash momentarily brightened the dimly lit room as other investigators busied themselves with setting up halogen lights on tall tripods.

Sam saw a person come out of the basement and walk toward the van, a large plastic bag in his hand. Evidence. He was wearing a white jumpsuit that covered his entire body and included a hood, clear goggles to protect his eyes, and a white mask that covered his nose and mouth.

Sam wondered what could pose such a threat to the investigator. He scanned the crowd of onlookers. Luke wasn't there.

Twelve hours earlier:

A strange sound, low and guttural, pierced the eerie hush of the church basement as the fire crackled softly nearby. More than a groan, the noise increased in volume until it became a penetrating scream of human agony. Luke's body jerked and his eyes cracked open. His clothes hissed as small flames licked at the burnt edges of his shirt. He rolled repeatedly, stopping as he lay flat on his back. He reached to the concrete floor to push himself erect. His fingers stuck there. As he yanked his hand away from the surface of the floor, flesh pulled off of his fingertips. They were shriveled and black. His left hand and face were charred. His abdomen and lower back stung fiercely as Luke shrieked again in even greater pain.

The cardboard box containing the letters wicked up much of the accelerant and diverted the fire to its paper, material easily consumed.

Father Jacob was on his telephone with the 911 emergency operator. He heard the strange noise, a call from the grave, the awakening of a zombie. The sound caused shivers to chill on his spine. He paused and listened intently for more, even a clue to identify it. The wind whistled outside as tree branches screeched across a glass windowpane. There was a bang somewhere behind him, probably a loose door on an outbuilding. That first noise, the eerie sound, he quickly deemed must also be from the storm.

Luke managed to stand, his vision blurred, his surroundings spinning around him like the view from a tilt-a-whirl. But he wasn't in an amusement park. His mind began to register with an account of the struggle he just had with Jacob. And it wasn't a nightmare. Reality set in. Adrenaline surged as the veins in his neck popped and throbbed with the vigorous pumping of his vascular system.

Luke took a cautious step and grimaced as he completed two more. He headed for the outside exit. Near the door on the workbench was a roll of nylon cord used in the weed trimmer. It was a job unfinished: several days before he was attempting to refill the trimmer base. A piece of cord, just about the right length for what he was considering, about four feet, and already cut, laid there. Without a second thought, he grabbed it as he headed up the steps. He wrapped the cord around his right hand and then his left, where it cut deeply into his blistered skin.

The pain was agonizing but Luke's brain was consumed with something greater. Nothing would deter him from accomplishing it. He was driven to finish the murderous task Jacob began, for great was the religious man's transgressions.

A few minutes later the priest heard another strange, unfamiliar sound. "Jaaacoob," the word was distinctive, the voice shrill, a high-pitched whisper. But how could it be?

He pushed his chair back from his desk and looked to the doorway of his office. No one was there. Was his caller invisible, perhaps a phantom, or maybe even Luke's ghost? Jacob often heard of such tall tales. He half believed them.

"Jaaacoob," the summons came again. He jumped up from his chair and started for the doorway. Cautiously he peered down the hallway, one way, then the other.

"Jacob, come here!" This time the words were quick, the voice raspy and demanding. Jacob noticed the door to the supply room was open. A light was on there. Slowly, he stepped inside.

Luke sprang from behind the door, and before the priest knew what happened, dropped the cord over Jacob's head. With inhuman strength, Luke tightened his stranglehold. The cord cut into Jacob's throat as he staggered backwards, grasping for it. Blood streamed down his neck.

Jacob was hacking and gasping for air as Luke pulled even harder, then upward, crushing his victim's larynx as he nearly lifted the priest off his feet.

In Luke's skull light was flashing, like that of an electrical short circuit. Blood trickled out of his ears. A noise was hammering in his head so loud that he could not perceive anything else, not even the thrill of the kill.

Jacob's body went limp and Luke let the unconscious man drop to the floor. He dragged it to the cellarway. Grabbing him under his arms, Luke groaned at the strain of lifting Jacob to his feet. It would be the priest's last stand. His head slumped; his bloody chin resting against his chest.

In a flash of unexpected clarity, Luke wished Jacob could know his final folly. He gave him a farewell kiss on the back of his head and then with a push Jacob's corpse fell forward, down the broken steps, and crashed onto the concrete floor below. Blood began to pool there.

Luke got another can of gasoline, poured it directly on Jacob, stepped back and ignited it. He used the lighter from the priest's vest pocket.

And so, it was completed, Jacob's murderous plan reversed. But had justice prevailed?

Luke walked quickly away from the church dragging one foot as he went into the woods. He still carried the can of gasoline used to douse his victim.

It was about noon when Gulyas drilled the police.

"I went and talked to Urban," he told the force of three. Officers Barney and Ken stood directly in front of the detective, taking the brunt of his fire. Chief Sabol sat behind his desk, nearly out of range.

"I understand your suspicions, but I'm not convinced he was involved in this arson/homicide. If his alibi pans out, and I believe it will, the timing is going to be problematic. So, who else could have a grudge large enough to want to kill the priest or his janitor?"

Blank stares were all that he received in reply.

"I still think it was Urban," Billings spoke first. Of course, he wanted it to be Sam, his election opponent. "By now they have figured out that Luke was the intruder at Culp's house." He paused at seeing Gulya's look of confusion. "She is Urban's girlfriend," he informed.

Gulyas suspected that the cop/candidate knew more than he was saying.

"Actually, Luke was probably their target," Barney clarified.

"You guys told me that Luke is the rape victim's boyfriend. Okay." Gulyas was establishing irrefutable facts. "So why would he break into this other woman's house, the one who is the girlfriend of the rapist?"

Observing their shifty eyes, and their excessive fidgeting, it was easy to see, they were hiding something. The detective already knew that Barney was the one who investigated the break-in, and the intruder had not been identified. If he knew, then why hadn't he acted on it? He needed documentation before making an accusation. He'd get a copy of Billings' report. But, he'd have to revisit that question at a later time.

"And when it comes to the priest, that's above my pay grade," Billings announced. His sudden comment seemed out of context and insinuating. "You need to go to the top with any questions about him."

"And who is that?"

Chief Sabol cleared his throat. "I believe the victim is Father Jacob," he inserted, urgent to change the tone of the conversation. He needed to preserve the credibility of his force, if that was even possible.

"What do you base that on?" Gulyas demanded, turning toward him. The chief had succeeded in getting his attention, to distract him away from Barney.

"The size of the corpse. Jacob was a large man, most likely over 300 pounds. Luke was less than 200, I'd say."

"Well, the victim was badly burned, partially consumed by the fire. You can still tell that it was him?"

"I know, it was gross, a terrible thing to see." Sabol looked toward the window. The sun was shining outside. It was a perfect spring day. He preferred to be elsewhere, anywhere unrelated to the fiasco at hand. "I just wish I could erase that image from my mind."

Barney and Ken, both flushed and nodded in agreement.

"So, you're pretty sure that it is the priest?" The question was repetitious, but Gulyas needed to be sure.

"Sorry to say so, but yes."

"Then where the hell is the janitor?" the detective demanded. "Could he have been torched too?"

It was then that Billings had an idea. "He might be hiding at his girlfriend's place," he noted, looking for approval from the top cop. "That's Faith. We should go and check it out."

"Then go! And don't leave until you're sure. Tell her she must cooperate with your search. We're not waiting for a warrant," the detective directed.

Barney hesitated. "Um, well, I thought Ken could do it. I still have an election to run…"

"You're the police first," the chief shouted. "We have a serious crime here. Now get going Barney!"

"I'll go too," Ken finally spoke, "for backup."

The chief nodded in approval. The two junior cops nearly ran for the exit door.

"What do you think?" Gulyas turned to the chief. "Could Luke have done it?"

Sabol shrugged his shoulders. "Who knows? Their relationship was tenuous at best. We need to search the priest's house and office for clues."

"Well, for that we will need a search warrant. It's too far from the scene of the crime. We can search in the basement, but we're limited to that space right now."

"Police! Open up!" Officer Billings hit Faith's apartment door with his billy club and then pounded on it again with his fist. "Faith, I know you're in there. Now open the door or I'll bust it down!" He banged on it for the third time.

Ken kicked at the bottom of the door, just for good measure. With the force from his foot the door bowed. "We can get through this easy," he told his partner. But just then they heard a bolt slide on the inside and the door opened a crack. Faith peered out of the narrow space. A chain hung across, in front of her face.

"Faith, where is Luke?" Billings demanded. "Is he hiding here?"

"No, he's not here."

"Open up, we need to check."

"No! You can't come in."

"Faith, we're coming in. Now move away!"

Billings took a step back, raised his foot high and kicked at the center of the door. The inside latch dropped to the floor; its screws forced from the thin plywood as it splintered into pieces. As the door flung open, it hit Faith in her face.

Barney and Ken charged in like soldiers on the front line of an attack: Pickett's Charge at Gettysburg.

"Where's Luke?" Billings demanded again.

Faith was rubbing her forehead. "He isn't here…" Her eyes drooped, darkened from mascara applied days before and smeared across her face. She was in the midst of enduring a bad hangover. Cans, liquor bottles, and pills littered her coffee table. She wore a thin terry cloth bathrobe tied at the waist.

"Dam you Billings!" she yelled. "I told you, he's not here. He left yesterday."

The big cop pushed her aside. "Check the bedroom, the closet, and under the bed… anywhere he could be hiding," he ordered Ken, who stepped away quickly in obedience.

Billings grabbed Faith at the shoulder and began shaking her. "You better wake up, you damned bitch. Tell me where Luke is, or I'll…

"Go to hell!" she fired back. "I'm going to file a complaint. This is abuse."

Billings gave her a shove and she fell onto the sofa. Her robe came open and she was exposed.

"Like what you see?! You pervert! Oh yeah, you're going to eat shit for doing this to me!" She pulled her robe closed and held it tight.

Billings raised his hand and was about to strike her when Ken interrupted. "He's not here."

"You sure?"

"Yes! I looked everywhere… Barney, stop it! You've got to get a hold of yourself."

"She's just a damn whore," he chided. "Next time, Honey, and I'm sure that time will come, we'll finish this. I look forward to our little dance."

Barney grabbed an unopened can of beer and headed for the broken door. He threw it against the wall.

++++

I arrived at Sam's apartment at 5:50 PM and we resumed our conversation from earlier that day.

"Sam, you and Father Jacob are both connected to Darcy." I watched for his acknowledgement. It was the foundation of the case I needed to establish. "That is something you and he have in common. Darcy."

"What do you mean? And what does that have to do with Faith and her trumped-up charge against me?"

"Jen says that her brother, the priest, has been consumed with guilt for raping Darcy. He was never able to right his wrong because she was killed in the crash, her life suddenly snuffed out," I paused as I weighed my words carefully, "and you were the driver of the truck that hit her car and took her life."

"He thinks I killed her? …and, you're saying the priest raped her?"

274

Sam's words were methodical. I could see that he was beginning to get my drift. "Yes, then she became his mistress."

"Could the priest be doing this to me?" he finally asked, deep in thought.

"Darcy wanted Jacob to marry her," I explained. "He was the father of her baby boy. He gave her support but would not accept the child as his own. That's JP… Poor guy, he must be really rattled."

"But what evidence do you have? Isn't it all just Jen's suspicions, the words of a jousted sister?"

And there was my judge, pressing for proof, he was back. Finally! "Jen got letters from Darcy," I explained. "It was all documented in those letters, the ones she wrote to Jen. But I lost them… Sorry."

"I can't believe Faith got so involved in all of this. It's not like her."

"Well, if Luke was recruited, she was his best pick, the bait to lure you in."

"But why would they do it… and how were they so convincing?"

Sam raised a relevant question, and I pondered on it. "Money," I answered with one word. "I'll bet they were paid to do it."

"And there is the state legislator." Sam seemed suddenly enlightened.

"Who? What?"

"Karen Jackson. She is the sister of the priest. Didn't you know?"

"Oh…" and then I understood.

"She's got the clout to pull it off." He paused, paced across the room and returned. "So, what do we do now? Someone died at that church last night. I saw them loading the corpse into the ambulance."

"I don't know. I've already tried everything I could think of. What else is there to do?"

"If Luke died in that fire… we may have just lost our best witness," Sam said. "But tell me about your visit with the priest. You said before that you went to see him."

"He was just awful! He was drilling me. He was happy about our predicament, and… he enjoyed rubbing it in my face… he humiliated me!"

"Like my brother did to me. He had some real good insults for me on Sunday."

++++

It was then that both were quiet for a long moment of reflection, each looking deep inside, evaluating their feelings about those things that individually confronted them, personal issues still unresolved. And Sam felt a new sadness at realizing the loathing malice of a clergyman. Jacob was a discredit to the church, even Christianity, on a broader scale.

Expressing the carnal nature and living for the flesh, this man fell unto the persuasion of evil. The temptations he yielded to quenched the Holy Spirit, and his actions became unjustifiable.

For love cannot be regulated.

In her apartment, Faith was crying softly to herself after being accosted by the police.

Fifteen: she had been counting the number of days since that night, the ominous time she acted to frame Samuel Urban, the judge. It was easier to take down an elected official in the judicial system than she expected.

It would be her detailed testimony that would convince a jury to convict the judge of rape. Faith would have to be a good actress and she was to be well compensated for an Oscar performance.

She had been reluctant to comply, but in the end, agreed to participate, mostly for the money. Because, she needed it.

Although she was once close to Sam, their recent relationship was causal and bumpy at best. Now she was jealous of his romance with Jodi, and protective of her new boyfriend, Luke. Initially, the sum she was to be paid was enough to make her willing to abandon an old friend. And Luke was in a tight spot as Jacob could have his bail revoked if he refused to follow an order. That meant a reservation at the Big House.

They had to toe the line. The priest held all the cards

Rohypnol, a tranquilizer ten times more potent than Valium was the key to their plot. She called them Roofies, and didn't know how Luke got his hands on them, but assumed it was the priest that provided them. Luke warned her to be extra careful. She was afraid that Sam would remember, so she gave him an extra one, two of the small white pills, crushed so that they would quickly dissolve. It was so easy – he had asked to use the restroom and left her alone with his drink.

She then drugged herself with one-half a pill, watched him fall asleep, and quickly called Luke. What happened next was difficult to remember, but it seemed like Luke enjoyed their romp a little bit too much. He got rough, then dropped her off on the street near the police station, and soon she was in an ambulance headed to the hospital where they would examine her for signs of sexual assault. Their plan was for Luke to take care of the need for such circumstantial evidence, bruising her before she went to the police.

But in reviewing the events that brought her there, Faith began to realize that they would never be forgotten. Her life was changing and she feared what might be coming next. She was guilty of lying to the police and falsely accusing Sam.

He was, you see, completely innocent.

She was full of regret.

++++

"I wouldn't have ever suspected a priest. This is a real mess," Sam finally revealed his thoughts to me. "In fact, I think my whole life is screwed up. Joey was right. I messed up again. Williams saved me last time, but… who is going to do it now?"

"Well, it's not going to be Father Jacob, I'm sure of that. There's a lot you still don't know about him."

"God… You mean it's not going to be God?" he clarified with a suggestion that took our conversation to a deeper place.

"My faith is very weak right now. I don't even know what I believe anymore." I paused and then remembered, "But hey, you got another letter from the Advocate. I brought it. Should we open it now?"

++++

This final note from the Advocate was lengthy and perhaps the most difficult to understand, even a tad troubling.

Jodi handed the letter to Sam, he opened it, and read:

"It is not just faith – which is of the mind – but devotion, which is of the heart, that sustains us in the midst of a struggle. True devotion, dependency on God, moves us beyond ourselves."

278

"The great delusion: it is religious claims of salvation brokered and determined by membership rules and status. If the message of religion has become deceptive, then only a greater understanding can reveal truth to those who still seek it."

"The sin of humanity is rebellion against its Creator, the rejection of a Loving, Holy Father. To be empowered by His Spirit we must confess this sin and repent of the many ways we have lived in opposition to Him."

"Only hope will facilitate a purposeful life. Hope comes in belief, actions of faith (devotion) exercised toward God. It is only in longing for life beyond mortal limitations, that we find the avenue in which faith can be fully exercised. The eternal life of resurrection, true life now, is this place: life through his Spirit who dwells in you."

"Suffering is purifying. God's transformation forms a mind with knowledge and wisdom, a heart of compassion, and spiritual life that leads to true healing."

"Practically, you can understand this way: reasoning and feeling, along with sensory perception of physical conditions, determines our actions. Our mind tells us what to do after evaluating it all. But without a spiritual element, we are greatly limited by our dependency on the physical. It causes us to act selfishly: shortsighted, without understanding, often foolishly."

"But there is an additional component of our being that is often overlooked: it is spirit. Spirit can be stronger than thoughts or feelings."

"Learn how, and train yourself to live in relationship with God. It requires spiritual discipline."

"The power of Holy Spirit will give you mind control, and victory over the hateful human nature. Choose to live in union with God: submit, rely, and depend on Him. The spiritual mind has the ability to know God."

"Are you striving among the living dead or are you truly alive? To know God is to experience God. Peace that passes understanding. He will sustain you."

"Dead or alive? Now you must decide..."

"Your Advocate"

++++

Sam was quick to reject the advocate's message.

"I don't get it," he complained. "What is this truth that he writes about? If not religion, what is it?"

I looked intently into his eyes and seeing hurt there, remained silent.

"I don't know what is wrong with me," he paused, "or if there is any hope for me now."

I gently rubbed the top of his hand hoping to give him some comfort.

"It's our parents that really messed us up, right? That's where it all began."

He was obviously deep in thought, perhaps seeking a scapegoat.

"My father was a deeply religious man, but I always felt like there was contention between us... like a dispute unresolved."

I frowned sympathetically as I remembered his father's passing.

"He always preferred my brother, you know... his firstborn. I was second... if he even desired my company at all."

280

"Maybe," I hesitated as I searched for words that would be gentle. "Maybe we shouldn't go there... maybe we should... I don't know, try to be more positive and not let the past dominate our thoughts right now?"

"Is that what the advocate means?"

"I don't know," I answered with a shrug.

"But what is our future? Do we even have one?"

++++

Both being emotionally drained, their discussion that night before they separated set the stage for what happened next.

Sam was confronted by his rebellious spirit. Convicted for his lack of devotion, the rejection he felt was overwhelming. It all seemed so hopeless. As he went to bed and fell asleep, questions of self-worth seized his mind.

Before closing her eyes for the night, Jodi was thinking about her mother, a woman entrenched in religion and faithful to keep its sacraments and observe its holy days throughout her entire life. Jodi feared condemnation for her lack of commitment.

++++

I knew in my heart that my mother's faith was deeper, anchored to more than the requirements of the church. Somehow, it was very personal to her. I was trained by her caring spirit, deeds of generosity that revealed a love greater than spoken words, and there was her commitment, unfaltering and unquestionable. I knew that my mom thrived there, in that special place of fellowship with God and his people. It sheltered her.

++++

The customs of her childhood home were centered around those observances. Christmas and Easter were especially eventful. A platter with a sampling of the holiday feast was taken to church mid-day, for a blessing. Once, Jodi stole a slice of ham while her mother's back was turned. Her hand was slapped, in a teasing way, as it came down from her mouth. She did not realize that one slice was placed on the platter for each person who would participate in the holiday feast. Hers was replaced before the plate was taken to church.

On Christmas Eve they attended midnight mass before returning home for a special treat: plum pudding, apple cake, many types of homemade cookies, and punch.

++++

It was unexpected, but just then I decided to call my mom. A weak, tired voice answered after many rings.

"Hello…"

"Mom, it's Jodi."

"My darling, Jodi, it is so good to hear from you."

She seemed to suddenly be energized. Mom was always happy to receive a call from me… and I didn't call that often. "I know Mom, I should call more frequently."

"Well, yes, but is everything okay?"

"I can't lie," I knew my mother was perceptive beyond her years, "it has been really tough for me this past week." I choked back a sudden sob, hoping she hadn't heard it.

"Life is hard sometimes, but I raised you to always do the right thing… and I know you will."

Her words felt a bit judgmental as my mind did a retake, flashing back to the events of the last few days. My fling with JP –

282

that was unforgivable. "I can only hope that I did," I hesitated in correcting myself, "that I am doing the right thing." JP was a drunken whim – it was Sam that I was struggling for.

"Oh, I have the utmost confidence in you!" my mother said with assurance. "Give it time honey; you will know… it comes clear with a little patience."

"Thanks Mom, I needed to hear that. But…" I paused as I gathered my thoughts, not wanting to sour the sweet moment, "I feel disappointed with my pastor, and the church," I admitted almost fearfully. "Have you ever doubted God?"

I felt like there was a gap in my faith, in my religious teaching and upbringing. I knew the right thing to do, but lacked the desire to do it. I still believed in God, but He was far from me.

"No, of course not. He has always been faithful to me, and He is also to you."

"I guess so…"

"Always remember Jodi, there is only one true God, and his Son, Jesus Christ, but…"

I recognized the break, a technique my mother mastered in making her main point in a conversation.

"But there are many pastors and churches," I interrupted. My comment was controversial, but still, I hoped not to offend.

"Some are better than others." My mother's tone was thoughtful. "I'll admit that," she continued, "and, sometimes we need to make a change… But Jodi, don't blame God for the shortcomings of others. People will always fail, and let you down, but our God won't."

"Were you always happy in church? You must have gone to almost every service. You were so committed."

"Oh my gosh, no! Sometime, when we have time, I will tell you some funny stories… things that happened with the people in my church and our pastors," she chuckled. "There are many distractions, but if you seek the truth, He will reveal it to you. Look beyond regulations. So much of it is just tradition."

"But weren't you hurt by their hypocrisy? Didn't that discourage you?" I persisted.

"Truthfully, at the time, some of it did. I have to admit, there were a couple of pastors, well, let's just say that I didn't really care for them."

"Then why did you stay?"

"I had many friends, good friends… the years go by so fast, and dear ones pass on. Time changes your perspective. It was foolish of me to be angry then, and looking back, so much of it is laughable now."

"I get it, I guess," I tried to agree. "We put too much emphasis on the now."

"Oh, my sweet daughter, don't let today's struggles take you too low. The Son will rise again tomorrow, with a new beginning in store for you, a blank canvas. Paint something beautiful."

++++

Jodi heard *the word* she spoke but thought of its other meaning: the sun will rise.

++++

"Thanks, Mom, you're a great encourager, as always. But I better get going. A big day tomorrow and I'm really exhausted. Love you…"

284

"Sleep tight my darling. Don't let the bed bugs bite. I love you to the moon and back."

They were words from my childhood, sweet assurances, that still tugged at my heart strings.

"Bye," I said as tears filled my eyes. Precious moments. I had known so many. And yes, I hoped there would be more.

"Bye Sweetie."

Blame. I know that it doesn't help to blame God. I know that I am supposed to learn something from times of trials. It's discipline, isn't that what they say? It's hard, but how else will I be changed, to become a better person?

I'd like to be more like my mom.

I hear everyone blaming God for everything that goes wrong in their lives. A woman lost her niece, a beautiful four-year-old, to a malignant tumor. She prayed for God to heal her. Now she blames God for taking her.

I heard an evangelist elaborate on this. He said that God did not take the child, but He received her. The little girl will forever be with the Lord, in a place without pain: no tears, no illness. And with that perspective, life here is short, and the daughter will soon be reunited with her loving mother, even though she is now consumed with grief.

We have a spiritual opponent, the preacher says, that takes great pleasure in human suffering, even as God grieves for us when we are hurt. Evil causes the pain, but God rescues us.

The hardships, trials, and pain of this life will lead us to blame God. But He is not the cause of it all. A spiritual war rages, and we are easily misdirected.

It makes sense to me. Gives me hope. Purpose. Resolution.

++++

Their dreams that night were initiated in their minds by lingering thoughts, concerns still unresolved, and the visions they received were generated by a spirit that visited them in the realm of slumber. Perhaps it was a guardian that whispered into their ears. Maybe the angel had always been there. But whatever, the spirit was invisible and hovered above, swirling with psychic energy as its message was transferred to their human minds in lucid dreams. The spirits' intent was to assist them, troubled souls as they were, to better understand what was about to happen… and to prepare them for it.

Like vehicles caught in a traffic jam, their minds were stalled. But even as they despaired, their receptors remained open, seeking a way of escape, just as the anxious driver frets while waiting for his way to clear.

++++

Jodi's recalls her dream:

A man is running toward me. I feel like I know him.
 "Look over there," he urges.
I suddenly realize that he must be the Advocate.
"I see a campfire," he suggests. "Go."

His appearance is not clearly seen. Although I still can't identify him, I'm not disturbed by his coming. He stands nearby, waiting for my response.

The fire is burning low with hot embers. A few bright yellow and orange flames dance over charred logs. As I watch other green branches are placed on top of it. They begin to hiss and smoke.

Nearby, a fisherman is finishing the task of cleaning several large fish. He carefully places them over the hot coals. The heated meat quickly provides a sweet aroma, a smell tantalizing to my taste buds.

My stomach is growling, but I am hungry for more than just food for the body. My spirit is weak. The man at the fire sees me and motions for me to come to him.

"Don't hesitate. Don't refrain from his invitation. Go and sit with him near the fire," the Advocate admonishes. "There is nothing to be afraid of. He is the Teacher."

Somewhat reluctant, I walk with the Advocate as we approach the campfire and those sitting around it. My heart is heavy with sorrow, but throbbing in anticipation. Guilt clouds my thoughts because of the many times and ways I have rejected the concept of Him.

The Advocate affirms my doubt. "He knows, he already knows everything."

I wonder, exactly what that means.

"He knows about your desire to be married," the Advocate continues. "But why do you not trust Him to provide the man, even prepare a husband for you?"

No, I don't believe he cares enough for me to do all that. It was an honest confession in response to his question.

"And He knows of your desire to have a family of your own. But why," the Advocate admonished me gently, "why don't you trust His timing? Do you not believe that He is the creator of all things, even the little ones you will be commissioned to love tenderly as you mother them?"

The truth is cutting deep, even to the scars of my heart. I feel an urge to commune with the Teacher, the one who already knows my future.

I see another person holding back. Is he also struggling with fear, or is it guilt? The Teacher addresses him directly with a provocative question. It pierces through the tough outer coating the man who followed Jesus covered himself with.

I feel that I am unworthy of being in such company.

Now the Teacher is speaking the same question, the one asked of his disciple, to me. He asks, **"Do you truly love me more than these?"**

++++

The inquiry is effective, intending to lead Jodi to new heights of awareness, to unite her heart with His.

++++

"What is your honest answer? Do you truly love Him more than these?" the Advocate persists. "Do you love truth more than the lies of self-gratification: desire, success, possessions; do you love Him more than the most important people in your life? Will you give Him first place?" he asks with explanation.

Suddenly the Advocate quickly advances toward me. He looms above me like a giant. His voice reverberates in my head as it echoes off a distant mountain. "Do you not know the first and

288

greatest commandment: to **love the Lord your God with all your heart, and with all your soul, and with all thy mind**?"

I look up and strain to see the Advocate's face. His hair is on fire. His eyes are bright red. I begin to tremble.

"What about your doubts and fears, Jodi?" he continues. "Is your pain His fault or is it the result of the grudges you nurture? Do you love anger for self-justification, pride for self-recognition? What do you truly desire the most? What is the essence of your faith: expecting that only good things will happen, or are you trusting in a higher power to rescue, change, and strengthen you?" He paused, knowing that my mind was reeling. "You must choose: religious condemnation or merciful love."

"Now is the time; talk to your higher power. Jesus is waiting for your answer. You must choose… now!"

And the man who was speaking to me suddenly vanished, right before my eyes.

++++

And with a deep breath, Jodi was jarred back awake, suddenly inhaling as one who had stopped breathing. As she returned to the stark reality of her existence, she recounted the dream to herself, like a video in replay, repeatedly making its declarations in her conscious being, not to be forgotten.

Sam's dream after reading the advocate's letter:

Sam peered through an open door into a long, darkened hallway. A tall man wearing a top hat and a long cape approached slowly, but stopped short of the bright light that shone through the doorway from beyond. Blocking the light and standing in his own shadow, his face was not visible, despite Sam's determined effort to focus on him there.

With a soft but distinctive voice, the Advocate challenged, *"Can you understand the mysteries surrounding God All-Powerful? They are higher than the heavens and deeper than the grave. So, what can you do when you know so little, and these mysteries outreach the earth and the ocean?"*

With increased volume, the Advocate continued to speak in verse:

"If God puts you in prison or drags you to court, what can you do?"

"Surrender your heart to God, turn to him in prayer, and give up your sins-- even those you do in secret."

"Then you won't be ashamed; you will be confident and fearless. Your troubles will go away like water beneath a bridge, and your darkest night will be brighter than noon. You will rest safe and secure, filled with hope and emptied of worry."

"So, this is what it's all about… God?" Sam retorted. "Isn't this the same religion that you so masterfully reject?" he demanded an explanation from the Advocate who seemed to be caught in a contradiction.

"He knows even your thoughts," an angry face appeared directly before Sam's, but then twisted and changed, again, and again, and still was not recognizable, "and your unspoken words," the Advocate shouted while no longer quoting God's Holy Word. "Are you a fool?!!!" The words echoed back to Sam, "…a fool!! ..a fool! .a fool."

Sam began to tremble. His entire body shook violently as fear consumed him. Then suddenly a seraph appeared, holding a golden grail. In it a coal glowed, red hot with intense heat, an ember taken from the altar that burned always before the Sovereign Lord. The seraph's face glowed, lit by the holy fire that radiated from the cup it held. It had human characteristics, but was distinctively not human. It took the coal and reached for Sam, gently touching his lips. A purifying, hissing sound was heard, but no burn was felt. And then, quicker than it came, the winged creature was gone.

"Go ahead," the Advocate instructed. "Your words have been cleansed. You can now talk freely to the Father of All Creation."

Sam felt a calm envelope him, an unearthly peace. A beam of light from above fell upon his face, brilliant, but manageable to the human eye. Sam peered into it, upward, and then still farther. There he saw the Lord God sitting on His throne.

"Why," Sam said in a whisper. "Why have I given up on myself? Haven't you also given up on me?"

God's answer came in a symphonic voice, echoing softly throughout the realm.

"People have a propensity for dislike more than like, for hatred more than love, because they are influenced by their knowledge of evil, that which now inhabits the earth."

With God's holy words, wisdom fell upon Sam, filling his mind with a vision:

At the time of a baby's birth, the father looks upon his second-born son and is troubled because he already has his heir. He wonders if two sons will compete for his affection. Does he have the capacity to love them both, equally?

It is his first-born son, this heir, that he treasures the most. In his heart, this new baby boy is already less valued.

As the second son grew up, there was always friction between him and his older brother. The second was regarded as a servant more than a son. The father's provision was provided, but with some reluctance. The second would never be given a full blessing. That belonged to the firstborn, the heir.

Sam suddenly understood that "The Parable of the Prodigal Son" was told for correcting beliefs that resulted in such rejection.

In the Savior's story, the second son demanded his inheritance, his portion of the family estate. It was granted and he willingly left, for he had become a problem for the family, perhaps even an embarrassment to their good name.

Finally, the second son was dealt with, according to the authority and custom of their time; and then was gone, hopefully forever.

The father had been influenced by his heir, his firstborn, for he was weary of the tension between his two sons. It was better to let the younger one go, to find his own way.

But in his second son's absence, the father realized his mistake. He should not have banished a young man, sent away without regard, without commitment; for love never fails.

He longed for his son's return and began watching and waiting, hoping for a chance for reconciliation. When the father saw his second son approaching, still a long way off, he felt compassion, ran to his son, and embraced him with kisses.

As the prodigal returned, the repentant and wiser father held back nothing, even to the offense of his heir.

Consider this father's extravagant display of true love.

Sam realized that God did not endorse the policy of parents having a favorite.

Because of their tradition, while realizing his second son's discontent, the father who cherished the single heir, would seek a covering to establish and reinforce his position of being correct in all that he did. Being patriarchal, he fortified his heart against self-doubt. Religion anchored in self-righteousness was born.

Legalism – it is the sin of generations.

But surely, there must be a better way, even if it is more difficult.

And Sam was that second son. The child of a religious man.

"But how do I contend with such a lifetime of rejection?" Sam pressed God further for the answers he needed. "I deserve to be punished for those I have hurt."

"Without love you are nothing. Understand and accept the sinful nature of man."

"And how do I overcome regret; how do I become a better person: is there any hope for finding a good life?"

"I AM light (understanding). I AM love (fulfillment). I AM life (purpose). Let me expose the failings of man to cleanse you of their effect. I will fill you and love you as my precious son: chosen and cherished. I am a father to the fatherless."

"Many fathers of this world have not truly known me, choosing instead to depend on religious teaching. Therefore, you

must first be emptied of all such things: primarily your pride. Let go of your striving. Only a new and empty vessel can be filled. Allow me to recreate you. I will be your life. You are complete as you are fulfilled in me."

"I am sorry."

The shaft of light that was so distinctive began to fade as heaven's door closed slowly.

Sam awoke suddenly with full knowledge of the vision he had just received. He found himself in darkness but felt a profound peace, an unearthly calm as the light of knowledge shone within his soul.

He believed. He accepted. He received.

And in the awareness of such Truth there was healing, freedom from pain long endured: a simple man's prideful knowing of himself, sacrificed to be resurrected as he became a new creation founded in the Father's Presence, red-hot, blazing Love. No longer dead in sin, but finally, truly alive!

Now, for the sake of your perception, an understanding of what Sam experienced, the question must be asked: "Had he attained spiritual life?"

Pre-eminently, this life is hidden. It is a mystery that defies ultimate definition. It is not understood or acknowledged by the world. It is not something we merely carry about us, even as we carry a religion.

It is a life that motivates with heavenly desire in denial of selfish aspirations. There are few among us that possess it.

Perhaps, the Advocate was one such person.

No, Sam had not yet attained it fully, but the door to his heart was opened to the Lord, and his journey to such an awakening, unity with God, had begun. Henceforth, the Holy Spirit would guide him to an experience in the Life of Christ… all for the glory of Jesus, our Risen Lord!

CHAPTER TEN: Revelation

Wednesday, May 15, 1985 – day eight.

HEADLINE: "Urban Wins by a Landslide"

It was an emotional day.

After a long, fitful and restless sleep, Faith panicked. She called her mother about 7:30 AM.

"Mom, did you hear about the fire at the church?"

"Of course, don't you think I hear the gossip in this town?"

"I haven't seen Luke," Faith's hand was beginning to tremble. "Not since Monday morning."

Her short factual statements expressed concern, and sought understanding. "What if he is the one who was killed in the fire?"

"I was beginning to wonder about that too… I heard that it was the priest though," Mrs. Culver noted, and qualified the rumor with, "I couldn't stand that man. When I heard that it was him who was killed, I was actually glad."

Faith wasn't interested in her mother's opinions. "But what… what if it wasn't Father Jacob? It could have been Luke that was burned up," she stammered. "Why hasn't he contacted me? He was there. He had to be involved."

A cry was coming.

"If I was you, Honey, I'd get the hell out of Dodge!" Her advice was rash, inconsiderate. She recommended Faith's departure without hesitation.

"What are you talking about?"

"It was a famous saying from a cowboy shooting out west." She was a fan of television western movies. "Well, in your case," Mrs. Culver continued, "guess I should say, 'girl, git the hell out of Walthem!" Clever with trivia, she smiled to herself. But Faith didn't appreciate her mother chronicling times of yore.

"C'mon Mom!" she yelled. "This isn't a joke. Don't be trivial!"

"Who's joking?" Her mother paused. "There is a distant cousin of ours, my grandmother's - sister's - daughter's girl. Lives in South Barrington. I think they'd put you up for a while."

"South Barrington? Where the hell is that?"

"Chicago! A good place to blend in and get lost in the crowd. I don't know how to reach them… in fact, I don't even remember her name, but I can make some calls for you, if you'd like. I'll call Aunt Dorothy… I think she is still alive… anyway, didn't hear that she kicked the bucket yet."

"Yeah, call her. Will you do that for me?" But it was unlikely that her mother would act quickly. "Mom! I already have my suitcase out. I'm packing. I just need an address."

"Well, okay… guess I'll have to see what I can do…"

Faith analyzed her wardrobe, calculating what was worth taking and what she would leave behind. It was limited by the size of her suitcase.

"Mom! Call me as soon as you have something, or I'll call you. I'm getting a bus ticket to Chicago. I'm movin' on!"

"I'll call as soon as I know something. Happy travels… and… good luck."

Faith's next call was to Greyhound Bus Lines. The first stop would be in Pittsburgh. The coach left in 40 minutes. She ran to her closet, crushed the hangers together, got her arms around a bundle, and tossed it onto her bed. Some blouses she flung to the floor. Others she tossed toward her luggage.

State Representative Karen Jackson had been trying to reach her brother, Father Jacob, since Monday. She needed to know if he retrieved the letters.

At first, Mrs. Thomas, his secretary, was evasive. Jackson called the priest several times that afternoon, but no one was answering any of the phones at the parish.

She was shocked by Tuesday's headline and immediately called Chief Sabol demanding answers. For some reason he was coy, standoffish, as if he was beginning to distance himself from her, and yes, she wouldn't stand for it: being treated with disregard, not even a tad bit. She intended to use her influence like a sledgehammer.

When she raised her voice, he became abrupt. "Thank you," was all he said, and quickly hung up the phone.

She nearly blew up. She dialed other numbers. Why wasn't anyone taking her calls?

It was late Tuesday when the local chief finally called back. She didn't answer as she was inconvenienced at the time of his call. His recorded message stated that preliminary tests by the county coroner identified the victim as Father Jacob, however, they were waiting for confirmation with dental records.

This Wednesday morning, the day after the vote, Karen Jackson raged, but it wasn't because of election returns. She wanted a perp walk with Urban on display, handcuffed for the cameras. He should be charged with murder.

She called William Dupont, the Pennsylvania State Police Commissioner. He was, of course, courteous and professional, as he spoke in a subdued tone. Yes, he heard about the fire but wasn't yet privileged to the details. He would ask for an update and promised to keep her informed. But when she couldn't control herself and raised her voice, even he became curt and quickly ended their conversation by promising to have the investigating office call her with an update.

Thirty-nine minutes later, Karen received that call. She had been pacing and watching the clock like a hawk. It was placed on hold by her secretary who used the intercom to inform her.

"Hello!"

Already her tone was tempered with disdain.

"Ms. Jackson. This is Captain Anthony Gorgone, with the State Police, Unit Thirteen, South Central Division.

And she was annoyed with the formal introduction. "Well, it's about time you called me!

"Good morning, Ma'am." Startled by her impertinence, he spoke inappropriately. "How are you today?"

"Oh, just great! I'm just fine and dandy!" Her sarcasm was intentionally insulting. She heard the man on the other end of the line clear his throat.

"The Commissioner asked me to call you," he began, "but I don't have much more to report. I already know that Chief Sabol updated you on the investigation." He could hear heavy breathing coming from her. "I'm sorry."

"Well, that's not good enough," she began to rage. "What's taking so long?"

"I assure you, Ms. Jackson, that we are giving this incident our full attention. A detective from our Harrisburg Bureau has been assigned to the case. Detective Gulyas…"

"I want action. A quick arrest!" she interrupted.

It became obvious to the captain that he was not going to lead the conversation and that she needed to vent, so he yielded. "Yes, of course."

"By brother is dead! A reverend! He was a holy man of God!"

"I'm very sorry for your loss." But his expression of condolence lacked the tone of sincerity needed to calm an angry woman.

"He was my brother, dammit!" she began shouting. "Why haven't you arrested Urban yet?! I want him arrested! Do it now!"

"As I tried to explain …" the captain was beginning to lose his patience, "Detective Gulyas is one of our best. His investigation will be very thorough."

"Humph! I don't think you know what you're doing. Urban is a rapist, and now a killer!"

"Ms. Jackson, please… please try to be calm. This matter must be handled in a very professional manner. Surely you can understand that protocol and procedure must be followed to the finest points. The crime lab is still collecting evidence and processing the scene."

The captain wondered why she would accuse the local magistrate. He made a mental note to follow-up with a question to Gulyas. But more than being curious about her charge, he just wanted to conclude the conversation as quickly and politely as possible.

"Dam your professionalism! Urban must be made to pay for what he did! He robbed my brother of his chance at a good life…" And as stone cold as she was, she struggled with a sudden surge of emotion. It was fired like a shot from a loose cannon, nearly overcoming her.

When she paused, the captain seized the opportunity to end the call. "I understand your concern. And again, I want to express my condolences for your loss. It is a terrible thing." And with that he quickly added, "Ms. Jackson, I promise to keep you apprised of our progress."

She choked and coughed as a brief feeling of sadness vented through her throat. It was very dry.

"Have a good day and goodbye for now." **Click.**

Before she could say another word, the connection was gone. She heard the dial tone and slammed the receiver down onto the telephone's base. She opened the bottom drawer of her desk and reached for the bottle of whiskey she stored there. She rubbed her right eye. It itched. But there was nary a tear.

++++

I was feeling relieved that morning, waking early and arriving at Sam's apartment by 8 AM. I greeted him with a peck on his lips.

"You seem to be in a good mood today," he welcomed me.

"I'm fine, well… better, I guess." I walked past him. "Today, I feel like everything is okay, no, better than that. Good." I turned back toward him and smiled. "It's a nice feeling, the first time I've felt like this in a long time." I went toward the kitchen. "I don't know, maybe it was the dream…"

"What did you say?"

"The dream… I had a really strange dream last night."

"Me too…"

Sam looked at me with intrigue on his face.

"What was yours about?" he asked.

"The Advocate. He introduced me to the Lord. How about you? How are you feeling today?"

"Better, too."

He answered quickly, his eyes dazed, apparently deep in thought, and distracted. But I sensed a change in his demeanor, different from even before his arrest.

"Resolved. I think things are more resolved for me now," he explained.

"That's interesting. What was your dream about?"

"I also dreamed about the Advocate."

He was enthusiastic, willing and anxious to confide.

"In my dream I saw God on His throne. I conversed with Him…" Sam noted.

Strange. I thought his admission to be very strange, even stunning. "Guess those letters had an effect on us?" I paused, and decided to pry deeper. "So, what did you say… to God on His throne"?

Buzzzz… Buzz.

"Someone's at the door. I'll get it," he interrupted. He pressed the intercom button. "Who's there?"

"It's me… JP."

I quickly stepped forward and nudged at Sam to move.

"Hi," I answered. "I'll let you up. Sam's here. Press on the door when you hear the clicking noise."

++++

Three minutes later, JP knocked softly at the entry to Sam's apartment. After brief introductions and a hearty handshake between the two men, JP took the lead.

++++

"Congratulations on the election," he began.

I watched their interaction, feeling a little uncertain, even insecure.

Without answering, Sam returned a surprised look.

"Surely, you must have won… didn't you?" JP asked.

"It looked good last night, according to reports on exit polls," Sam noted, "but I still haven't seen the paper today." He looked at his wristwatch. "Comes in about an hour…"

Buzzz– Ring –Ring – Buzz.

"Wow, guess I'm popular today," Sam reacted. "I'll get the phone."

"And I'll get the door, again," I offered.

"Hello," Sam answered. Pause… "Jared, how's it goin'?" Pause… "Really?!"

Sam looked at me and motioned with his hands, but the gesture was something I did not understand. I shrugged my shoulders and shot back with a puzzled expression: eyebrows raised, head cocked to one side, and hands open, empty as they were, wanting more. "What? What are you trying to tell me?"

Sam spoke into the receiver, "Yeah, okay," then looked at me again. "Jodi! You've got to hear this…"

He appeared to be confused and happy at the same time.

"Great news…" he said to his caller. "Thanks, Jared. Thanks for the heads up."

Someone was knocking. It couldn't wait. As Sam placed the phone in its cradle, I answered the door. He was still grinning, ear to ear.

"Yes, he's here," I said to the visitor. "Please, just a minute…. I'll get him."

Sam saw the young woman standing in the doorway.

"Who is it?" he asked as he came toward me.

"A reporter," I informed in a whisper.

"Who…?"

"Hi!" The woman stepped forward to quickly greet Sam; her hand extended. "I'm Maggie Johns…"

At first, there was no recognition on his part.

"…with the **Morning Herald**…"

"Oh yea… I remember you," Sam finally answered.

"First of all, I want to congratulate you on your election victory." She slowly dropped the hand that was rejected. "Do you have a few minutes? I just have a couple of quick questions."

Sam stood squarely in front of her, blocking her entrance into his home. The rejection was palpable. She looked at me, but I wasn't about to intercede on her behalf. I realized who she was too.

"So, I won?" Sam asked, "I really won the election?"

"By a landslide," she answered with a warm smile. "If I could come in… for just a few minutes…"

"How much?"

"How much?" she repeated his question. "How much what?"

Sam was uninformed of the vote.

"I won by how much?" he clarified.

"Oh, you don't know?"

Sam shook his head.

She grimaced and answered. "By a lot. It's estimated that you got 95 percent of the vote." She took half a step toward him.

Again, Sam didn't move. JP and I were watching with interest.

"Oh, so now you want to interview *me*." Sam was shaking his head. "Thanks for the information, but now I seem to recall that you were the one who wrote that scathing article about me a few days ago.”

“Well, yes, but…”

“Oh yeah, I remember you,” he spoke louder. “The interview and front-page headline you wrote with the state representative. Guess it didn’t accomplish what you hoped.”

He was bragging and rebuking her simultaneously. And it felt good to see him that way, his confidence restored.

“No, I don’t want to talk to you,” he announced boldly. “Tell your editor to send Susan… Susan Kasper. I’m only talking to her.”

And with that he advanced, forcing her back, and began to close the door in her face.

“But… but if only…” she raised her hand in protest.

“Nope. Sorry. Send Susan.”

And she was gone. And, I didn’t feel sorry for her. In fact, I felt jubilant. “Wow, that was something!” I acknowledged his aggression. “So, we won… we really won!”

“Yes! And there’s more,” Sam began. “That was my attorney on the phone. Jared said his snitch at the D.A.’s office is hearing that they are in an uproar over there. Seems that their star witness is expected to back out.”

He was animated in sharing the news.

“They’re debating if they should drop the charges against me.”

I was astonished.

“Jared thinks they will…” he concluded, “it’s finally going to be over!”

“Oh my God! We did it, we won again!”

JP was standing in silence, taking it all in. Because of his presence, I held back, and Sam noticed the slight.

JP offered him a handshake. "Now congratulations are truly in order."

I thought he was sincere, but not really happy for us.

Uninterested in him, Sam was watching, waiting for me.

I ran to him and we embraced. I looked into his eyes; he pleaded for more.

"Sam, we're free…" I threw my arms around his neck and kissed him passionately.

I was already thinking of what would be next, ideas that inquired about our future. For until then, I hadn't allowed myself to consider such things.

"Well, let's take a seat at the kitchen table and relax," I suggested.

JP's presence suddenly seemed like an intrusion. Whatever he was up to, the purpose of his visit, it now felt like a threat.

"Good idea," Sam confirmed. "Who wants a cup of coffee?"

++++

All the while, JP was troubled in his own way, trying to form his questions and waiting for the appropriate time to spring them on Sam. Suddenly, he couldn't wait any longer.

"Sam, I have to ask you," he charged ahead as he placed his hands flat on the table and cleared his throat. "Wasn't Judge Williams overly lenient on you?"

Sam returned a surprised look.

"Sorry, I don't mean to be demanding," JP said, "but this question has been eating at me for a long time. The judge was, almost merciful…"

++++

"JP is Darcy's son," I reminded. "He survived the crash." Sam seemed to understand, so I continued, "He asked me about Williams… but I didn't know what to say… so, I told him he'd have to talk to you."

"Well, sure. Yeah, of course. It's okay," Sam nodded. "You're right. Now is the time to finally come clean. You deserve to know what really happened."

He went to the kitchen sink and filled a glass with water. We watched and waited, for an explanation, further commentary on the incident that haunted us both.

Sam leaned back against the sink. It looked like he was stalling. Finally, he began to recall the details of that fateful day.

"There's something I've never told anyone. It's the secret I kept with Faith."

And his was an intriguing story.

++++

Staring out the window of the Greyhound bus, Faith was forlorn. Her eyes didn't follow the movement of houses, cars, people, even children playing in the front yards of their happy homes. It all passed by quickly, in a blur. She was dazed, analyzing and remembering, but mostly regretting.

Her memory shifted to another time, that day in June, early in the month, seventeen years ago. Although he wasn't her first crush, back then, she was hot for Sam. She had already been with several other boys. She had experience, but just then, desired and needed Sam's attention more than anyone else's. Yes, it was infatuation.

They were high school juniors. Sam was already driving with a license. She was studying for her learner's permit. He often chided her about the rules. For them, driving was liberation, the freedom they so desperately sought, for many years as yearning juveniles.

She had been sitting around a swimming pool, at a graduation party for a person who was an acquaintance more than a friend. Presently, she could not recall the graduate's name. It was a girl, probably competition for Sam.

Faith was wearing a short sundress, strapped over the shoulders, and sandals. The outfit, she clearly remembered.

Then the rest of the memory came almost as a vision, broadcast into her thoughts with surprising clarity. It was Sunday, mid-day, and she was bored. She had been there for nearly an hour and Sam still hadn't arrived.

Then she heard the roar of an auto engine.

Back then, a young man always revved his motor while parking, after first shifting to neutral. He held the brake with one foot and jabbed at the accelerator with the other. Next, he had to move both feet, and be quick or the car would drift. The left foot went from the brake to the clutch, as the right foot followed to the brake. Sam did all this before putting the transmission back in gear and shutting off the engine, finally releasing both pedals. It was a tricky maneuver, refined with practice.

The male ego needed to flaunt; it was a demonstration of his control over the many horses he harnessed under the hood. He was the big man with raw power at his disposal. Of course, it was important to have an appreciative audience, one that would acknowledge his status in the kingdom of motorheads. And the female was usually willing to accommodate, although for most, that whole thing with the clutch and the pedals was something she'd rather not do, preferring an automatic transmission instead.

Except for Faith. She was determined to impress.

She turned to see the dust settling as Sam parked his father's pickup. The old man seldom let Sam drive it, his pride and joy: a 1960 Chevy C10 Fenderside with a 327-cubic-inch V8 engine, a big upgrade ordered directly from the factory. The pickup had a three-speed stick shifter mounted on the floor in front of the bench seat. Its color was bright blue with metallic flakes that sparkled under the sun. For some reason, Sam was privileged to borrow it that fateful day.

Faith ran to the cooler that sat near the edge of the pool, grabbed a can of beer, and took off for her man. She had already consumed several alcoholic drinks, but who was counting? She was determined to be the first to greet him.

She saw Rachel, his current interest, stand after hearing and seeing Sam's dramatic entrance. Determined to beat her at her game, Faith nudged Rachel, nearly pushing her into the pool, as she sprinted by. The girl swayed, regained her balance, and with a "Hey, watch where you're goin', you bitch!" made a gesture of contempt. But Faith didn't care. She smiled at the thought of Sam seeing Rachel and thinking her middle finger was meant for him.

As he tinkered with the radio in the truck, Faith approached, a broad smile on her face. Sam jumped out, his thick hair falling into his face. As soon as he closed the door, she threw her body against his, pushing him back against the vehicle. She planted a quick, wet kiss on his lips. It wasn't entirely unexpected or unwanted.

Taking the bait, Sam lingered and didn't move until he felt her hand in his pants pocket. He lifted her elbow. "Faith, stop! You know I'm not like that."

She pushed her hand farther in and reached for the bottom of the pocket. "I just want the keys," she teased.

His body stiffened.

This time, Sam yanked at her arm and removed her hand. "Oh, no you don't."

"But I just want to go for a little ride."

She said it with her pout face. And it was young and pretty.

"Faith…" Sam corrected, "I just got here."

"It's boring," she whined. "Let's just go for a little ride."

She coaxed with her full charm on display.

"But I need to at least say hi," Sam protested.

"Then take me home. Would you Sammy, please…" she smiled as her brown eyes twinkled under the afternoon sun. He hesitated, so she continued, "please… Sam, please…"

"Well, guess I can come back."

Rachel had come onto the driveway and stood a short distance from them, watching Faith's performance. She had her fists on her hips, her elbows flared at her sides, and a disgusted look on her face. She appeared as the aggravated hen, about to take flight.

"Hi," Sam said as he looked beyond Faith to wave to his girlfriend. He appeared like a little boy in trouble, caught with his hand in the cookie jar.

She snorted and turned away, walking briskly, headed back to the party.

"Rachel, I'll be back soon."

He wanted to appease her with his failed promise. "Faith just needs a ride home. It's not far..." But the other girl did not acknowledge his insincerity.

Faith ran to the passenger side, climbed in and sat in the center of the bench seat, close to where the driver would be. She pulled her dress up, positioned the shifter between her knees, and held the top of it with her right hand.

Sam chuckled when he saw her. "Well, I'm not sure that will work."

"But I know how to drive a stick shift," she bragged.

"Oh, you do?"

"Yes, of course. I drove my grandfather's John Deere once. It's not that hard."

Sam pushed on the pedals, placed his hand on top of hers and moved the shifter back one notch. His hand rubbed against her inner thigh.

"Now this is neutral," he noted, and was determined not to be distracted. "First gear is up, now neutral, and then down to second gear." He enjoyed being the instructor. "Third is a little bit harder. Up from second, across neutral and up again. Do you think you have it?"

"Like getting to third base?" she suggested slyly. But Sam remained suspicious. "Easy peasy," she concluded and snuggled even closer.

"Okay, I'll tell you when to shift." He looked to her for confirmation and their eyes met. They shared an excitement that was unexpected.

She nodded and giggled. "Okay then, let's go Mr. Big Truck Driver!"

On the bus, Faith remembered driving several miles as she watched Sam's every move. They proceeded without difficulty through several stops and intersections.

"Stop the truck," she suddenly ordered. "I want to drive." She had an idea and changed her strategy.

"I don't think so. You have to use both feet and press in the clutch," he advised.

"Sam, I know about the clutch. Now don't act like I'm a little dummy." She placed her hand on his leg. "Please," she begged, as she slid it closer to his crotch. "You don't want to hurt my feelings… Do you?"

It was against his better judgment, but he saw a wide berm ahead and pulled the truck over. His hormones had surged, and he was beginning to feel jumpy. More than anything, he wanted to cool things down; he needed to get some space between himself and Faith, who was being a big tease. He could feel an arousal coming.

She quickly jumped out and ran in front of the pickup, skipping, smiling, and waving at him as her dress flitted in the breeze. Reluctantly, he slid over, all the way, against the passenger's side door

With a few more instructions she got the truck moving on the road after three stalls and a fast-jerking motion that squealed the rear tires on the edge of the pavement when she popped the clutch. Sam sighed. But she seemed to know the shifting pattern.

He frowned as she took the engine to a high rpm before moving it into second gear. Their speed kept increasing. They went faster… and faster.

"Faith, slow down," he warned. "There's a four way stop ahead."

"Oh, this thing has some real torque. I like it."

"I said, slow down. Now!"

She turned to see his expression, expecting that he must be impressed with her driving skill. "Sam, relax. We're just having a little fun."

His face held a stern look, his eyes fixed ahead. Suddenly he yelled, "Faith, stop! STOP!!!"

She pressed on the brake and accelerator at the same time, completely forgetting about the clutch. The sure power of the V8 overcame the braking system.

"The clutch!" Sam was panicked now. "The clutch!!" he yelled again. He reached for the steering wheel, but it was too late to avoid a crash.

++++

"Yes, Faith was in the driver's seat when we crashed. I was her passenger." Sam looked to me for recognition.

"You mean all this time…" he watched as I spoke, "All these years…" But I couldn't complete the thought.

Still, he nodded in agreement. "I had a bad cut on my leg."

Sam placed the edge of his hand halfway between his knee and hip on his right leg to indicate where it had been.

"Somehow, I think it must have been a miracle," he continued, "that Faith wasn't hurt… really, just bumped her head on the steering wheel. She cried for a moment… then, seeing the car we hit and the lady in it, right there in front of us…"

Sam grimaced and swallowed hard to choke back emotion. "That was your mother," he said to JP. "And you were in the back of the car in a baby seat. Sorry… I'm so sorry."

313

"It was a long time ago," JP moaned.

His voice was flat and unemotional, a near whisper. I reached over and squeezed his hand, then looked back to Sam. "So, what happened next?"

"Faith got the idea and started yelling at me to switch seats with her. I didn't know what to do."

He paused as I felt the horror of the returning memory in a vivid way.

"Later I realized why" Sam explained. "She had been drinking at the party before I got there and probably had one or two too many. Besides, she shouldn't have been driving. I mean, it really was my fault. She didn't have a license to drive, and she wasn't experienced with a standard shift."

Sam looked at us, saw blank stares, and continued.

"Before I knew it, she jumped out of the truck, came around and was pushing me toward the steering wheel," he shifted on his feet, "to the driver's seat. But it really didn't matter. Once the fire started, we both jumped out. But by then, another car stopped and there were witnesses. They saw me as the driver."

"Oh my God…"

"But that's not all," Sam demanded our attention. "They took me to the hospital and stitched up my leg. My mother asked them to keep me for observation because they also suspected that I might have had a concussion. Faith was the first to visit me that night. She made me promise to keep our secret. Then the police came to take my statement. I told them that I was the driver. They had found an open container in the truck and ordered a BAC."

I wasn't sure what that meant.

"That's a blood alcohol content test, but my level was well below the legal limit," Sam noted. "I don't think they even checked Faith for an alcohol level."

I sat erect, intrigued with his tale. "But you still haven't explained why Judge Williams dismissed the charges against you."

"Oh, yea. That's the rest of the story." He raised his glass and took a couple swigs of water.

"The day of the accident, that evening," Sam continued, "the judge got a call from my father. He had the truck towed to our house and was looking it over. He found blood under the dashboard where it cut my leg, but it was on the passenger side. He showed the judge and told him of his suspicion: that I had to have been the passenger – not the driver. Then Williams came to visit me in the hospital, early the next morning."

I was growing impatient with the many details. "Well, tell us. What did he say?"

"I didn't have to say anything, because he had already figured it out. But I didn't go back on my word. It was important to me, back then, to keep our secret and protect Faith."

"Why?"

"I was all shook up. One young woman was badly injured, about to die. My life, and Faith's were on the line too. I guess, I just needed to do something noble… maybe it seemed like that would justify the wrong."

And it was then that I suddenly realized what must have been in the letter I delivered. "Oh," I blurted. "So that's what you wrote about in the note to Faith?"

"Well, not exactly, but almost," he answered. "The note asked a simple question. It said…" he rolled his eyes, "now just a minute, I want to get it right… oh yeah, it said: **'If this is the way**

it's going to be – why shouldn't I tell them everything?' And I think it worked. She obviously knew what it meant."

"Okay, okay… you were talking about the judge…" I prodded to put him back on track.

"I told him, Judge Williams, that I already gave my statement and that I wasn't going to change it. Even if the evidence indicated otherwise, I wouldn't testify that Faith was the driver. I was. It was just that simple."

"But why?" I was beginning to tear up.

"It was my fault. I wanted to shoulder all the blame and the punishment for it. I'm the one that put Faith behind the wheel."

"Well yeah, but…"

"Until I got to the hearing," Sam interrupted, "That was when I found out that they were charging me with vehicular homicide, and…" he swallowed hard, "I just turned seventeen, so they decided to charge me as an adult. They were throwing the book at me."

I shook my head in disbelief. "You would have gone to jail?"

"Oh yeah, for sure." Sam spoke with authority. He knew the law. "It's a felony, third degree. For at least a couple of years, probably longer."

A stern look seized his face as he continued to speak.

"It would have ruined me, for sure. My plans for a career in law – it was over. I'd be a jailbird, a convict. That's all I would have ever amounted to."

Sam scratched at the base of his neck, behind his ear.

"You know… I checked on the statute of limitations."

I wasn't sure, but he seemed to be changing the subject. What was the 'statue'? I didn't know.

"Faith can still be charged, and I think, maybe, she knows it."

His eyes narrowed as he peered at me. Was he asking for permission?

++++

The statue determines the maximum number of days, after a crime occurs, that a person can still be charged. For some crimes, there is no limit.

++++

I wasn't sure how I felt about Faith finally answering for the wrong she did, but the irony of it all hit me with a gut punch. She was accusing him of rape, and he was still protecting her?

"But of course, you won't tell anyone," Sam concluded. "Now it's *our* secret. And… I'd deny this conversation if a word of it ever got out to anyone else. It's my decision." He focused directly on JP. "But I decided that you deserved to know."

JP seemed a bit uncomfortable with his demand, so I spoke before he could. "No, of course not. We wouldn't tell a soul." I looked over at JP. He nodded.

"I'm sure that my dad was putting pressure on the judge," Sam resumed, "so what else could he do? At the hearing Williams announced that I was not intoxicated, said that the homicide charge was a far overreach and that there was no intent for harm."

Sam swallowed a surge of emotions. "That's what he said… and I'll never forget it… that it was just a tragic accident." He choked on a sob. "Williams slammed down the gavel, and that was the end of it. I walked out of his courtroom a free man."

"Unbelievable… that's quite a story." I stood, darted to Sam and gathered him unto my bosom in a firm embrace. "I'm sooo sorry," I whispered into his ear. He tried to pull away, but I

317

held him firmly and pressed against his body, squeezing even tighter. "I shouldn't have ever doubted you," I confessed as I looked into his eyes, peering deep into his soul, before relaxing my grip.

"Jodi, you fought for me, and I am eternally grateful."

Sam held my shoulders as tears filled his eyes.

"You did the battle," he acknowledged.

His emotions were running out of control.

"And we won," I suggested.

"Yes, we won… *we* sure did!" Sam hugged me again.

++++

And in that tender moment they were reconciled but still had much to talk about as the desire to share intimate thoughts and feelings with each other was finally, fully rekindled.

++++

Mercy. On my way home I thought about Sam and his story. He was such a great example. He had the power to punish, and Faith certainly deserved it. Yet somehow, even after all she put him through, he still chose to forgive. But how can one so disparaged not need retaliation? I was dumfounded. He had something I sorely needed and desired, and I wanted him more than ever before.

My heart swelled with pride. Our victory… Sam surely deserved it.

CHAPTER ELEVEN: Confirmation

Thursday, May 16, 1985 – day nine.

HEADLINE: **"Charges Against Urban Dropped"** and **"Father Jacob Identified as Victim in Church Fire"**

Sam began this day feeling chipper, even energized. With questions about Faith and Luke still lingering, he decided to swing around and stop at her apartment on his way to the office. Sam was not yet reinstated to his position as District Magistrate, but he needed to visit his courtroom just the same.

He quickly climbed the stairs to Faith's apartment. There was a spring in his steps. He found that her front door was already open. He saw evidence of a quick and shoddy repair. Cardboard taped there. He slowly pushed on it while calling her name.

"Faith… Faith, are you here?"

He peeked inside and saw that the place was disheveled. Then suddenly, another door opened on the other side of the hallway. An elderly woman stepped halfway out with one foot and peered at him with evil eyes. Her hair was long, stringy, and gray. Her face drooped to one side, ghastly white. Her voice was raspy low.

"She's not here!" she rattled.

"Oh," Sam was startled at her appearance. "I'm sorry to bother you."

"I don't care nothin' about that," she growled. "And I don't think you should be snooping around here either."

"No, of course not... I didn't go in," Sam noted in his defense. "Just wondered if Faith was still here... You know, I wanted to talk to her."

"Nope. Like I said, she is gone! Left in a hurry. Yesterday."

Sam turned to leave quick. "Thanks," he managed back to the lady.

He approached the church, slowed his car, and pulled to the curb, far enough away, so as not to be seen. Others had stopped in front of the cathedral; its side was blackened by the smoke from the fire. A makeshift memorial was taking form on the lawn. Sam saw crosses, photos, and flowers. Several people stood around it, as some bowed their heads, but no one seemed to be praying or eulogizing for the deceased. They were shocked and dismayed by a reality which they could no longer deny, even though they still did not know the extent of the evil that had resided there, finally exercised in a violent crime. Most likely, they would never know.

Sam quickly scanned the crowd, examining each face, searching for Luke. But he wasn't there.

As he entered his office Jill brightened immediately and greeted Sam with enthusiastic congratulations. "I knew all along that you were innocent," she announced. "They kept the office open," she noted. "And I've been holding down the fort."

"Thanks Jill, I knew that I could count on you."

"There's some mail, it looks to be personal for you, so I didn't open it. It's on your desk."

Sam nodded as he walked by. "Thanks, again." and he stopped near her. "Really, I appreciate all that you have done."

A handwritten note lay on top of the stack of envelopes. "Glad you're back," it said. "I've been rooting for you." It was signed by Judge Art Gregory. He was the magistrate in the adjoining district that pulled double duty while Sam was out.

He smiled and set the note to the side of his desk. He flipped through several envelopes, unusual sizes and colors, obviously greeting cards. Each would have special meaning for him. But before he began to open them, he came upon that familiar envelope, the one with the simple hand writing.

This note from the Advocate simply said, **"Show mercy."**

Sam looked at the handmade plaque that hung on the wall. It was still there. It also said, "Show Mercy – With Cheerfulness." A coincidence? He doubted it was so.

But there was more, handwriting on the back of the note. **"Act as one judged under the law of liberty. For judgment is without mercy to one who has shown no mercy. Weeping may endure for a night, but joy cometh in the morning."**

Sam understood the meaning of the message, for he truly had been shown mercy. The events of his life shaped him. And these messages helped sustain him during his lowest times of fear and regret.

He looked at the plaque again. *So… that was the Advocate's first message?* But who was this person that kept sending these messages? Sam pondered on the merit of discovering his identity. Finding him might be good… or perhaps, it would be the wrong thing to do. Just as a superhero must preserve and protect his anonymity, the truths taught by this mentor might be minimized once his mask was unveiled.

Would Sam expect too much of the Advocate in a personal relationship, once they met and talked freely? Besides, it was unlikely that the Advocate would consent to such exposure.

No, it was not necessary to find him, Sam decided. Best to leave well enough alone. At least for now.

A Few Days Later:

Sam was awake before dawn. Another day arrived with glory, evident from his rear porch that faced east. Sam sat there, holding a hot cup of coffee between his two hands as he warmed them against the morning chill. The sky was glowing like fire, a bright orange color that extended into the horizon, both to the north and to the south, and changing to become hues of violet, red, and blue. His ordeal was finally over. He was free. Even his reputation could be repaired.

These ideas fell into his brain like the approaching high tide, waves rushing in, one after the other, and then retreating to reveal the bottom of the ocean. Remnants of sea creatures deposited there were like the rumors that still lingered in Sam's town. But he was establishing a new base. Much had been revealed. The beach would be groomed.

He won the election. Justice prevailed. God is good. Love endures.

Judge Williams came to mind. Did his old friend and mentor somehow intercede for him once again, maybe from heaven?

Sam thought about the accident, how he lied for Faith, and the hearing before Williams. Then, the rape charge, but he didn't deserve it, and finally, the overwhelming number of votes he received from the electorate. That was unexpected. But generally, people are real.

Sam felt confirmed and fully received the blessing of mercy first proclaimed by his benefactor. Williams was right all along. Sam realized that he never should have doubted himself. Confidence came to establish itself in the vacancies of his heart where the tortures of rejection were finally evicted.

And then, the dark cloud of condemnation that clung to his soul was released and dissipated.

It was gone. Gone for good!

He wondered if he should make a statement to finally set the record straight: tell Susan, the reporter, that Faith was the driver? It would make a great headline.

Show mercy. The words crashed on him like those blurted from a loudspeaker at full volume. No, he would still guard her secret. That was the merciful thing to do.

A saying came to mind, one that he thought was in the Good Book. **"Blessed are the merciful: for they shall obtain mercy."** He considered the adage to be true. It was his experience.

Sam had a job of great responsibility. How could he ever be free of its intent, demand, and consequence? But now he had a new beginning. His spirit soared in freedom. He determined to walk with God and seek His ways. A greater power. Strength beyond his own, in union with the Holy Spirit.

And so, in the end, in consideration of the great plethora of human suffering, we come to the simple conclusion, a realization, of how much we need Him to heal and transform us; for this is how we cope in this life, truly live now, even as we prepare for the next.

But Sam needed support in his new quest. He hoped Jodi would be his partner. He wanted to share his new found passion with her. She stayed by his side despite the accusation of rape. His heart was drawn to her.

He called and they agreed to meet at the Three Way Diner for breakfast.

++++

As I entered the diner, I immediately saw Sam sitting alone at a booth in the back. No one was nearby. *Private. Good, we can talk.* I saw several familiar faces at the counter.

"Hi, Jodi. Good to see you again."

It was a voice I recognized. Dennis Canton, the college professor.

"Oh, hi Denny. Good to see you too." I paused not wanting to be rude to a friend. "It's Sam, he's waiting for me." I pointed ahead.

"Oh yeah, sure. Tell him I said hi."

As I approached Sam, he sat his coffee mug on the table and rose to greet me. He reached for a kiss. "I love you," he whispered in my ear, and we hugged briefly.

"A beautiful day," he noted.

I smiled in agreement.

"God is good. His mercy endures."

"I am grateful."

"I think I'm different, after going through this whole ordeal."

He waved his hand in a circular motion to emphasize his point. The experience was of a global significance for him. It changed his world.

"Yes, but how?" I prodded.

"Baggage… the monkeys on my back. I feel like it is all gone."

"That's great!"

"I've been reflecting on it all. The false accusation, but mostly the notes from the Advocate, and my dream, or vision, or whatever it was." He paused, "I'll never forget it."

"Yeah, tell me about it."

"You understand?"

"Yes, that's what I mean… I had a similar experience, and, you already described your dream to me."

"Yeah, well, I've learned that God is loving and kind. A father to the fatherless."

"A father to the fatherless," I repeated. "I like that."

A waitress placed a cup of coffee in front of me.

"I'll be back to get your orders," she noted and left in a hurry to refill other cups at booths nearby.

I was glad to see her go, because I wanted to resume our conversation. "I like what you said," I continued, "I think God is all about relationships… more than religion, in fact, religion can ruin the relationship."

We both took a sip of coffee and Sam nodded.

"I can trust Him… we can trust Him," he admonished.

"I think, He is real, and we must be real too," I suggested. "I mean, God is supreme. He sets the terms of the relationship. He has to be first. We have to love Him, first and foremost." I paused.

"And like any relationship, insincerity is a breach of the intimacy that is needed to stay close."

"We will have to be dedicated."

I nodded but then unintentionally corrected him. "I think you mean devoted." But I didn't want to be abrasive. "Sorry, I didn't mean to…"

"No, you're right," Sam interrupted. "No offense taken." He smiled. "We need to give Him our minds and hearts… Do you think we can do it?"

"We can try…"

Sam nodded again as the waitress returned. We ordered breakfast and vibrant conversation resumed. I could see that he was different. He laughed with ease, and frequently. He was so sincere. His eyes were intense, so much so, that I had trouble looking away. He held my gaze. My heart leaped with joy.

Leaving the restaurant, we had to wait at the cash register. "Oh no," the hostess said, "you're all paid up."

"What do you mean?" Sam inquired.

"It was the man sitting over there, by the window. I don't know his name."

I turned to look that way. The seat was empty.

"He already left," she noted, seeing the inquest of my gaze. "Oh, almost forgot. He asked me to give you this. She handed a napkin to Sam.

A note was written there. It said, **"Don't be a slave to fear, remorse, or even religion. In Christ you are adopted to <u>BE</u> <u>A</u> <u>SON</u>. You are truly forgiven, to be free indeed!"**

Sam smiled, gently folded the paper, and placed it in his jacket pocket.

"The Advocate?" I pondered aloud.

"Maybe…"

I looked at the counter. Dennis was also gone.

EPILOGUE

Monday, February 17, 1986

HEADLINE: Urbans Announce Birth of Daughter

Jodi Urban sat upright in the hospital bed, pillows stuffed behind her back, hoping for visitors. The image she portrayed was picture perfect for a new mother holding an infant. Visiting relatives would hardly believe she had just given birth three days before. Her little angel, a bundle of love, appropriately arrived on February 14, Valentine's Day.

Jodi's hair was styled and her makeup was applied with perfection. She looked bright and cheerful. She wore one of her favorite pieces of jewelry, the cross necklace.

She finished nursing the infant and asked the father if he would like to hold his new baby daughter. Sam was waiting for the chance. He carefully supported her head as he reached for his little girl and held her against his chest, gently cradled in his arms. With her powder blue eyes, she was looking into his face, cooing softly.

"What will we name her?" he asked his wife. "Have you chosen a favorite yet?"

"Yes, I think I have," Jodi smiled broadly. "Have you?"

"Well, looking at the list that we narrowed down, I think I do have a favorite, but I want you to tell me first."

Sam sat on a chair that was at the bed's side and reached for Jodi's hand in a tender expression of unity. They were now a little family of three. Links in a chain, closely connected.

"I think," she paused for dramatic effect, "that we should name her Mercy."

"Mercy," Sam repeated as he looked into his baby doll's face. She smiled with approval. "Mercy it shall be! That was my first choice too," he winked at his wife. "But is it Mercy with the letter 'y', or Merci with an 'i'?"

"Mercy is a girl's name of English origin meaning compassion. I looked it up." Jodi smiled immodestly, but there was no need to impress.

Sam was full in, adoring his bride, and head over heels for his new daughter. "Okay, that's appropriate."

"But Merci with and 'i' means 'thank you' in French, I believe."

"I believe you are correct, my dear."

"I have… we have, much to be grateful for."

Sam squeezed her hand and gently kissed his daughter on her forehead. "Yes, we certainly do. So, it's final. Merci with an 'i'."

"And you certainly are," Jodi said.

Sam returned a puzzled look.

"Mercy's man. And you are a wonderful father to our little Merci."

"Oh, but you are the best! And together we are blessed!" Pride swelled in his heart.

"But… what is her middle name…?"

#

Shortly after Sam's acquittal, the couple, greatly relieved and once again hopeful, went on a weekend trip to Niagara Falls. It was in the spirit of celebration. They returned as husband and wife.

Jodi's mother complained that they had eloped but the blushing bride claimed that the ceremony had been unplanned, a spontaneous expression of joy. She promised to hold a banquet in recognition of their marriage that would be attended by family and friends. No definite plans were made. Then suddenly, the newlyweds became aware of her pregnancy, and the party was postponed.

But who was the father?
She never told him. (You do the arithmetic.)

\#

Luke was never seen or heard of again. He may have travelled to a distant place and changed his name, assuming the ID of another person already deceased.

However, many years later, the decayed remains of a corpse was discovered several miles from Saint Patrick Church in a remote area of State Game Lands. It was on a ridge under a rock ledge at the edge of a ravine. The forensic pathologist who examined the remains believed there to be evidence of a fire. That may have been the cause of death. The identity of the deceased was undetermined, still a mystery many years later.

Long before the discovery of the human remains, in the month of November, 1985, during deer season, a hunter came upon a gas can in a narrow canyon. It was still usable, so he took it back to his hunting camp. It was his only catch for the day.

If you have a desire to reach others with this vital message, share by going to:
 www.UpdykeBooks.com/readers-respond/

On my web site: www.UpdykeBooks.com/addendum-1 , the reader is offered links for additional consideration of the book's theme.

Reviews on Amazon and Barnes & Noble will also greatly help for reaching others.

Please give us a review: If you find this book insightful, please know that our success depends on your review.

Go to Amazon.com and search the author's name, "Alan Updyke."

If searching by title, in the search box write:
"The Tarnished Cross - Romantic"

Or, simply scan this QR Code: